Five for Freedom by Underground Railroad

Five for Freedom by Underground Railroad

Elaine Wentworth

FIVE FOR FREEDOM BY UNDERGROUND RAILROAD

iUniverse books may be ordered through booksellers or by contacting:

iUniverse
1663 Liberty Drive
Bloomington, IN 47403
www.iuniverse.com
1-800-Authors (1-800-288-4677)

Because of the dynamic nature of the Internet, any web addresses or links contained in this book may have changed since publication and may no longer be valid. The views expressed in this work are solely those of the author and do not necessarily reflect the views of the publisher, and the publisher hereby disclaims any responsibility for them.

Any people depicted in stock imagery provided by Thinkstock are models, and such images are being used for illustrative purposes only.
Certain stock imagery © Thinkstock.

ISBN: 978-1-4917-9897-3 (sc)
ISBN: 978-1-4917-9896-6 (e)

Library of Congress Control Number: 2016916340

Print information available on the last page.

iUniverse rev. date: 11/01/2016

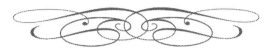

Contents

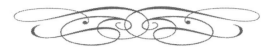

Preface

I was initially inspired to write this historical fictional when I first visited the Jackson Homestead some years ago, around 1993, with my late husband, Murray Jackson Wentworth, who had not been there since he was a child. He was the great-great-great-grandson of William Jackson, who lived there with his large family before and during the Civil War. The homestead has now long been a famous museum belonging to the city of Newton. Many adults, as well as schoolchildren, visit and are fascinated by the deep root cellar hole below the basement floor that was used to hide fugitive slaves passing through on their way to Canada and freedom.

William Jackson helped start the first bank in Newton and owned a soap and candle factory. The museum features exhibits of this long-ago industry. What caught my imagination was a tiny beaded bag, as well as the caption that went with this display. The caption noted that William allowed his youngest daughter to work in the factory just long enough to earn her own money to purchase the bag.

From this tidbit of information, I began to weave my own story about this house that had long ago become a famous stop on the Underground Railroad. Besides these two facts, everything is historical fiction. I imagined a young slave girl coming to this homestead on the way to freedom along with a group of grown-up slaves, all of whom could read and write. I set the story in 1860, one year before the start of the Civil War, with Lincoln having been elected president and hoping to end slavery.

As a well-known visual artist, I first planned to write only a short story with many illustrations. But somehow, my grown-up fiction characters took over and urged me to also include their tragic but inspiring stories! The first two chapters are similar to my picture-story manuscript, which has not yet been published.

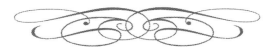

Introduction

Come gather round, my reading friends! Open your imagination to a faraway time in America, back in 1860. It was one year before the beginning of the Civil War. By then, the Northern states and the Southern states were close to the breaking point over the issue of slavery. In December, the United States would dissolve as South Carolina seceded, followed in a few months by the rest to become the Confederate States of America.

Cotton-growing plantation owners were furious with the Northerners who were helping slaves to escape by the thousands. This escape plan was called the Underground Railroad. No eerie train whistle was carried along on the night wind to announce its arrival or departure, and no clackety-clack of the wheels over rails could be heard in the land. No steam engine hissed billows of smoke into the air. This train was made up of one single thought and purpose, expressed in action—that of people helping people. Both white people and free black people worked for the "railroad."

Because it had to be accomplished in secrecy, it was named "underground." And because it involved transporting many folks great distances, it was called "railroad." The people spoke in railroad terminology, using terms like *depots*, *stations*, *passengers*, *conductors*, *tickets*, and the like. During the years that this Underground Railroad existed, more than fifty thousand fugitive slaves escaped because of it.

Close your eyes now on today's world, and open your imagination to the sights and sounds of such a train in operation. At first glance, there is nothing at all to see except the pale moon passing in and out of misty clouds over a dark forest. Move in closer, down at the level of the forest floor, and you will just barely make out a worn path through the woods, swamps, and fields. Nothing is marked, but many hurrying feet have trampled the twigs, needles, and grasses underfoot. Listen for footsteps; you cannot hear them. You'll hear only a thud or crackling sound now and then, spaced out at intervals.

Look carefully now through the confusing pattern of trees and night shadows when the moon rides clear of the clouds. There is a train just taking off from the station. The lower trunks of some pine trees have peculiar shapes. All of a sudden, the shapes emerge, spaced out at intervals, one at a time, to form a single file line. The silhouetted shapes come in different sizes. At the head of the line, a tall, striding shape walks along, and the others must keep up. There are shorter shapes, and if you peer carefully into the mysterious shadows, you will notice that three of them are wearing long skirts. Each carries a wrapped-up bundle. Then follows a shorter, thin shape with long legs. At the end of the line is another taller form, also wearing trousers and carrying another small shape high on his back, piggyback style. Can you see? It's not a bundle; It's a young girl, with her head nestled into his neck, already fast asleep!

Without this secret railroad, this story could not have happened. This one little girl could never have traveled such a long distance, all the way from South Carolina up into New England. She could never have met another little girl, just her own age, who lived in Massachusetts. The chance of their meeting would have otherwise been impossible to imagine. It wasn't just the long distance between them in those faraway times of difficult travel that might have kept them apart, for their differences were far greater than the miles that separated them.

Chapter One

Taffy's Long Day

Taffy walked along, ever so slowly, down the long carriage driveway. It was still early enough to be cool. Overhead, the morning sunlight flickered through the oak trees casting purple shadows across the pink gravel. The birds sang as they swooped down from the tall oaks onto the magnolia trees. It was a morning to make the heart sing like the birds, but Taffy's slow footsteps were only in tune with her sad, young heart.

The closer she got to the big white house, the more slowly she walked. Everything in front of her looked the same. The tall white columns that lined the front were dappled with sunlight. The covered veranda behind them was as cool and inviting as ever, with its swinging settee padded with bright cushions. Taffy sighed, kicking a pebble with her bare feet. Everything looked the same, but nothing really was the same. Over and over, the same questions ran through her mind. Her mother and father were gone. Where were they? What had happened to them? Why had she been left behind? Would they come back soon and get her? How long had they been gone? It seemed like such a long time. How long had it been? Days? Weeks? She had no way of knowing.

She finally reached the three steps up to the shady porch. Engrossed in her sad questions, she stopped and stood there awhile. Her arms were folded in front of her, and the questions with no answers pounded through her head. It was still too early for anyone to be relaxing on the swing. Probably no one was even up as yet. Except for the singing birds, it was quiet.

Still pondering, Taffy aimlessly did something she never would have done if she had been more alert. She walked up onto the long porch and sat down in the swing settee. It was just too comforting to resist. She leaned back against the plump pillows. She pushed her feet against the floor, and the swing began to move with no creaking sounds at all. She pushed again, and the swing started back and forth on its own rhythm. For a long while, Taffy sat there, feeling contented once again, lost in her daydream. She imagined that she was sitting there in a long, full dress, printed with pink and green flowers, with white shoes peeking out from the ruffles along the hem. Instead of the pillows, she imagined the comforting warmth of her mother sitting close beside her. All of a sudden, Teddy, the family collie dog, bounded around the corner of the porch; saw Taffy sitting there; and began a loud, continuous barking!

"Ssshh, Teddy, come here," she whispered, holding out her hand.

The big dog ran to her. He stopped his barking but leaped up onto the swing beside her.

"Teddy, no, no, you're not supposed to sit on these cushions and pillows. You're as bad as I am—I'm not supposed to be sitting here either."

Just as she said that, the front door opened, and a voice called out, "Here, Teddy, sssshh. Whatever is the matter out there?"

Just in time, Taffy slid off the swing, ran to the end of the porch, and jumped off into the flower beds. Teddy followed right after her, starting to bark again. Taffy ran to the rear of the big house and entered the kitchen door just as quickly as she could.

Susie was there in the big kitchen alone, mixing up a batter for breakfast biscuits. There was only Mr. Davis, the master of the plantation, and his older sister, Miss Sarah, to cook for. Big Sally, the head cook, had gone to the mountains with Mrs. Davis to help open up their summer lodge. The two children were still away at boarding school.

It suited Susie just fine to have the kitchen work all to herself. She was only sixteen, but she had been a house slave in this kitchen since she was twelve years old, assisting Big Sally and Della, Taffy's mother. With Big Sally away, she could make up menus on her own and try out her own ideas. There was nothing Susie would rather do than cook. Every day, she said a prayer of thanks that she did not have to pick cotton in the hot fields with the other young slaves.

"What took you so long, Taffy?" Susie asked, wiping her forehead with a towel. It was already getting hot in the big kitchen with the woodstove oven going. "Did you have to wait all that time for Sam to come by in the wagon?"

Before Taffy could answer, Susie gave her a hug.

"Never mind, Taffy honey, just give me the package Sam handed you while I sit and cool off a minute. Plopping into the chair, she pushed her dark, curly hair away from her forehead.

Taffy's brown eyes went wide with fear as she clapped her hand over her mouth. The package? What had she done with the package? Then she remembered. While she had been daydreaming, she had put it beside her on the swing. Teddy had probably sat on it and squashed it.

"Taffy, what is it? Where is the package?"

"I left it on the swing, Susie, I'll go and get it!"

"The swing on the front veranda? You never sit on that swing! Never mind, go find it. And be quick about it!"

Taffy ran to the side of the long porch and peeked around the corner. No one was out there. She tiptoed to the back of the swing and looked down on the cushions. No package in sight! She leaned over and moved one of the loose pillows, and there it was, slightly squashed, but it was still there! It was wrapped in brown paper and tied with twine.

Susie was waiting with the kitchen door held open. She grabbed the package from Taffy and dashed to the pantry with it. She took the lid off a wide crockery jar and stuffed the package inside. It was not unusual for Sam, a slave from the next plantation, to come by with grocery supplies, which he delivered to several places along the way. Sometimes he had special gifts of berries and herbs for Susie to cook with, but Susie had never before hidden the packages away or seemed so nervous about it. In fact, Taffy noticed that Susie seemed nervous all morning long.

Finally, all the morning chores were done. Susie sat down on the back steps and called Taffy to her side.

"See how smooth my hands are?" she said as she took Taffy's soft brown hands in her own. "My hands are not all hard and bruised like the hands of the women and girls who pick cotton in the fields all day. If you grow up to be a good cook like your own mama was, you'll never have to pick cotton."

Taffy listened, but the mention of her own mama made her ask once again, as she did many times a day, "Susie, when is my mama coming back again? Where is my daddy?"

Once again, Susie evaded answering Taffy's pitiful questions about her missing mother and father. "Hush, child, don't fret about it. One day, they will come back for you."

Susie managed to change the subject by having Taffy peel and chop up apples, shell walnuts, and set out raisins to add to the batter for a spicy cake for the family's evening meal. Master Davis and Miss Sarah were very fond of Susie's cakes and desserts. They were pleasantly surprised that, even with Big Sally away and Della gone, the cooking was still excellent. When the cake batter was smoothed out in the baking pan and ready for the still hot oven, Susie told Taffy to sprinkle spoonfuls of brown sugar over the top and then add dabs of butter. Taffy carefully followed the instructions, but somehow, a few spoonfuls of sugar strayed past the batter and onto Taffy's tongue.

Taffy was nine years old, going on ten, and Susie wanted to teach her all she could about fine cooking; and she was in a hurry to have Taffy learn just as quickly as she could. Becoming a valuable cook could be the only thing that might one day save her from becoming a field slave. That was the worst fate of all, thought Susie, who had always been a house slave. Taffy's mother, Della, had been a very valuable cook, and she was also a fine seamstress. Susie was certain that wherever she was living now, she would at least be working inside the house, not toiling in the fields.

But what if she and Taffy were separated before Taffy had learned enough? Susie worried about that. They might be together in this kitchen for years; then again, it could all change in a short time. What about herself? She was hopeful that she, too, would be considered too valuable as a cook to waste in the hot cotton fields. But what would happen to poor little Taffy if they were separated? She was still a child, with her skills undeveloped. She could likely be sent to live at slave row under the care of a field slave who had many other children to worry about. Susie could not bear the thought of it.

Della had been like a mother to Susie when she'd first come to this plantation four years ago at age twelve. How frightened she had been, moving to a strange new place, knowing no one. She did not remember her own mother or father. But Della had immediately treated her like a beloved daughter. Under Della's loving care, Susie had become confident and skilled as a cook. More than that, she now knew what it felt like to have a loving mother. Susie had also come to love Taffy as a little sister. So now, more than ever, she was fiercely devoted to her little helper.

"Now we are going to make something extra special while the oven is still hot," said Susie. Then she went into the pantry room, which was quite large, the walls lined with shelves. On the floor were rows of large crockery jars for flour, sugar, and grains, plus jars that were empty. She took out the hidden package and opened it. Inside were a smaller package and a long, sealed envelope that Susie dropped on the floor. Susie quickly picked it up and hid it back in the jar again. The other package she brought to the kitchen to open.

"Look, Taffy, Sam brought us a big slab of chocolate today, and I'm going to teach you how to make a real Devil's food cake! Miss Sarah has invited her embroidery guild over for afternoon tea tomorrow, and we know how they all love chocolate."

All the other ingredients were set out on the table. Susie carefully explained each step to Taffy. First up was how to melt chocolate so it would not burn and taste bitter. Then, she had Taffy dribble the melted chocolate mixed with a dab of butter into the well-beaten eggs and sugar. Taffy stirred the swirls of chocolate around until the mixture was an even, deep brown color. Then they alternated adding the flour mixture and the milk. Last of all, they added vanilla.

But just when the huge bowlful of batter was ready to pour into the greased cake pan, Susie suddenly asked Taffy to run to the outside storehouse and look for something.

"Don't worry." Susie laughed, looking into Taffy's disappointed eyes. "I'll save the bowl for you to lick when you return."

While Taffy was gone, Susie quickly greased a tiny cake pan and poured some of the chocolate batter into that. Then she popped the tiny cake pan into the oven first, so it was hidden behind the large cake pan. When Taffy returned, the cakes were already beginning to rise and fill the air with the smell of warm, baking chocolate. Taffy carefully licked the big bowl clean. Susie seemed more relaxed, and Taffy felt happy and contented for a while.

Then Susie asked her to do something she had never done before. "Taffy, I want you to go back to our own cabin early today. I want you to spend some time making it extra neat and clean, and then I want you to take a nap. We may be up extra late tonight, and I don't want you to be tired."

Taffy opened her mouth to protest, but Susie quickly said, "Don't ask questions. You ask entirely too many questions. Just do as I say."

"But, Susie, I wanted to help you frost the cake. Will you save some frosting for me to lick?"

"Yes, my honey child, I'll bring you some frosting to lick. I promise I will, if you will just go now and do exactly as I say."

After Taffy was away from the kitchen and the two cakes were cooling on the table, Susie mixed up a bowlful of white sugar frosting. When the cakes were cool enough, she covered both of them with swirls of frosting, all over the tops and around the sides. She placed the big, round cake in the pantry under a glass dome, ready for the tea party tomorrow. The tiny cake she placed in a deep bowl that hid it from view and covered it with a plate. She opened a box in the pantry and took out one small candle and stashed it in her apron pocket. In a cup, she had already spooned frosting bowl scrapings for Taffy. Susie hoped that, distracted by the treat of eating frosting, Taffy would not pay any attention to the covered bowl, which she would slide under the table in their cabin.

For the second time that long day, Taffy walked slowly. She made her way alongside the large vegetable garden that was already producing peas and lettuce. On the other side were the smokehouse, the outside kitchen, and the cold storage shed. Beyond that were the orchards—full of peach, apple, and pecan trees. On her side, there was now a thicket of bushes bordering a narrow brook. A wide plank made a crossover place and was the entrance to a pine grove. Clustered under the pine trees were three small log cabins. These were the living quarters of the slaves who worked in the house. Big Sally's cabin was now empty. The largest one had been where Taffy had lived with her parents. That was empty. Just looking at it made Taffy feel sad and lonely once again.

Taffy lingered awhile at the brook, splashing her feet in the water. It was hot now, in the middle of the afternoon, and it would be stuffy inside Susie's shack cabin. Paddling around in the brook was a pleasant distraction.

I'll just wait awhile before I start to clean the cabin, Taffy decided. Instead of crossing over and entering the pine grove, she continued on down beyond the gardens to the edge of the open fields where the cotton plants grew. Alongside were the living quarters for the field slaves. On each side of a central clearing was a row of connected shacks. They had no windows, but that didn't matter much, for the openings in the chinks of the logs let in some light, as well as heat or cold, from outdoors. The floors were hard-packed dirt. Crude ash hearths were used inside. Most of the cooking was done outside in a campfire pit and grate in the central clearing. There was a covered lean-to where the slaves could eat in rainy weather and be near the fire. Next to that were the sheds for the chickens, and just beyond, the pig stys. All in all, it was not considered a large plantation.

Taffy knew she would find someone to talk to down at slave row. Sure enough, there at the campfire was Aunt Crissy, already laying many sweet potatoes on the grate while she kept her eyes on four small children playing nearby. She wasn't really Taffy's aunt; she was everybody's aunt.

Aunt Crissy held out her arms to Taffy and pulled her onto her lap. Taffy snuggled up against Aunt Crissy's plump body and immediately began to cry in soft whimpers. Crissy held her for a long time, rocking back and forth and singing, "Hush-a-bye-my baby, hush-a-bye."

Crissy knew why Taffy was so miserable, but no one wanted to say in words what Taffy would, by forces of reality and time, eventually come to know. Once they told her, it would dawn on Taffy that her parents would never be coming back for her. After a while, Taffy felt better, just from sitting there, and she wiggled away and went off to play with the children. It felt good to have little children to laugh and run and tumble with for a change.

After a while, Taffy remembered that she was supposed to be cleaning her and Susie's cabin. "I have to go now, Aunt Crissy. I'm supposed to clean before Susie comes back from the kitchen."

Aunt Crissy gave Taffy a final hug and kiss. "You and Susie better come down and eat with us tonight. I reckon some company would do you both better than eating those fancy leftovers alone. You tell Susie she ought to start going down to the swamp cabin dances again, too. There's some mighty fine music now, what with new folks coming over from another plantation. One of them even has a real banjo, besides all those handmade things to bang on. Susie's not been there since_." Crissy looked away, but the sadness only flickered in her eyes for a moment before she was smiling down at the little girl again. "And Taffy, you can jus' stay with me while she's gone. You two, all alone up there now in that pine grove, it ain't right No good at all, settin' there lonesome." Crissy gave her another hug as she released her. Taffy knew what Aunt Crissy had not finished saying. Everyone down here was extra kind to her since her parents had disappeared, but no one ever spoke to her about what had happened to them. Taffy gave her another hug as she squirmed off her lap saying more cheerfully "I'll tell Susie what you said, or I won't have time to clean the cabin."

This time, as she crossed over the brook and entered the pine grove, she felt better about going into the empty cabin.

It wasn't a shack; it was a cabin. The three separate cabins in the pine grove were so much nicer than the shacks the others had down at slave row. Having just come from there, Taffy was more aware of the difference. First of all, there was a real door with a wood hinge so they could lock themselves in at night. There was even one tiny window with a hinged shutter so it could be closed. Taffy's father had made them for all three cabins from leftover lumber in the carpentry repair shop. Best of all, there was a real wood plank floor. That meant the cabin could be kept clean by real sweeping with a broom and scrubbing with a brush and soap. Taffy knew that was exactly what Susie had in mind for her to do before she came back from the kitchen.

"Home," Susie called it. Now it was supposed to be "home" to Taffy, too. If she had not been still grieving over the loss of her mama and daddy she could have been happier about living with Susie.

But everything was different now. Even Susie was different. She had always been full of fun before. Now she was more serious and quiet.

Like this afternoon, Taffy thought to herself. *"It just wasn't like Susie to send me home to clean before she frosted the cake."*

Taffy sighed and took a pail off the hook by the door. She filled it at the brook. There was a well for drinking water closer to the house. After she swept and scrubbed the floor, she scrubbed the top of the table under the window. On it was a jar with wilted flowers. Taffy walked back through the pine grove to the edge of a meadow where wildflowers grew. "Susie likes fresh flowers on the table for Sunday", she said half aloud, as she gathered the flowers.

After she put the flowers into fresh water on the table, the room really did look spruced up for Sunday, their special day. Taffy's mother's handmade quilt was already smoothed out across the bed in the corner. It had been pieced together with scraps of printed cotton. It was what made the plain room look like a cheery home. There was only one bed, but it was wide enough for both of them. Taffy knew they were fortunate, indeed, to have a real bed. For at slave row, the beds were only planks set off the floor on old crates. And most of the children slept on straw-filled mats on the hard-packed dirt floor.

Now she was supposed to take a nap, Taffy remembered. What she wanted to do was run back to the kitchen to see if the cake was frosted. But Susie had been so serious all day long; she did not dare go against her orders. Taffy stretched out on the quilt, but she knew she would not be able to fall asleep.

"I wonder what Susie meant about us being up late tonight. Maybe she does want to go the swamp dance, and I'll be up late waiting for her with Aunt Crissy."

Once again, Taffy's mind started going around in sad circles, thinking about her missing parents and wondering why they had left her behind. Not even Susie had explained it to her. One night, she had gone to bed in the cabin behind this one. But when she'd woken up, she had been all alone. Susie had come to get her, but she hadn't explained anything except to say Taffy's parents had to go away to work for a while.

"But they had not even said good-bye." Her mother had always explained so many things to her. "Don't do this, Taffy, because" and, "We're going to do this now, because".

Now there was no "because" at all. Susie had just kept saying, "Hush, hush, don't fret. It won't be too long."

But every day, it was longer and longer. A late afternoon breeze suddenly stirred through the pine grove and came in through the window and open door. Taffy began to relax a little, and her mind turned from fretting to daydreaming. She pretended that tomorrow, when she awoke, it would be just like Sunday's used to be. *Before she went to bed on Saturday nights, Mama would give me a real bath in a wood tub with pails of warm water carried from the indoor kitchen stove. It felt so good to crawl into my own little bed after that," she sighed.*

In the morning, she would dress in a printed cotton dress, and her mother would braid a ribbon through her thick, curly, clean hair. After she and her parents were dressed as special as they could manage, they would meet up with Susie and walk to the church meeting down on the deep woodland.

Finally, they would come to an old cabin the slaves from several plantations used as their own church. A slave who knew Bible verses was the minister. Here, they could listen and sing their favorite hymns and spirituals just as loud as they pleased, while they clapped their hands and swayed to the rhythms they created. Afterward, everyone gossiped, sharing news about the plantations. There were other slave children for Taffy to run and play with. It was such a pleasant memory Taffy relaxed enough to fall asleep for awhile.

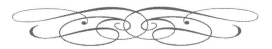

Chapter Two

The Birthday Wish

Susie's long day in the kitchen did not end until Master Davis and his sister, Miss Sarah, had been served their evening meal. On this particular night, it seemed to Susie they lingered an extra long time over their coffee and spice cake dessert. Miss Sarah even requested a second serving of cake, which she nibbled ever so slowly.

Finally, they left the dining room. Master Davis went to the library, and Miss Sarah took an evening walk. Susie cleared the table and washed and put away the last dishes. While waiting for them to finish, she had already packed a basket with leftovers for her and Taffy's own meal, later, in their cabin. There was always the choice of eating down at slave row and being able to laugh and gossip with the other slaves or staying by themselves and having better food to eat. Lately, however, Susie was less inclined to be sociable. She was not certain who she could trust.

Susie listened at the kitchen door for a moment, but she heard no footsteps heading for the kitchen. Sometimes Miss Sarah came in with special requests for the next day's dessert. Satisfied, Susie went to the pantry room and took out the sealed envelope. She tucked it into the basket that held their supper and the tiny chocolate cake.

As she entered their cabin, Susie called out, "Here's frosting to lick, Taffy. You can have it right now before supper if you like."

Just as she had hoped, Taffy was easily distracted by the cup of frosting. Susie unpacked their supper and set it out on the table. Then she quickly shoved the basket under the table.

Before they sat down to eat, Susie took off her starched white pinafore and her printed cotton dress and hung them carefully on a hook in the corner. She put on a gray homespun dress similar to the one Taffy was also now wearing.

Susie looked around the room with pleasure—everything in its place, flowers on the table, a few dishes and discarded silverware from the main house set neatly on a wall shelf made by Taffy's father, and a pair of printed curtains strung across the little window. Taffy's mother had made these as well as the bright quilt on the bed. The wood floor was still slightly damp from being scrubbed and smelled of pine and strong soap. Having a wood floor was not so much for their personal comfort as it was to help house slaves maintain cleanliness.

"You made everything look nice, Taffy. Now we can relax and look forward to tomorrow, going down to church meeting and seeing everybody. I've left muffins for breakfast, and I don't have to be back in the kitchen till noontime. But right now, until then, I'm home in our little private place." Susie sighed and plopped down on one of two small benches, also made by Taffy's father. She had never minded living alone in this tiny cabin, because Taffy's family was right behind her, and Della had helped her fix it up in such a cozy way.

"I guess you'll be walkin' and talkin' with Sam tomorrow morning," Taffy said while they were eating.

Saying that reminded her of what Aunt Crissy had said. "Susie, I saw Aunt Crissy today, and she said you should start goin' to the swamp dances again. She said they have new musicians from a plantation on the other side of the river, and one of them has a real ban-banjo. I can stay with Aunt Crissy while you go."

"I'll go again some Saturday night, Taffy, I will. Sam always asks me on Sunday mornings why I don't show up. But not tonight. I don't feel like goin' down there tonight. I'd rather be right here with you. I tell you what. Sometime this summer, we'll both go! Sometimes there's a few children there, just sittin' and watchin' the dancing. I'll fix up your hair with a ribbon like we do Sundays, and I'll see you get a piece of cake."

"Oh, the chocolate cake we made—did it come out good?"

"My, yes; it's in the pantry, all ready for tomorrow's party."

"Can we sneak a piece after the party's over?"

"We'll see what's left. Miss Sarah will know, and she's bound to want a piece for dessert on Monday." "What about the spice cake? Did you bring some home for us? "No, I didn't dare. Miss Sarah dawdled over two big pieces. I thought she'd never finish. That's why I'm so late. She might ask if there's enough to serve at the party. I guess you have a sweet tooth tonight, Taffy!"

After they finished their meal, it was still light. Usually, they would have gone for a walk through the pine grove, meeting up with other slaves to chat as they walked.

Susie said she was too tired tonight. "I'm goin' to pull the curtains across the window so we'll be private but still have that cool breeze comin' through." Then she shut and locked the door.

"Now, Taffy, I want you to sit down at the table again." In hushed tones, she continued. "Taffy, there's something different about today—something special. I want you to do exactly what I say. Close your eyes tight shut, and keep them that way till I tell you to open them. And no peeking!"

Susie poked the tiny candle into the thick frosting, and then she lit it and placed the cake in front of Taffy. "Now, open your eyes!"

Taffy's eyes opened wide in amazement.

"A cake for me?"

"Yes, just for you, because today you are ten years old, and that's a very special birthday."

Taffy sat staring at the candlelit cake, speechless for once.

Susie continued, "First you have to make a birthday wish—a special, secret wish that you tell to nobody or it won't come true, and then you blow out the candle. I wish it was ten candles, but I didn't dare take that many."

Taffy was still silent, her big brown eyes blinking. Finally, she decided on her special, secret wish, and then she blew out the candle. They finished every crumb of the cake before Taffy spoke again. "Susie, how do you know it's my tenth birthday today?"

"Because your mama told me just before she went away. She wanted you to have a birthday cake if I could manage to do it."

Taffy sat quietly, thinking again. "But Susie, how did you know my birthday is really today and not some other day?"

"Well, there's a special reason why I know. But that's part of a special secret. Now that you are a big girl of ten, I think I can tell you. I think your mama would want me to. It was the very last thing she said to me. She said, "Wait till Taffy seems old enough to keep a secret. Be sure; and then you can tell her." Are you a big enough girl to keep a secret? I think you are. What do you think?"

"Oh, yes, yes, I can keep a secret. I know you think I talk too much sometimes and ask too many questions, but I only do that with you, nobody else."

"Well, your very life, and mine, too, depends on your being able to keep this secret, and that's why your mama wanted me to be sure."

Taffy was so excited about the idea of a special secret and that it came from her mother, that she didn't think to question exactly *when* Susie had last talked to her mother.

"Part of the secret is something I have to show you," continued Susie. She put a finger to her lips, and then she peeked out through the closed curtain just to be sure no one was snooping around.

"Big ears can have big mouths, too" she said and went to the door and listened for a moment.

Susie went over to the bed and got down on her knees and reached underneath. She uncovered a loose board in the floor and pulled out a small box. She opened the box and carefully took out a worn, leather-bound book. She placed it on the table and smoothed the cover as if it was something very precious. There was still something else in the box—a pencil and a few sheets of paper. Taffy looked at these things with more wide-eyed wonder than she had shown over the surprise birthday cake. Slowly, she reached out gingerly touching the book. In a whisper she asked, Susie, can you read this book? "Yes, Taffy, I can read it. That is the secret. I can read! Your very own mama and daddy taught me to read. They secretly taught other slaves how to read, too. Then, finally, some blabbermouth told on them. We don't know who. And that is why they were both punished by being sent away from you." Susie still could not bring herself to say the awful word, *sold*. But she gulped and narrowed her eyes.

"Slave owners never want slaves around who can read and write. They know their whole way of life depends on keeping slaves ignorant."

"Was that why they didn't say good-bye? Was that part of the punishment?"

"Not exactly. Not even Master and Mrs. Davis wanted you to be punished, too, is my guess. She looked away as if searching for an answer, then saying," so they made them leave in the middle of the night. Slaves have to do as they are told to do and go where they are told to go. Your parents had no choice in the matter at all. That's the only thing you must remember about this—they never would have left you if they had any choice."

"I don't want to be a slave anymore, Susie."

Susie began to fear that, after all, telling Taffy anything about these things might have been a mistake. She tried to divert her attention back to the leather-bound book on the table. "Taffy, this book belonged to your mother. She learned to read this book of beautiful poems when she was a child like you. She's kept it all this time. She would want you to have it. And that's the best part of the secret—I am now going to teach you how to read!"

Taffy immediately perked up at that part of the secret. "I'm really going to be able to read?"

"Oh, yes, indeed. You'll see how fast it goes when you really want to do something special, even when it has to be done in secret. And, Taffy, this book really is yours, you know. See, here in the front, your mother and father have both signed their names, and under that, they wrote your name and also the date of your birth."

Taffy sat there, silent with new wonder. Her own mama and daddy could both read and write!

"Will I be able to write, too?"

"Yes, you will. They both go together. See this pencil and paper in the box? That's what we will use, and Sam can get me more paper. In fact, I think he already has."

Susie reached under the table and took the long envelope out of the basket. She carefully slit it open and took out four sheets of folded white paper—crisp and new, ready to be written on.

There was another small yellow sheet, and on it was written with a pencil, "Happy Birthday, Taffy." Under that, it said "Sam." Susie read it to Taffy.

"You see. Sam can read and write, too, and it was your father who taught him how."

Taffy looked worried again. "Will Sam be punished and sent away, too?"

"I'm afraid so, if he is found out. That's what I mean about it being an important secret. Remember, you cannot tell a living soul about any of this—no one at all. Susie held Taffy's gaze for a moment before saying," Do you understand why? If we are ever found out, we will be sold away from here, and the next owners might not treat us as well as they do here. At least these owners do not whip their field slaves. We could be sold away separately, too, and never see each other ever again. And we might have to work in the cotton fields instead of in a nice kitchen, and our hands will get all bloody and sore—"

At that point, Taffy had heard enough, and she threw herself into Susie's arms. "No, no, I don't want to lose you, ever," she cried. "I want to stay with you forever, Susie." Her shoulders heaved, and she managed to gulp out between sobs, "I promise—I'll never tell a single soul our secret, never, never, never." Taffy could not stop crying. All the fears and sorrows about losing her parents engulfed her, and she hung onto Susie tightly and went on sobbing.

Susie felt like crying, too. It was supposed to be a happy day for poor little Taffy, and here she was, causing her more grief than pleasure. Susie rocked the little girl in her arms until Taffy calmed down.

"There, there, Taffy. I didn't mean to upset you like that. We will all be very careful. Sam, you, and me—our secret will be safe. I don't intend to teach anyone else to read, only you. I'm too afraid to teach anyone else. Sam says he won't either. You must not be so frightened that you don't want to learn to read at all. I never meant to scare you that much."

"I do want to learn to read, Susie! You don't even know how much I want to learn to read." As Taffy said that, she suddenly clapped her hand over her mouth.

"What's the matter?"

"Nothin' nothin'. Can we start the lessons right now, tonight, before it gets too dark? Can we read and write by candlelight when it's dark?"

"Um, if we're careful not to keep it burning too late we can. Our cabin can't be seen by the main house or by slave row, so we won't be noticed unless someone is walking in the pine grove. Here we go. Let's get started."

Taffy and Susie both sat close together on one side of the table, and Susie opened up the book and read the first poem in hushed tones. She pointed out some of the letters and showed Taffy how to copy them on paper. The letters she had her copy were "T A F F Y."

"There see, already you have learned to spell your own name!"

Taffy was so excited now about learning to read and write she wanted to stay up all night long. But Susie said it would look strange if anyone should just happen to notice the candle burning too late, so they carefully put the book, paper, and pencil back in the box and returned it to its secret hiding place under the bed.

After they were both under the quilt and Susie had kissed her goodnight, Taffy lay there, wide awake, thinking about all that had happened on her tenth birthday—surprise gifts and important secrets that had to be kept. Did all secrets really have to be kept? she wondered. Susie had said a birthday wish was a secret, too, or it wouldn't come true. Well, her own secret birthday wish had already started to come true, and she wanted to tell Susie what it was. It was more than she could bear not to tell Susie about her birthday wish.

"Susie, are you still awake? I want to tell you my birthday wish."

"You can't even keep a secret over one night? You must learn how to keep secrets. Our lives depend on your being able to do this."

"But it won't be dangerous to tell you my birthday wish."

"No, but you must practice what it means to keep a secret, no matter how much you want to tell it. Go to sleep, now."

Taffy still could not fall asleep. It was hard to believe, that her birthday wish had come true in a matter of minutes! It just seemed that Susie should know, since Susie herself had brought about the answer to her secret wish. For Taffy had wished to learn how to read!

It seemed to her that she had been secretly wishing she could read for a long time. In the house, she had seen books on shelves and books on tables—beautiful books with pictures of flowers and birds and animals. Sometimes Susie and her mama had let her use the feather duster in the parlor, dining room, and library, and that is where she had seen the books. If only she could read them! That thought had come to her this past year, but she had never thought of speaking about it to anyone.

To think that all this time her own mama and daddy could read. She had never seen them reading a book. They had kept this a secret from her, too. What had Susie said? She had to be old enough to keep a secret before they could tell her. But now they were punished and gone, before they could teach her themselves. But they had already taught Susie to read! And now Susie was going to teach her! And the book they were using belonged to her own mama. It even had her own name in it, and so now it was her very own book!

Taffy said the letters of her name over and over until she finally fell asleep. She dreamed she was standing in front of a huge, chocolate cake, taller than she was. The cake had white frosting, and there were birds flying over the cake holding tiny cups of melted chocolate in their feet. The cups were tipped, and the chocolate dribbled down onto the top of the cake, spelling out the letters "T A F F Y."

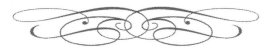

Chapter Three

Daisy's Tenth Birthday

The morning of her tenth birthday, Daisy awoke very early. The songbirds were back from the south, singing in the elm trees outside her open window. Down the hall, her mother was still asleep. Her father always left very early to open up his soap and candle-making factory, and Saturday was no exception.

Her sixteen-year-old sister, Cornelia, was asleep, and Frank, her eighteen-year-old brother, was home from college and would probably be the last one to get up. There were two still older, a brother who was working in another state, and Alice, the oldest girl, who was now married and lived too far away to visit home often. Daisy was definitely the baby of this family, and sometimes she thought they would never get over thinking that.

She dressed quickly in her Saturday clothes and tiptoed down the back stairway to the kitchen. Aunt Mary, their cook who came by the day, had not arrived yet, so Daisy went outdoors to wait for her. She sat down in the rope swing under the elm tree by the side of the house. The trees were now in their late springtime green, and red and yellow tulips lined the brick walkway up to the front door of the white Colonial-style house.

Aunt Mary always made the "birthday child" a special breakfast. Daisy could hardly wait for her personal order of hush puppies, bacon, and hot chocolate! Aunt Mary wasn't really their aunt; it was just that she had been cooking for the family for so long that they had taken to affectionately calling her "Aunt."

Mary had been born a slave down South, but she had been freed many years ago. She still carried her legal freedom papers with her every day, as she said, "Just in case some Southern agents come snooping around, looking to find runaway slaves and think I'm one of them."

She liked to tell her own story—how her long-ago slave master had been saved from drowning by one of his own slaves, and it had given him a change of heart about owning slaves. He had given up growing cotton and freed all his slaves. Then Mary would tell about the struggle of finding their way up North, using the secret Underground Railroad. Even with their freedom papers, she and the other runaways were terrified of being captured and forced back into slavery on another plantation. All along the way, there were secret homes of white people and also of free black people who hid and fed them and gave them directions to the next "station" on the "railroad." Once Mary found herself in New England, she was moderately safe, since that was now over ten years ago, before the Fugitive Slave Act was made the law in the United States, in 1850. After that was enacted, the slaves had to escape all the way to Canada to hope to be free from slavery.

Daisy's home was a secret station on the railroad. Even though almost all people in New England were against slavery, the plight of the slaves there was dangerous. That law of the United States Constitution stated, "It is illegal to steal or keep another man's property." Southern slave owners considered their slaves to be just that—"legal property" that could be bought and sold as they wished. It was no different to them than selling a horse. In fact, when they sold a slave, the new buyer often would examine the slave in the same way one would examine a horse, peering in his or her mouth to examine the teeth and so on.

The Southern agents who scouted around the Northern states to track down runaway slaves took advantage of this law by insisting that the local sheriff accompany them to legally search a house under suspicion. They were not allowed to search in the middle of the night, but during the day, they might turn up at any unexpected time. No slaves had ever been found at Daisy's home, but it was widely rumored among the agents that this peaceful-looking Colonial house was indeed a secret stop on the Underground Railroad.

"Someday we'll catch someone there," the agents vowed among themselves.

There was money to be made in returning runaways to their owners in the south—especially if the slave worked in the house and had special skills, such as cooking.

Daisy was, so far, unaware of this secret about her own home. Sometimes strangers did walk through the house with either her mother or father right behind them, along with the accompanying sheriff, but she did not know why. Once, when she had been sick in bed with the chicken pox, they had opened the door to her own bedroom, but her mother had not allowed them to enter. Daisy had never seen any runaways, either, as they crept in silently in the dark of late night, and were safely hidden in a secret hiding place during the day.

There she came, at last. As Aunt Mary made her way along the path to the kitchen door, she carried a bulging shopping bag in her hand. Daisy ran to her for a hug.

"Aunt Mary, it's my tenth birthday today Do. you remember that?" Daisy looked up, her eyes soft and gleaming.

"Is that a fact, child? Why, no, I didn't know that!"

Daisy's mouth opened wide in dismay.

Aunt Mary chuckled and said, "Don't you know when I'm a-teasin' you? What do you suppose I'm lugging in this bag?

"I've got everything extra to make your special birthday breakfast. Come on. Let's get started before everyone else gets up hungry. This breakfast is only for you, my honey lamb." She tousled Daisy's hair lovingly. Daisy was Aunt Mary's special child of the family, for she had arrived just before Daisy was born, the last baby of this family. Instead of sending Mary on to the next stop on the Underground Railroad, the family to Mary's pleasure decided to keep her with them. Since she had legal papers, it was safe in the North for her to be seen in public. Eventually, Mary had married and moved to live in her own house and came to cook by the day. She'd never had any children of her own.

Aunt Mary bustled around the kitchen and soon had the steaming hush puppies and bacon strips to serve to Daisy. Kissing the top of her head, she said, "I can't believe my honey lamb is ten years old today. How fast the years go by!"

It was going to be a long day for Daisy. The family tradition was to celebrate birthdays in the evening when their father arrived home from the factory. Being a Saturday, Daisy hoped he would arrive earlier.

In the afternoon, however, her sister, Cornelia, came to the rescue. "Come on, Daisy, I'll take you downtown for an ice-cream soda at Mr. Bailey's drug store."

As they passed Mr. Drake's General Clothing Store, Daisy stopped in front of the display window.

"Cornelia, can we just go inside and look around?"

From inside, Daisy was able to touch what had caught her attention outside—a beaded bag. The brilliantly colored beads were glassy and ice-cold to her touch. They were strung tightly together to form a starburst design. Daisy's best friend had a bag similar to it. Daisy wished now that she had one, too, but it was too late to add that to her birthday list. The gifts for tonight's party were probably already wrapped and hidden away in a closet.

After the girls had cleared the evening meal from the dining room table by the girls, Aunt Mary carried in a chocolate layer cake with fudge frosting. Ten candles circled the big cake, with one to grow on in the middle. The candles were already lit, and everyone said, "Quick, Daisy, make a wish before they all burn down into the frosting!"

Daisy shut her eyes and quickly wished she could have the beaded bag in the window. Then she took a deep breath and blew out every single candle, all by herself.

After the gifts were opened, her father took his youngest child on his knee, asking, "Well, did you receive everything you wanted for your birthday?"

"Almost everything, Father."

"Hmmm, What else could a ten-year-old want, I wonder?"

Daisy didn't give away her secret birthday wish, but she did admit she would love to have the beaded bag in the window.

Her father raised his brows, looking earnestly at Daisy. He thought a few moments and answered, "Daisy, you are a fortunate little girl. You have everything you need and everything you want. Some children are not so lucky in this world. I think you are now old enough to realize that. You know, some poor children have to work long hours in a factory. I would never hire children. In fact, I am fighting right now for child labor laws to protect children from such unfair abuse. But everyone, no matter how fortunate, should learn the value of earned money. How would you like to come down to the candle factory on Saturday mornings and work at some easy task to earn the money for your beaded bag all by yourself?"

"Can I really do that? Oh, yes, I want to, Father."

Daisy was excited about this idea. She had visited the candle-making factory and thought it was an exciting place, with all the hand dipped candles hanging on wooden racks. Besides white candles, there were many beautiful shades of rose, red, blue, green, and yellow.

A sudden knock sounded on the kitchen door. Aunt Mary, now ready to go home to have her supper with her husband, went to the door. She called Mr. Jackson into the kitchen to speak to the man at the door.

"We just got word there's a small group coming through on the railroad late tonight. We can take three, can you take the other three here?" he said in muffled tones.

Mr. Jackson said yes, and they spoke in low tones for a few more minutes, and then the man left. Mrs. Jackson hurried out to the kitchen and talked to her husband and Aunt Mary who was putting on her coat to leave.

All of a sudden, the birthday party was over. Cornelia and Frank were sent upstairs to get quilts. Aunt Mary put her apron back on and began to light the stove again.

For a while, Daisy was completely forgotten. When her mother next noticed her, she told her to hurry right up to bed.

"What is going on? Why is Aunt Mary peeling all those sweet potatoes and apples now?"

Her father spoke to her mother in whispers, "I don't think we can keep this a secret from Daisy any longer. She's ten years old today. She's old enough to be able to keep a secret herself now, and you know she won't get to sleep. She'll probably sneak down the back stairs later and see for herself what is going on here, so better she understand it."

Her father sat Daisy on his knee again, saying, "Daisy I'm going to tell you a special secret about this family and this house. You must promise never to tell anyone—not a living soul. Do you understand? People's lives will depend on you being able to keep this secret."

Daisy nodded her head solemnly. Secrets, so far, were fun, but this seemed very serious.

Her father went on to explain to her, as simply as he could, the meaning of the Underground Railroad. Then he told her that their very own house was a secret stop and that they had a special hiding place in this house that no one would ever be able to find.

"Come with me, Daisy, and I'll show you the secret hiding place."

Daisy followed her father down the stairs to the cellar. The cellar had a hard-packed dirt floor. But in one section, boards had been laid to make a rough floor. There were shelves with preserve jars lined up on them, and there were old chairs in need of repairs, hanging from hooks in the ceiling. A worn rug covered part of the wood floor. On top of the rug was an old sea chest with dusty boxes piled on top, plus an old oil lamp in need of repairs. Mr. Jackson took hold of the rope handle on the end of the chest and pulled hard, inching it out to the middle. Then he rolled back part of the rug and lifted up a square-shaped section of the floorboards. Under that was a round, cement cover. He lifted that next, and then they could peer down into a deep, black hole. It was lined with fieldstones set into cement. It made Daisy shiver just to look down into it.

"Is it an old well, Father?" she asked.

"It's really a root cellar, but it's not used anymore for storing anything. There's never any water in the bottom of it. Look down, Daisy. You see there are rungs to climb down to the bottom. Four people are the limit it will hide, with two standing on the bottom and two hanging on above to the rungs."

As he covered it over again, he went on to tell her, "People just like Aunt Mary are going to come here late tonight, exhausted from walking through the back woods with nothing to eat for maybe a day and a night. We will give them food and rest down here in the cellar. But if any Southern agents show up in the daytime when they are sleeping down here, we have to quickly hide them in the hole." Then he folded back the rug, pulled the other side of the chest back over the place where the hole was, and smoothed out the rug.

Late that night, tucked under her puffy quilt, Daisy lay wide awake with excitement, thinking about her happy birthday and its surprise ending. Except for that, the family celebration had been the same as all the other birthdays.

But not quite, she thought to herself, for there was something that felt different about this one. Somehow, she felt older and more grown-up! She had been the baby of this family for so long. All of a sudden, she felt just a little more on equal footing with her almost grown-up sister, Cornelia, and her very grown-up brother, Frank, who now lived in a college dormitory and only came home some weekends and vacations.

She was going to earn the money to buy the beaded bag! She was going to work in her father's factory! Cornelia had never done that! Only the boys worked there on vacation times, helping with packing and shipping.

And she was now included in the family's deep, dark secret—that they helped people like Aunt Mary escape from slavery. She blinked her eyes, yawned, and tried very hard to stay awake until she heard some noises from downstairs. Then she intended to sneak down the back stairs and peek into the kitchen and see what was going on.

But she never heard any suspicious sounds at all because she fell fast asleep before the three runaway slaves crept silently into the kitchen, were given some food, and then followed Mr. Jackson and Frank down the cellar stairs in the middle of the night.

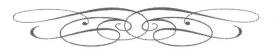

Chapter Four

Taffy's Secret

Soon after Taffy's birthday, the long, hot days of the Southern summer set in, but Taffy's naturally high-spirited nature was returning, and not even the steamy weather could dampen it. She no longer cried in bed at night, begging Susie to say that her parents would be back soon. Still, the hardest part for her to understand was that they had not said good-bye to her.

Gradually, however, Taffy was beginning to grasp the terrible truth of why her parents had left her, and why they had not even said good-bye.

The truth was that they had no choice—no control over what happened to their own lives. Worst of all, they had no choice, no control over what became of their own little girl.

This terrible truth could be explained in one simple word—*sold*. Her parents had been sold, in the same way people sold off horses, cows, and pigs. They had been forced against their will to leave in the middle of the night, never to see their child again. Neither would they have the comfort of each other, as they were sold to separate masters.

To comfort her, Susie had tried to reassure her that someday her family might be reunited again. At first, Taffy had clung to this hope, but now she was resigned that this vague "someday" was too far away to constantly yearn for.

Following her tenth birthday, two activities filled her mind and helped ease the pain of losing her parents.

First, now that she was learning more about cooking every day, the long hours in the kitchen passed more quickly. Before, she had only run errands—out to the smokehouse and the outside cooking shed, to the well for fresh water, to the vegetable garden. But now she was making special dishes from start to finish and could take pride in her finished accomplishments.

"What am I going to make today, Susie?"

"Today, I'll show you how to make the best chicken salad in the whole county. It's the same way your mother made it. Then we'll make the lightest buttermilk biscuits in the entire South, and for dessert, we'll make a peach cobbler topped with whipped cream. That should please Master Davis and Miss Sarah tonight and help them forget how hot it is."

Mrs. Davis and the two children were settled in for the summer at their lodge high in the North Carolina mountains. Along with them to take care of all their meals was Big Sally, the elderly head cook. Also with them were three women slaves who were accustomed to washing and cleaning chores for the "big house," plus an elderly male slave to do outside chores and drive the horse and buggy. Mrs. Davis had fragile health, and she feared for her children's health as well during the hot weather in the cotton-growing lowlands. Fatal diseases were sometimes of epidemic proportions and could sweep through an entire county of plantations, killing slaves and masters equally.

There was another, more fascinating reason why the long days passed more quickly for Taffy this summer. Her birthday wish kept her mind alert. Even as she went about the daily work of helping Susie cook and maintain a clean and organized kitchen, her mind was focused on learning to read and write. She eagerly looked forward to the twilight hours, secure in their own cabin, when she could sit by the window with her mother's book and pencil and paper. Every evening, Susie helped her to spell out and write down a few more words. Every night, the list of words was growing, and she was able to read more and more at a glance. This was so exciting to Taffy; she would sit there until the fading light made her squint and hold the book closer to her eyes.

That the book had belonged to her own mother made it all the more special to Taffy.

"Susie, I wonder who taught my mother to read. Do you know?"

"We never had much chance to just talk together, alone, but I sort of remember that she did say she had learned to read when she was only a child. Yes, she said it was always easier to learn the younger you was. That's why she kept pushing me to spend all the time I could, in learnin' as fast as I could.

"Taffy, the other slaves will wonder what's the matter with you, staying inside these hot nights. Put the book away, now, and go join the group for a walk. I can hear them now out in the pine grove passin' by. I'll follow along in a little while with the next group I hear going by out there. We don't want no folks pokin' around here being curious about us. Remember, we can never be sure who we can trust. Somebody had to have tattled to Master Davis about your parents' knowin' how to read and secretly teaching others to read as well. You and I have no way of knowin' who that could be—if it's somebody right here on this plantation or someone from another place."

Sam was worried, too. The next time he went to town for his own master, he also had supplies to deliver at the Davis plantation, so he pulled up by the hitching post near the kitchen entrance. Taffy was on an errand out to the smokehouse, so he had a chance to talk to Susie alone. Sam sat down at the kitchen table and slowly ate a big piece of pecan pie Susie placed before him.

"I don't like it. There's lotsa rumors going round now about slaves secretly learnin' to read. You better have a safe hiding place for your book and writing papers. There's more in the newspapers, too, about the North goin' to war 'gainst the south over slavery. There's a lot of tension, and who knows what that means for us?

"The paper I picked up in town this morning for Master Shelton says some white masters are thinkin' of selling off some of their slaves soon, just in case there's really a war comin'. Far as I can tell, they are scared that, if slavery is abolished, they will be stuck with all their slaves as free American citizens they can no longer sell. In fact, they will have to pay us wages, just like white folks, if that ever happens.

'Susie, this is mighty fine pie. You would be gettin' some fancy wages up North as a cook if you was free, do you know that?"

Susie didn't answer, and Sam continued talking while he ate smaller bites to make it last longer. "Susie, I think you better start thinkin' about escaping to the North by the Underground Railroad. I'm helping a group make plans right now. There's four who say they are ready to be "runaways." I'm thinkin' I should go myself this time, but I don't want to leave you behind; you know that."

Susie had a strong feeling that Sam, who was maybe four years older than she was, really cared for her as a girlfriend, not just for her good treats. "I'm not sure yet, Sam. I got it pretty nice right here now. But of course, when Big Sally comes back, I won't be the one in charge of this kitchen then. If I do try to leave, I want Taffy with me. I'm not ever goin' without her, less I'm dragged away."

"I'm afraid she's too little to keep up. She'll hold the rest of us back, and that's very dangerous. Until we get out of the lowland plantation country, we have to walk almost without stopping. Once we hit the mountains, search parties usually give up trying."

"Well then, I'll stay here and take my chances."

"We don't have to decide yet, Susie. Just be thinking about the idea. Meanwhile, you should start coming to the swamp dances again. That way, I can talk to you easily without any others being suspicious. Even on Sunday mornings, I think we have to be very careful from now on. We both can read, and we don't know who might know that. There's danger in our going off alone to talk in the daylight—never know who's watching and getting suspicious."

"All right, I'll come to the dance this Saturday night. I promised Taffy I'd bring her along. I hate leaving her alone, and if I leave her with someone down at slave row, I'm afraid they might ask her too many questions. It's hard for a child as friendly as Taffy to hold back when someone is being nice to her, but we don't know who can be trusted."

Sam finished the last crumbs of the pie as he gazed at Susie, now mixing a batter in a bowl by the window. *How pretty she is now*, he thought, *from the skinny kid she was when she first came, shy and scared, her clothes and hair a mess.* The sun shadows from the window behind her and the apron tied tight around her waist revealed her now curvy shape and pretty, dark, curly hair, similar to the older girls who came to the swamp dances.

Sam was now a tall, thin, but sturdy young man, maybe nineteen, or even twenty—he didn't know for sure—but he knew the grown-up girls there liked to have his attention. But he never wanted to lose Susie, and he knew that's what leaving as a runaway without her would mean. *I will just have to wait awhile longer.*

Taffy returned to the kitchen with a thick slice of smoked ham and sweet potatoes in her basket as Sam was just scooping up the last bite of pie.

"Well, I better be heading on, or they'll wonder what took me so long to do the errands in town. Come on, Taffy, you can ride down to the end of the driveway with me."

Taffy eagerly climbed up onto the driver's seat beside Sam.

"Susie promised me she'd come down to the swamp dance this Saturday night, and she says you're comin' with her. What do you think of that?" said Sam, jerking the reins.

"She is? I am? She hasn't been in a long time. Aunt Crissy said she should start to go again, that they have more musicians than ever before."

"That's right. They have two fiddles now and even a banjo, as well as all the homemade drum skins, sticks, and other things they always had. It's somethin' to see and hear, all right. Now, I want you to promise me that you make sure Susie doesn't back out. She won't go without you, so don't you back out, Taffy. You do want to go, don't you?"

"Oh yes, Sam, I can hardly wait."

"Fine. It's a long walk through the back woods—several miles. Are you a good, strong walker?"

"Oh, yes we go for walks every night almost." Taffy grinned with pride.

"That's good. I'm glad to hear that. All right, Taffy, this is where you get off. I'll be alookin' for you both on Saturday night, all dressed up smart as you can, you hear?" Taffy ran all the way back to the kitchen.

"Am I really goin' with you to the swamp dance?"

"That's right, honey child. Didn't I promise you I'd take you along?"

Finally, Saturday night came. The kitchen was all organized for Sunday breakfast.

"Can we go home, now, Susie, and get ready for the dance?"

"Wait, Taffy. I'm thinkin' 'bout somethin'. The stove is still hot. We can heat water quickly here … Yes … This is what we'll do. There's no one around at all. Instead of carrying pails of hot water back to the cabin, we'll have a bath right here in the pantry, where we can shut the door. You can be first."

Susie fetched a wooden tub that was not big enough to sit in but was big enough to stand in and scrub down with a sponge bath. Since they did not have to carry water back to their cabin, they enjoyed washing themselves with really hot water. When Taffy was sponged and toweled dry, it was Susie's turn.

"Now you just stay outside the pantry door and guard me," she said.

Then they put their clothes back on and went home. "Now, we'll change into our dancing clothes." Susie laughed. Taffy put on a blue, cotton, printed dress, and Susie a yellow, printed dress. These were the clothes they wore on Sunday mornings to go to the church meetings, and it was as dressed up as they could ever be.

"Oh, there's one more thing we can do," Susie said, reaching under the bed for a small wooden box that had been Taffy's mother's. Inside was an assortment of ribbons. Susie selected a blue ribbon for Taffy and a yellow one for herself, to braid through their clean, dark, curly hair. Now they were ready to go to the dance!

The woods were already cooled with twilight shadows when Susie and Taffy started out through the pine grove, along with other slaves from the Davis plantation. They crossed the wide meadow and entered the deeper woods, where they were joined by another group, coming in from the other direction. It was dark when they finally were close enough to the old swamp cabin to catch the first strains of music wafting through the trees. The musicians were already in fine form. The pounding beat of assorted handmade drums backed up the dancing melodies from the fiddles and the banjo. Even at a distance, the sound was too full of lively rhythm to resist. The slaves at the front of the group began dancing and singing along the path as the music grew louder. When they reached the swamp cabin, they were all singing a familiar song together:

Rabbit in the briar patch,
Squirrel in the tree,
Wish I could go hunting
But I ain't free.
Rooster's in the henhouse,
Hen's in the patch.

Love to go shooting,

But I ain't free.

Taffy knew that one well. Her daddy had often sung it as he worked in the carpentry shed.

In the dark, the shabby old building looked festive with the door open and two windows that glowed with the light from two oil lamps hung from the ceiling. There was room inside for about seventy-five people to dance in the middle and sit around the edges on assorted planks across crates. The floor was only dirt, but it was packed hard from the constant slapping down of feet.

By now, even the usually serious Sam was in a dancing mood. "Come on, Susie, let's start to set the floor!"

"Wait, Sam, I have to take off my shoes. They're too heavy for dancing!"

The other slaves were out there dancing in their bare feet, too, slapping down hard at every step.

Susie put her shoes over in the corner and found a place for Taffy to sit, right over them. Two young boys, about twelve years old, were already sitting in the same part of the room with a good view of the musicians. One boy had a makeshift drum made from a piece of tree trunk hollowed out and a piece of sheep's skin stretched over it, attached with horsehairs. The other boy had a mule's jawbone that he beat on with a piece of iron. Their rhythm was in perfect beat with the three drums they watched.

Taffy thought of the wooden flute like instruments her daddy had carved and given away and wished she had one to blow through. Instead, she started tapping her feet and clapping her hands to the beat of the drums.

There were two small drums out there, but one was a big barrel with a piece of hide stretched across one end. The musician sat astride the barrel to play on the drum head with two sticks. The fiddler with the almost white hair seemed to be in charge of calling out the different dancers, one at a time, dancing inside a circle. After a while, this fiddler came out into the center and drew a better circle on the floor with a piece of charred corncob. Then he called up one after the other to come and dance inside the circle. Everyone crowded close around and clapped to the music, as the individual dancers competed to be the one with the most complicated steps. But if just one step touched the edge of the circle, the dancer was out of the contest. The contest was finally down to two dancers, a young man and a plump, older woman. Everyone was crowding around so closely Taffy could no longer see who was in the circle, so she squeezed herself through the crowd up to the edge. It was Aunt Crissy who was winning the dance! Taffy had never seen Aunt Crissy dance before, and she began to clap and stamp her feet and holler out cheers just as loudly as everyone else.

Aunt Crissy was the winner!

Then someone called out, "Crissy, set the floor with water!"

Aunt Crissy was wearing a wreath on her head with two big bows on each side. Someone brought a tin cup filled with water and handed it to Crissy. Carefully, she set it smack in the middle of the top of her head. Then she started dancing in the circle again, stepping high and fancy but ever so smoothly that not one drop of water spilled onto the floor.

Then some others tried it, but no one lasted more than a few seconds before the water was sloshing out and the cup falling onto the floor.

"Aunt Crissy is the winner!" they all shouted with glee. "Crissy wins the cake!"

Someone escorted Crissy over to a bench, and another slave appeared in front of her and handed her a large round cake while everyone clapped again.

After that, the fiddler called out another dance. And this time, Sam found Taffy in the crowd and twirled her out into the middle of the floor.

"Come on, Taffy, you can do this one!"

The fiddlers and the banjo player started "Going to the East; Going to the West." And all the couples paraded back and forth, bowing and circling and bending forward from the waist, their hands on their hips.

"That's the way, Taffy! Step high and lively now!"

Breathlessly, Taffy did her best to keep up and do what everyone else was doing in time to the music. Besides herself and the two boys who sat in the corner playing their own instruments, she noticed no other children there at all.

Susie, meanwhile, sat down on a plank along the wall to catch her breath and just watch for a while. There were so many people there she didn't know. Had it really been that long since she had been to a swamp dance? she wondered. Perhaps Sam was right—that slaves were being bought and sold, shifted about more than usual these days because of the fear of war and the possible end of slavery.

As she watched the dancers twirling around, an open space appeared, and Susie could see across to the other side of the room. She saw a very tall man with thick, silvery hair standing there. He just stood there, not clapping or swaying to the music at all. Aside from being so tall, he looked different than the other slaves. They all tried their best to get cleaned up and dressed as well as they could for the swamp dances, but the fact was that even their washed clothes were very worn and shabby. The tall, gray-haired man seemed better dressed and, even at that distance, Susie sensed a special dignity about his bearing.

Just as quickly as he had appeared to her, he vanished as the crowd closed in again. Sam came back to her side right then, guiding a very out-of-breath but delighted Taffy. Taffy plopped herself down on the bench beside Susie. "Did you watch me, Susie? Did you watch me dancing?"

"Of course I watched you, Taffy. You really are some dancer, sweetie pie."

Sam leaned over and whispered into Susie's ear. "Susie, you may not see me for a while. Don't worry. I'll be back to walk you home. I've made a new contact, and we need to go off into the woods where we can discuss some important plans without being noticed."

Susie nodded, and to herself, she thought, *It might be that tall man who was dressed better than anyone else here.*

Sam disappeared into the dancers as he crossed the room. A space opened up once again, but Susie could not see Sam. Nor was the tall man in sight.

On and on the musicians played, and the later it became, the better they played, making up new tunes as they went along. The fiddler called out for a cakewalk, and then for the broom dance. The slaves sang and danced away the pain and sorrow of their everyday existence, while those too tired stood around the edges and clapped their hands and swayed to the rhythmic beat of the makeshift drums and the lively melodies, some with words that expressed their own lives:

Massa sleeps in the feather bed;

Nigger sleeps on the floor.

When we get to heaven,

There'll be no slaves no more.

Once again, Sam appeared before Susie.

"Look at Taffy, Sam. She's nodding her head and falling fast asleep, leaning against me, in spite of wanting to stay awake the whole time here. I better start back right away."

"Don't worry, Susie, I'm going to walk with you the whole way so you won't be alone. No one else is about to give up here for another hour at least," said Sam.

Taffy was so tired on the walk home that her feet dragged. "Here we go. Up on my back, Taffy, or we'll never get there," said Sam.

As soon as she was hanging on with her arms around his neck, her head drooped down, and she fell fast asleep. From then on, Sam and Susie could talk softly without waking her or being heard by anyone who might be following along the same way.

"I guess you noticed how long I was gone," Sam said. "I'd never met George before tonight; he comes from the other end of the county, and he had new information about the railroad. There's a swamp dance cabin over his way, and he has contacts there. Besides that, I have news you will be mighty interested to hear."

"What is it, Sam? Tell me quick."

"There's a fair chance we may have found out where Della is. We're not sure, but there's a chance it's really Della."

Susie stopped walking and grabbed Sam's arm.

"Oh, Sam, tell me, quick. How do you know?"

"I got this news from George, from the swamp dance he goes to over there to get information—you know, plans for escaping, how many we dare let be runaways at one time, and when it's just too dangerous to even try to make a run for it."

"Yes, yes, Sam. But what about Della? What did he say about Della? Is George that tall man with silvery hair?"

"Yes, very tall. You noticed him then. He tends to show up too well wherever he goes! He's very smart, is a house servant to some important official, I think. I know he can read and write."

"Sam, please hurry up and tell me—you said he found out something about Della!"

"Yes, this is it. He made a new contact last week with a slave from a very large plantation, way over across the river from where he is. That slave somehow happened to tell George that there is a new cook in that big kitchen who came several months ago. The reason it came up is because anyone new might be either a good contact for new information, or they could be someone not to be trusted at all. George asked him to find out more details about the new cook and where she came from."

Susie was disappointed. "There could be almost anyone new in a kitchen somewhere. Why is that so special?"

"Well, after George mentioned it to me, I thought of Della, so I asked him questions, and it seems this is a big plantation where there is a lot of formal entertaining, and they only have exceptional cooks in their kitchen. George also had the information that the new cook lives inside the big house. It seems that all the house servants there live inside the house. They have special quarters there for their house servants. He also had the information that the new cook is short and slender. He wanted to know in case she eventually shows up at a dance sometime. But so far, she has never left the house, so it's hard to make any contact."

"Well, it might be Della. Oh, I hope so. To think we may soon know where Della is! At least then we'll know she is safe, and not way down in Alabama or Louisiana. She doesn't like hot, humid weather. If it's really Della, can we get a message to her?" Susie's voice trailed off into softly weeping.

"It's too dangerous right now. What if the message got into the wrong hands? Then it's a dead giveaway back to all of us, and all my hard work to keep secret messages going will be lost. The main purpose of my contacts, you know, is to help slaves run away by the Underground Railroad."

"What if we ever become runaways? Is there any way we could tell Della so she could escape with us?"

"Oh, Susie. I wish we could, but I'm afraid it won't work. That plantation is too far away from where we would be taking off. By the time she ran away to meet up with us, they would have a search party out hunting for her, and it would get around to the other slave owners that an escape plan was in the works. The runaway groups are safest kept small and not spread too far apart. Right now, we may have five all set for the next escape. Pretty soon you'll have to decide, Susie. I really want to go myself this time."

"Taffy has to go too, or I won't go, Sam. I just won't. They'll have to drag me away screaming before I leave Taffy all alone."

"Susie, I do know how you feel. I don't want to leave without you, for sure. In fact, I probably wouldn't. I'd just help the others get started on their way North and wait till another time. But know what, Susie? I'm just finding out that Taffy is light as a feather on my back. I could carry her this way for hours of fast walking. I've changed my mind! Taffy can come along, too. That makes eight of us now. What do you say now about making the next escape?" Sam slowed down and took a deep breath.

"Then we'll go. It's settled, Sam. We'll be ready whenever you give us the word. I'd be so lonesome here without you coming by the kitchen; it would be terrible for me, too."

As they entered the pine grove, Susie asked, "What about telling Taffy, in case it does turn out to be Della over there? Do you think I should tell her?"

"I don't think you should. She's still a little girl. It must be hard for her to keep secrets and wonder who she can trust and who she can't trust. It's hard enough for us to do that."

"Yes. And Taffy would be so excited and then she would be upset all over again. And then she'd be reminded of her daddy, too, and wonder if we knew what happened to him. She may even think that they are still together. I don't talk about the details to her. We don't know anything about her father, do we?"

"Not a scrap of solid information has turned up about William Davis. But we did hear about a group of runaways who got away safely—way over on the coast. Seems a new slave owner was taking his newly purchased slaves to a plantation over there, but they managed to escape. Wouldn't that be something, if Taffy's father was in that group of runaways?"

"Oh, if only that is true—that he managed to escape. Perhaps he'll be lucky and get all the way north to Canada before we even leave here! But how in this wide world will slave families ever find each other and get together in our whole lifetime. That is what I can't figure out."

"Well, Susie, you can see what an advantage it will be someday to be free and also be able to read and write. Who knows, with the freedom to search and write openly, people may actually get reunited. We just have to keep hoping it could turn out like that."

Sam carried Taffy right to her bed, and she was still sleeping soundly as they tucked her in.

"Sam, you goin' to have good practice tonight with walking. It will be close to dawn by the time you get back to your plantation."

"Sure will. But it was worth it. We settled many things tonight. Will I see you at church meeting tomorrow morning?"

"No. I have to be in the kitchen for breakfast. Then, by midday they will be off to a barbecue at another plantation, so I'll come back here and rest for the rest of the day."

❋   ❋   ❋

Taffy didn't wake up until Susie returned from the breakfast chores. In the afternoon, Susie was so tired she took a nap. But Taffy was now wide awake and still so excited about all she had seen and heard the night before that she took out her writing paper and pencil and began to draw pictures of all the people dancing and the musicians playing their instruments.

When Susie awoke, Taffy had used up the last sheet of paper they had, and her drawings were strewn on the table and onto the floor.

Susie looked over all the animated little stick figures, dancing and playing music.

"These are wonderful, Taffy. But now you have no paper left at all, and Sam probably won't come by with more for another week. I only dare to snitch a few pieces of paper once in a while from the library desk, you know, or Master Davis might begin to notice how fast it gets used up."

Taffy was still too excited to care. "Susie, I need to know how to spell *fiddle* and *banjo* and *broom dance.*

After she carefully titled her drawings, Susie helped her put them away in the box and back in the hole under the loose floorboard under the bed.

You're such a fast learner, Taffy. I just wish I could give you all the books and paper you deserve."

"There's lots of books in the library, Susie, and hardly anyone around now. I could go into the library to dust, and then stay and read for a while. I can hear Master Davis or Miss Sarah if they are heading to the library. Master has heavy footsteps and Miss Sarah uses a cane."

"Hmmm, I have a sneaking feeling that you have already done some peeking into books on the sly. You better be careful, Taffy. Remember, learning to read is the most dangerous thing a slave can do. Still, you're right. There's hardly a soul coming and going these summer days. Just be sure you leave things exactly as you found them, because Master Davis does use the library, especially in the evening after dessert, and he'd be sure to notice any of his books were out of place on the shelves."

The very next day, Taffy had her first chance to spend two hours in the elegant library room, just reading, not dusting at all. With her feather duster close beside her just in case of unexpected footsteps, she curled up in the cool leather chair. There was something about this room that felt far removed from plantation life. The walls were a mellow, polished wood. The two longest walls were completely lined with bookcases. The outside wall had two long windows to the floor. A mahogany desk was by one window, and the leather chair was in the corner near the other window. Thick bushes brushed the windows, making it difficult for anyone to peek inside.

Taffy knew she must always be alert for unexpected footsteps or voices. Even if someone did sneak up close to the window, they could not see her curled up in the chair, turned away from the view. Miss Sarah was taking her usual afternoon nap, and Master Davis was off again to one of his political meetings. He had driven off by himself in the small open carriage. With the library windows open, Taffy was certain she would hear the horse and carriage coming back and crunching on the gravel, no matter how engrossed she was in reading. There were so many books to choose from, but she liked poetry the best. Poems had a rhythm that made them easy to follow along. If she didn't understand the subtle meaning, it didn't bother her, for it was fascinating enough to be able to read the words and get the idea of it!

Today was Monday, so no slaves would be coming inside to clean. The cotton picking season was now beginning, and with such a small household, only two slaves were assigned house duties. But today they were working in the laundry sheds. The slaves who regularly worked in the outside cooking and laundry sheds or in the smokehouse remained at their jobs instead of joining the cotton pickers.

Besides the library, Susie had decided to assign Taffy the regular dusting of the front foyer, the parlor, the dining room, and the sunroom with its many plants. She took special care to inform both Master Davis and Miss Sarah that Taffy would now be responsible for these tasks, at least for the rest of the summer. "Taffy is a big girl now and can be trusted to do this carefully and not break anything. Also, it keeps her busy when there's not much kitchen work to do."

Anything that kept a slave busy working was the way slave masters liked it, and Susie wanted Taffy to be considered as valuable a house worker as any grown-up slave.

Master Davis had agreed in an absentminded way. He was far too preoccupied with his own worries about the tension between the North and the South to care who did the dusting. Miss Sarah did not care at all who did what task or how the household of her brother was run, not as long as she was called to the dining room on time for delicious meals and special desserts.

This casual state of household affairs made it easy for Susie to take over Big Sally's place as head cook and also be more or less a housekeeper-in-charge as well. Now that the cotton picking season had begun, Susie also continued a custom that had been Big Sally's—that of baking goodies for the field slaves, who did not return to slave row until dusk. Since Big Sally had managed the kitchen and housework so well for so many years, even Mrs. Davis, when home, paid little attention to what went on. But now it was easier than ever to sneak in extra baking. Twice a week now, Susie and Taffy made large batches of cookies and muffins to give away to the tired field slaves.

Evenings, they went for walks through the cool pine grove, sometimes as far as beyond the meadow and on down to the river, along with other slaves. Susie wrapped up their treats in a burlap bag just as Big Sally had done. Usually, she gave the bag to Aunt Crissy to hand out. These night walks also gave Taffy a chance to run and play tag and hide-and-go-seek with other children. When the moon was full and a cool breeze blew through the trees, it was hard to return to the cabin to sleep until late at night. Sometimes they walked home by way of the cotton fields. By the light of a full moon, the fluffy cotton blossoms glowed with an eerie blue cast as far as one could see.

"Sure is different at night than by daylight," mused Susie, thinking of all those weary slaves, picking away at the thorny blossoms throughout the long, hot days.

Sam continued to come by regularly in the wagon with supplies for the neighboring plantations. Late in the summer, he had news for Susie.

"Where's Taffy?" he asked as he followed Susie into the kitchen for a hot muffin and a cup of coffee.

"She's in the library rea— uh, dusting, you know?"

"Be cautious about this routine, Susie. Don't get careless, not for one minute. It will be dangerous for all of us if a slave child is discovered being able to read. And, imagine—found sitting in the master's own favorite chair in his own library! Please be careful. Keep reminding Taffy how important it is to be alert all the time. But I'm glad she's gone right now, because I have news about her mother."

Susie sat down at the table across from Sam and waited breathlessly for him to speak.

"I'm certain it must be Della at that big plantation way over across the river. George found out from his contact over there that her name is Della! She arrived there about four months ago now. But George's contact hasn't been able to speak to her or give her any message to let her know we have a direct line of contact back to us. That place is much larger than this one, you know, or even than where I am, and it's run much tighter. The slaves who work full time in the big house even live inside the house in a side wing, so they don't mingle with the other slaves unless they go to a dance or a church meeting. They would never come across the river to go to our swamp dance or meeting place; there's a place over there. If the contact can figure out something, he'll let George know."

"Oh, Sam, to think Della is really over there, and now we know it! It's a comfort to me to know she is even that close. If we could only get a message to her!" Susie's eyes brimmed over with tears. "If only I could let her know that I'm taking good care of Taffy and that she is learning to read and write so fast. Why, Taffy could write her mother a note!"

"There's little to be gained by taking that risk right now. We have too much to lose—right down to the secret chain of contacts—if any message is exposed, showing that so many of us can read and write. Look at it this way, Susie. Della must be fairly sure that Taffy is still safe here with you to take care of her; and now *you* know that she is safe, working in a good kitchen, and living in clean quarters where she will come to no harm."

Susie sighed, wiping away her tears. "That's right. We don't want to make things dangerous for Della either. It must be terrible for her, missing her child and her husband gone from her, too. But it could be worse, couldn't it? What if, somehow, her new master had sent her out to pick cotton instead of using her as a cook!"

"Listen, as plantations go, it's a decently run place from what I hear. Be thankful for that. It's better organized and much larger than this place. The master is important in state politics, and they are very sociable people, often entertaining at grand parties, so you know they must value a fine cook like Della. She might be doing dressmaking for them, too. They would never waste Della in the cotton fields, Susie. You can count on that!"

Sam got up to leave. "Don't tell Taffy about this—not yet."

"I won't. I promise. She's so much happier now because of learning to read and write. She talks of nothing else to me at night now. She is learning so fast; it amazes me. And you should see how she can draw, too! I just wish I had more paper to give her."

"I'll bring you some paper next week. I know where I can get my hands on a block of plain paper. Just be careful you always hide the papers away in that hole under the floorboards or burn them up in the stove." He touched her arm softly as he held her gaze meaningfully.

Sam then left and climbed up into the driver's seat and took up his reins. Susie ran out after him and handed him a small package. "Something to remember me by, for later." She laughed up at him.

"Susie, I don't need food to remember you by, no matter how good it is," replied Sam.

He started the horse, heading around to the front driveway, and then called back to her, "Don't forget to come to the swamp dance Saturday night, Susie! I'll be looking for both of you, all dressed up with ribbons in your hair!"

❊   ❊   ❊

And so the long days of summer drifted by. Tensions rose, and problems deepened between the Northern abolitionists who wanted to abolish slavery, and the Southern white planters, who depended on free slave labor to make a profit in the cotton-growing business. There was nervousness, too, among the Southern planters about the growing popularity of a Northerner named Abraham Lincoln, who was definitely against the expansion of slavery into the border states. There was a possibility he might be elected president of the United States in the fall of 1860.

But for now, none of these political affairs affected the everyday lives of the slaves. For Susie and Taffy, their easygoing routine peacefully continued, day after day, while down in the hot fields, the other slaves picked cotton from early morning till dusk.

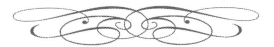

Chapter Five

Two Important Visitors

The last day of August was the hottest day of the summer. That was the day Mrs. Davis and the two children came home from the mountains. Hot and weary from the long carriage ride, they all went straight to their rooms until it was time for the evening meal to be served. Susie called in two slaves to carry pitchers of hot water up to their washstands. The carriage was unloaded and all their baggage carried upstairs by two young male slaves.

The large trunks arrived later on the wagon with the returning slaves. The wagon went around to the back of the house, where four slaves got out and went straight down to their own quarters in slave row. Susie didn't have a chance to speak to them first.

"Big Sally not with them, Susie. Do you think Mrs. Davis sold her?"

"I don't know Taffy, I don't know. Tonight we'll go find Aunt Crissy. She'll have found out what happened by then. She and Big Sally were good friends, I know that, Taffy."

A cold shiver of fear stayed with Susie the rest of the afternoon in spite of the steamy weather and the stove being on. The questions kept repeating in her mind: Could Mrs. Davis have really sold Big Sally? How could she have done such a terrible deed to an old loyal servant? Big Sally was getting old and had not accomplished much on her own the past year. Had Mrs. Davis noticed that, too? Taffy's mother and Susie had done most all of the work and often encouraged Sally to sit down and rest awhile. She became out of breath so easily; it had frightened them.

Just before Susie finished cleaning up the kitchen for the night, Mrs. Davis came in, carrying Sally's old suitcase.

"Susie, I have sad news to tell you. Sally died suddenly in the mountains, just a week before we left for home. It must have been a heart attack. She died in her sleep. We had her buried up there, on our own mountain property. This is her suitcase. I put her clothes in it, and you can take care of disposing them and anything else in there. Probably someone in the slave quarters can wear the cotton dresses."

Susie took the suitcase, too surprised to say a word. Mrs. Davis started to leave, and then she turned around to Susie again and asked, "Did you know Sally was ailing?"

Susie thought a moment before answering. What *harm could there be now in telling the truth about poor old Sally?* "Yes, ma'am, both Della and I knew she was not feeling well. She got so out of breath, and we often told her to go rest this past year. There wasn't that much work to do that the two of us couldn't manage easily by ourselves anyway."

"Hmmm, I see. She was too weak to be in charge of a kitchen alone. I never should have taken her up to the mountains. It was obvious that the kitchen was not run the same up there. Meals were often late, for one thing. On the trip home, I was thinking that I would have to find a new head cook for this kitchen. But now that I have talked it over with Mr. Davis and Miss Sarah, I have decided not to do that, at least not for a while. They both were very pleased with how you managed the kitchen all on your own, Susie, all summer long. They both remarked what excellent meals they had and especially the desserts. We are not a large family, anyway, and this year, both children are going away to boarding schools, so there will only be the three of us most of the time. When we have guests, you can always get extra help from the other slaves. But you will be the head cook, Susie, from now on, and we'll see how it goes."

Taffy was standing in a corner, listening as Mrs. Davis went on talking.

"Just continue as you are doing, Susie, and keep Taffy with you all day as a helper."

Mrs. Davis turned then and took full notice of Taffy. "You've grown taller over the summer, Taffy. I think you could use some new dresses that fit you better. When we sort out Melinda's things to get her ready for boarding school, we'll put some outgrown ones aside for you. Maybe shoes, too, will fit."

Mrs. Davis seemed like a friendly, kindly lady, Taffy thought to herself. She wanted so much to like her—even to trust her. But no, she must not think such thoughts. Susie reminded her often that she must never let such feelings take hold in her mind.

"It will only break your heart someday." That's what Susie had said. Susie had also explained, "You are only a slave to them. Remember that, Taffy. You are not even seen as a real person—the living soul that you truly are. They think they own you—all of you—just like they own their horses and cows and pigs and dogs, and they can do just as they please with you at a moment's notice. Without even telling you ahead of time, they can sell you off to another white master."

Thinking of Susie's harsh words and her own missing parents, Taffy did not move a muscle or smile. She just softly mumbled, "Thank you, ma'am."

Mrs. Davis looked at Susie again, as if thinking about something. "Susie, did you learn to cook so well from Sally or from someone at the plantation where you came from?"

"I was only a child and a helper in that other plantation. When I came here, it was Taffy's mother who taught me so much about good cooking and desserts and pies and all, ma'am."

"I see," replied Mrs. Davis, still looking very thoughtful. Then she turned and left the room without saying anything further.

That evening, they took Sally's shabby old suitcase down to Aunt Crissy. Crissy wept as she went through it and folded the clothes into a neat pile.

"So little she had, so little of her very own, and so much she always gave to all the rest of us down here," cried Crissy, "You know, she had a husband once, many long years ago, no children, but she did have a good man of her own. That was at another place, and he was sold away, and then she was sold and came here. She never knew what happened to him, but she used to talk about him, how good he was to the other slaves."

There was nothing Susie and Taffy could do to comfort Aunty Crissy except just sit there and let her cry and talk.

"We didn't get to go to her funeral. At least they gave her a little service up there. They told me Mrs. Davis even shed tears. But we need to do something for her, too. You know how she always took food from the kitchen to give away to all of us down here—especially in the cotton picking time, when we were all so tired at night. We'd send someone sneakin' up to her cabin after dark, and Sally would have a big bag all ready, with cookies for the little ones and pie and even sandwiches for the rest of us. I don't know how she sneaked all that food without anybody noticing, but Mrs. Davis never was one to pay much attention to the kitchen, with things being run so well up there. Well, we'll have our own service for her down at the Sunday meeting—we'll have ourselves a good time, just singing and crying and speaking out about old Sally, bless her heart. She's been around here a long, long time." Crissy wiped her eyes, and told them goodnight.

On the way back to their own cabin, Taffy was full of questions. "Do you think Mrs. Davis really felt sad about Big Sally dying up there in the mountains?"

"I don't know. She should have. Big Sally was a loyal slave for many years here. She said she was there when both of the Davis children were babies, and she loved those children. She was there when you were born, too."

"Do you think Mrs. Davis ever feels sad that Master sent my mama away? And my daddy, too?"

"I have no way of knowing what goes through her mind at all. She may very well have objected to the selling away of your mother, especially. After all, she lost an excellent cook and a slave who could also do plain sewing and skillful dressmaking. It might have been only Master Davis's decision, you know, and she just had to accept that, even if she felt bad about it."

Later, still thinking about all these things, Taffy announced, "I don't want Melinda's old dresses, Susie. I have a nice dress for Sunday, and my own mama made it for me."

"I know you do, honey lamb, but you will soon outgrow it. Never mind your feelings in this matter, Taffy. Just take the clothes and enjoy wearing them. You need new clothes. Think of it as pay for all you now do in the kitchen that is of service to this family. Just remember, you owe these people nothing. You work for them without any pay. Do you understand?"

Taffy nodded her head. When Susie got on this subject, she became very angry-looking, and her voice was harsh.

Susie stopped walking then and put both her hands on Taffy's shoulders, very firmly. "Taffy, never give your heart or your soul away to these people. Just go on being polite and keep your thoughts on other things. Just concentrate on learning all you can about useful things—learn to read and write and learn to be a good cook—in case someday you may be free. Sam says if there is a war soon over slavery, we might all end up free someday—even before you are a grown-up. Then, we can all work for pay just like white folks do, and we can live on our own and do just as we please. You just keep saying your prayers that this will happen to you and try to be cheerful. That's what your own dear mama said to me, over and over, when I first came here. I hardly knew what she was talking about at first, but it finally all sank into my stupid head."

❀ ❀ ❀

With the Davis family together again, there was a flurry of activity going on every day. There were end of summer picnics and parties with the other plantations. There were shopping trips with both Melinda and her twelve-year-old brother, Henry. Melinda helped choose fabrics and trimmings for new clothes to take to boarding school.

"Is Aunt Sarah going to sew my new dresses, Mother?"

"Not this time, dear. I've found out there is a slave over the other end of the county who is said to be an excellent dressmaker, and I've made arrangements for her to come stay here and sew for you."

"Good," said Melinda. "Aunt Sarah always stuck pins into me when she was fitting the dresses on me, and then they never fit right anyway."

The slave seamstress soon arrived by carriage with her own special trunk of sewing supplies. Melinda looked her over with keen interest, for she looked very young, and she was exceptionally pretty. While she was there, she lived in Big Sally's cabin, which was still almost the way Sally had left it. There was a handmade quilt on the bed and curtains at the little window. A table and bench just like the ones Susie had were by the window. Susie and Taffy placed fresh flowers on the table before she arrived.

Julia was very polite and thanked them for the flowers, but she did not encourage any further conversation. Every day, she went to the upstairs sewing room, and every night, she stayed inside her cabin by herself.

Then, one day, there was added excitement at the Davis plantation. Cousin Louise arrived from the North for a visit with her younger Southern cousin, Melinda. Everyone went off in the big carriage to meet her train. She had come all the way from Pennsylvania. Taffy was on an errand when they returned and had a glimpse of Miss Louise as she swished gracefully up the front steps. She was a small and thin grown-up, but she seemed to bound out of the carriage and up to the front porch with high energy. Under her green bonnet, her hair was a bright golden color.

From then on, the sound of laughter filled the house, and lively footsteps were constantly heard traipsing up and down the stairs or going in and out. Even the usually rather glum Melinda seemed happier with her sprightly, grown-up cousin around. There were more parties than ever to show off the high-spirited Louise.

One day, Taffy had a chance to show off, too. Susie let her take full charge of a special luncheon party just for the two cousins and their visiting friends. Six girls, all around ages fourteen to twenty, arrived by carriage in the middle of the day. Taffy had already been working in the kitchen for hours, and the luncheon was ready to be served. She had prepared a huge bowl of elegant chicken salad, and now she decorated the silver platter the bowl was placed on. First she put lettuce leaves around it, and then she arranged grapes and pecans in clusters. Puffy buttermilk biscuits were hot out of the oven. Tall glasses were set on a tray with a pitcher of fresh lemonade. And ready for dessert was a still-warm peach cobbler to be served with whipped cream.

The luncheon was served picnic style outside on a long table covered with a yellow tablecloth. Earlier, Susie had helped her arrange a milk glass jar full of fresh black-eyed Susans from the meadow, and that was in the center of the table. Taffy peeked through the dining room curtains while the girls walked around the table filling their plates, all the while laughing and talking. How pretty they looked in their hooped gowns, all ruffled and trimmed with ribbons and lace.

Miss Louise is the prettiest of them all in her green print dress and golden hair, Taffy mused to herself. She wondered what Susie would look like, all dressed up like that with layers of petticoats and ruffles and bows. Taffy smoothed her own crisp, white apron. At least she wore clean, printed cotton dresses and aprons every day. Young slaves, Melinda and Louise's age, who had to pick cotton wore ragged tunics that hung loosely below their knees. Only on Sundays or Saturday nights did they wear a decent dress.

"Time to serve the dessert," called out Susie from the kitchen.

Taffy ran to the kitchen and whipped a bowl of heavy cream until it stood in peaks. Then she added a sprinkling of sugar and a splash of vanilla and spooned the cream over the peach cobbler.

Susie proudly watched her do it, and then she lifted the bowl of cobbler onto another silver serving platter.

"There you are. It's beautiful, Taffy. Now remember, just place it on the table and then leave. Don't speak to anyone unless they ask you a direct question. Do you understand?"

"Yes, Susie, I understand." She sighed, but just the reminder made her wish that visiting Miss Louise, at least, would say something to her.

But of course, none of them did. Miss Louise was too busy talking and laughing to even notice that the dessert had arrived.

While Susie and Taffy cleaned up the kitchen and started preparations for a light meal in the evening, the guests played croquet on the side lawn. Their laughter wafted through the long dining room windows. Taffy could not resist running back and forth to watch them.

"Do you think they really liked their lunch?" Taffy asked Susie for the third time that afternoon.

"Of course they did, my pet. You notice there wasn't one scrap of anything left over. It's a wonder they are all so thin the way they can eat," replied Susie.

Susie put her arms around Taffy and hugged her for a long moment.

"Taffy, you are a very friendly little girl by nature, but your friendliness may bring you harm someday. You have to remember all the time that these people do not see you as a real person equal to themselves. You are just there to serve their every whim, and that is all. They do not ever think they should thank you for anything you do. Never. Put them completely out of your mind as much as you can and think of something else."

"I wish you were all dressed up and playing croquet out there, Susie."

"See? That's just what I mean. Such thoughts will only make you sad. If you insist upon wild daydreams, then you might as well start thinking about such grown-up affairs as a war between the North and the South and the end of slavery forever. We'll celebrate and play croquet all day!

Later, a carriage rolled up the front driveway to pick up the guests. There were about five minutes of more laughing and saying thank yous and good-byes, and then the guests were off.

Melinda ran right upstairs to her bedroom, but Miss Louise appeared in the kitchen doorway.

"I just want to thank you, Susie, for such a lovely luncheon."

Susie was so caught by surprise she just stood there for a long moment, saying nothing. After all, slaves were not expected to make comments, and receiving compliments was very unusual. But something about Miss Louise's beaming smile encouraged Susie to find her voice. "Thank you, Ma'am, but I didn't make this luncheon. Everything was made entirely by Taffy, all by herself."

Louise looked Taffy over with new interest. "Well then, I'll thank you, Taffy. You made a beautiful luncheon party for us, and for such a little girl, that is very special, indeed. Thank you very much, my dear."

Now it was Taffy's turn to feel speechless, but as soon as Louise left the kitchen, she couldn't stop talking about it.

Even as she was falling asleep, she mumbled to Susie, "I can't help it. I really do like Miss Louise a lot."

✳ ✳ ✳

Long skirts, fitted jackets, blouses, and two party gowns began to take form in the upstairs sewing room. Both Melinda and Louise were fascinated watching Julia run the sewing machine, pumping with her feet to make the wheel turn, and feeding the fabric into the needle's automatic stitching. But Julia's special skill was in the designing and fitting and hand-sewn details of the beautiful clothes.

The day Melinda had her first fitting, her Northern cousin Louise decided to take advantage of Julia's talents and have two new outfits made. That meant another shopping trip for fabrics and trimmings before Julia could begin. Louise deliberately bought much more fabric and trimmings than she needed. When she brought the package to the sewing room one morning, she told Julia, "There's more here than you will need for my clothes, I realize, but I want you to keep everything left over for yourself. Do whatever you like with it. It's yours."

Julia thanked her and folded the gift assortments away in her own small sewing trunk that traveled with her.

"Isn't it unusual for a slave to know how to sew so well?" Louise asked Melinda one morning after they had watched Julia for a while as she cut into a soft blue-gray flannel for a skirt for Louise.

"I suppose it is, but we had a slave who could sew like that. It was Taffy's mother, in fact."

"Taffy's mother could make all those complicated jackets and dresses?"

"Oh, yes. She made lots of clothes while she was here. My Aunt Sarah liked to sew for me, too, but they never fit as well or looked as stylish as the ones Della made. I wish my father hadn't sold her. My mother was very upset about that. She begged him not to do it, but he just wouldn't listen to her," replied Melinda.

"Why did he sell her?"

"Because he said he had to set an example to the other slaves—even to slaves at other plantations around here. You see, both Taffy's mother and father could read and write, and they were secretly teaching other slaves as well, and my father says that is the most dangerous thing that can happen on a cotton plantation—to have slaves around who can read and write."

"I see," said Louise, quickly dropping the subject.

Seamstress Julia was extremely quiet. She never spoke unless she was asked a direct question. Even with Susie and Taffy in the kitchen, where she took her meals, she was polite and pleasant of manner but did not engage them in any conversation that led to information about herself.

❈ ❈ ❈

The longer she was there, the more Susie couldn't help being curious about her. She guessed Julia was in her late twenties, although she looked younger, being delicate of figure. It really was unusual for a slave to be able to sew that well, and Susie wondered where and how she had learned to be as skillful as Della. Beyond that, there was something else about Julia that haunted Susie. In some vague way, she seemed familiar to Susie, as if they had met somewhere once. But where? Since she offered no conversational information, there was no way to find out anything about her past.

❈ ❈ ❈

The daily routine went by, and the beautiful clothes were now hanging up in the sewing room, almost finished except for their hand-sewn trimmings and final fittings. Susie realized that the time would soon be drawing near when Julia's work was completed, and she would be returning to the plantation at the far end of the county. Susie knew that, unless Julia returned the following year, she would not be likely to see her again. The persistent feeling that she had met Julia before would not go away. One night, after Taffy was asleep, Susie walked over to Big Sally's cabin and paid Julia a visit.

"I brought you some leftover pie from the family's dessert tonight. You left the kitchen before they had their dessert, so I couldn't serve you any then," Susie explained at the door.

Just as she had hoped, Julia invited her in. Julia was cordial, as always, and insisted on sharing the big wedge of pie with Susie.

After they had finished, with Susie doing most of the talking, Julia confided, "I keep to myself these days, even from other slaves, because I have discovered that I don't know who I can trust anymore. It's not that I don't like you and little Taffy. In fact, there is something especially appealing to me about that little girl that makes me feel drawn to her. But since I won't be here much longer, there's no use in becoming close to her."

For Susie, those remarks were a clue. When a slave felt frightened and distrustful of other slaves, it could mean that the slave was hiding a dangerous secret. And what was more dangerous than being able to read and write?

All of a sudden, Susie was convinced this was Julia's own secret, and she decided to risk telling her that she, too, could read and write.

For the first time, Julia offered information about herself. She admitted that, yes, she could read and write. She had learned a long time ago at another plantation, far away from here. Now she was in this state, and as far as she knew, not a soul at this plantation where she now was knew anything about her background and that she could read. She had certainly never intended to tell a living soul her secret, but now, somehow, Susie's friendly and trusting manner had caused her to reveal it.

"Your secret is safe with me, Julia. I promise you that."

Then Susie went on to explain how she had learned to read and write from Della, Taffy's mother, and how Della had been punished by being sold away, leaving her little girl behind and losing her husband as well.

"Della? Taffy's mother's name was Della? Could she sew well?"

"My yes. She did all the things you are now doing for them. They really lost a skilled slave when they sold Della."

"Did this Della have a good husband?"

"Oh yes. He was skilled, too. There's no one here now who can do all the things William Davis could do. Master Davis must very often regret his decision, because he lost a good carpenter who took care of all the repairs on this plantation. Besides that, he could make furniture, too. He had his own shop where he worked, and no one bothered him. So when he had spare time, he made tables and benches for us and toys for the children. He could sing, too, and he made a few wooden instruments to blow through. Everyone liked him."

Julia leaned forward, and with serious intensity, she asked, "How long was Della at this plantation? Were you here when she first came?"

"No. I came here about four years ago. Taffy was six then. But I know Taffy was born here. And her father grew up on this plantation, but Della didn't. She came from somewhere down in the lowlands of Louisiana I think. She never talked about the past. I only remember she said it was cooler up here, being closer to the mountain country, and that she felt better here—could breathe better, she used to say."

To Susie's surprise and distress, Julia covered her face in her hands and began to rock back and forth, weeping quietly.

"What is it, Julia? Did I say something to upset you?" Julia just kept rocking and weeping. Susie reached out and put her arms around her, but that only made Julia cry harder.

Finally, she managed to recover enough to speak. "It's not you Susie. It's about Della, and Taffy. It has to be the same Della—even her having problems breathing in the hottest weather— my dear, dear, very own sister, Della. To think she cooked and sewed right here, where I am now. Oh, I have longed to know what happened to her for all these long these years.

Thank God she never had to become a field slave, my beautiful, delicate sister. And to think she married here. What happened to him when they sold Della? Oh, of course, I understand— they were both sold separately as punishment because they could read and were teaching others as well. Poor, dear Della, how she must be suffering now, all alone, without her husband and without her little girl."

Again, Julia began to cry.

Susie hugged her again. "Yes, you are right. That is just what happened—they were sold separately. That is why we have to be so careful who we talk to. We have no idea who tattled on them—no idea at all. Now, at least you and I can share our secret together. It all makes me so frightened for Taffy, and for myself as well. I know just how you feel, wanting to stay by yourself and never say too much."

Thinking of Taffy, Julia wiped her eyes once again and stopped crying. "Poor little Taffy. Losing both her mother and father. Oh, will there ever be an end to this evil in this land?"

"Yes, she was heartbroken for a long while, but she is doing just fine now. She really is."

"Oh, Susie, I *knew* there was just something about that child's eyes that haunted me. Even some of her mannerisms are like her mother's. To think, Taffy is my very own niece. Susie, she is my own flesh and blood. Taffy and I belong to each other. We are family!"

Saying they were family started Julia sobbing all over again.

"It is all so hopeless for us. We can never manage to stay with our own families. The misery never ends. I shall never marry as long as I am a slave—never. I never want to bring any more slaves into this wicked world."

Susie tried her best to comfort Julia, but years of unspoken heartache and unshed tears were hard to stop.

Then Susie thought of something to distract poor Julia. "Tell me about your life together as sisters. I promise I'll never tell a soul—except, perhaps, someday it would be a good thing to be able to tell Taffy about her mother's past."

"Yes, when she's older, it would comfort her. Della and I don't remember our own mother. All we remember is being together, ever since we can recall anything at all. Vaguely, I think we knew she had died in an accident when we were very young. Della is older, but she never remembered any details either. About our father, I know nothing at all. We grew up together on a plantation down in Louisiana, and we were separated when I was sixteen—about like you, Susie, I guess—and Della was nineteen. That was the worst day of my life. No matter what else ever happens to me, that will forever remain the worst.

"However, our life together, growing up on that place, was very unusual for slaves; extremely unusual. Julia wiped her face, then went on," You see, we were owned by a white mistress who was against slavery! She had no children of her own, and she was married to a much older man, and he was not well. It wasn't even a working plantation. Well, I guess they did grow some sugar cane, but it didn't seem to be very important to either of them. They only owned a few slaves compared to cotton plantations, and mostly, they just took care of the vegetable and flower gardens and looked after keeping things repaired. Sometimes, they had houseguests who came and stayed for long visits, and they were always from far away places, either from up North or from Europe."

"Were you and Della cooks there?"

"Not at first. We were just children, you know. There was someone much older who was the head cook. We did learn to cook there, but not so much from the slave cook as from our white mistress! You see, she loved to cook, and so she would come down to the kitchen, and we would all be there together, concocting wonderful dishes! We cooked enough for all the slaves, too. We all ate the same food."

"That's not like any plantation I ever heard of," said Susie.

"Oh, I doubt there was ever a Southern plantation anything like it! That was the way she wanted to run it, you see. She was more like a teacher and a housemother to us than a slave owner. She told us that someday all the slaves would be freed, and we must be prepared to lead independent lives. She said, if she could help but a few slaves get ready to lead free lives, she would feel her own life was worthwhile. And so of course, she taught all of us to read and write."

"Did her husband know she was doing all this?"

"No, I don't think he did. But it wasn't difficult for her to keep this a secret, as he followed a very predictable routine. Every day, he went for a long walk, and then he would rest and read and write in his library all the remainder of the time, except for mealtimes. He was a writer, and he always was working on a manuscript. Sometimes he went to town to spend hours in a library.

"Also, it was easy for her to keep her own plans secret because she had Della and me upstairs most of the time, in her own private sewing room. You see, she was able to tell him that she was teaching us to sew. He didn't object to that. In fact, he might not even have objected to our learning to read. I don't really know how much he knew.

"So you see, our days were spent learning fine sewing, reading, writing, and cooking. We learned a lot about gardening, too. It was almost as if we were going to a very small and special private school. Her own children, if there had been any, could not have had better ways to spend their time, except they could have gone out together socially, which of course we couldn't do."

"What about the other slaves? Did they resent what you and Della were doing and learning?"

"Everyone was learning something. Any slaves who were there realized how fortunate they were, and no one would have ever said or done anything to upset our pleasant life. There was no white overseer around to check on us, because they didn't need to run it like a business. I think our master earned a living from writing, but I never did see any finished books lying around. Oh, we had some dusting and polishing chores, and others had their jobs to keep things up. But in some ways, we all sort of did things together. Mistress MacGregor would just gather us together and say, 'Let's catch up on the housework this week and get the ironing out of the way' or whatever she wanted done. It was almost as if we were helping to run our own home!"

"And where did you sleep? Did you have cabins off in the woods like we do?" Susie asked, listening intensely.

"We were inside the house, in a wing added on in the back. When they had houseguests, we didn't go upstairs to the sewing room. We stayed in our own section, or we spent more time in the kitchen making special dishes for her guests. We never minded that."

Susie still listened to Julia's story very intensely, so she would remember every detail of this strange plantation. Then it occurred to her. "If she was against slavery, why did she allow you to be separated? Why didn't she just free you both?"

"That's the tragedy of it all. She always said that, if her husband died, she would sell the place and move far away. But first, she would legally free all the slaves. No one ever thought that she would die first. But that is just what happened! She died very suddenly—of a heart attack the doctor said. One day she was there, good-natured and kind, and the next day she was gone!

"Her husband was so grief-stricken, he very quickly sold the estate and all of us along with it. Perhaps he thought we would all continue to live there. But the new owner had other plans, and so he just sold us all. Maybe he had slaves of his own he felt more safe having around. It was just like getting rid of a whole family—the way we had all been so happy there, all working along together. We hardly knew we were slaves at all until we were sold off. Then we knew all right. Then we knew!"

"And that's the last time you ever saw Della?"

"The very last time. I cannot bear to think about it, even after all this time. My beautiful, kind older sister—she was well enough most of the time, but she was not that strong, especially in the hot, humid weather. I just prayed and prayed she would never be placed in the fields picking cotton. She was not rugged enough for that awful life."

"Where did you go from there, Julia?"

"I lived at three other plantations before I came up this way. I was always a house servant, and I was fortunate indeed that I could sew so well. It has helped to make my days more bearable. I have only been up here about a year now, and no one knows anything about how I grew up.

"But enough about me; I've survived, and now I have Taffy to think about. She sighed resolutely. Tell me about Taffy. Does she understand what happened to her parents?"

"She didn't at first, and none of us could stand to tell her. But she understands now. She's grown up a lot in her understanding of the ways things are for slaves during these past few months. Before that, she was the way you described yourself and Della as children—you hardly knew you were slaves at all! Della was planning to begin teaching Taffy to read this summer. She just wanted to wait until she was sure that Taffy was grown up enough to keep it secret. Della owned a book of poetry that Taffy has now. I'll show it to you some night, and you probably will remember it as coming from the place where you grew up.

"After hearing your story, I can see why Della felt it was her mission to teach other slaves to read. She was the one who taught me when I first came here, and so when Della was taken away, I decided I should begin to teach Taffy. Already, Taffy can read better than I can."

"Oh, Susie, it is so dangerous. Are you certain Taffy is cautious? She's still a little girl". Her eyes looked terrified as she gulped in fear.

"I think she understands all too well these days. She loves learning, and she's going so fast, I can't keep up with her. But what shall we tell Taffy about you, Julia?"

"Since I will be leaving soon, and we may never see each again—at least not for a year, providing we are all still in the same places—I don't think it's wise to tell her."

"You're right. It might be different if you were going to stay here all the time. She's not unhappy anymore, but she still misses her mother and father. Taffy is a very friendly child, and she would quickly become very attached to you. Then she'd want to be running upstairs to the sewing room to hang around you as often as she could. Then you would leave, and she would be miserable all over again."

When Susie finally got into bed that night after her long talk with Julia, she could not fall asleep for thinking about the startling news. To think that Julia had turned out to be Della's very own sister! That made her Taffy's very own aunt! How sad it was that they could not share this amazing news with the one person who deserved to know about it.

"Sharing the news" made her suddenly think of Sam. She had promised Julia she would not tell a soul. Did that include Sam? She knew it was safe to tell Sam, but still, a promise was a promise. All of a sudden, it all came together in her mind, and she sat straight up in bed. Of course she had to tell Sam about Julia. But first, she would talk to Julia and tell her why and see how she felt about it.

With Julia staying in Big Sally's cabin, it would be easy to sneak over in the dark and talk in private. But she must not wait, for Julia was soon to be finished with the sewing, and then she would be sent away again. There was no way to predict whether they would ever meet again. The swamp dance cabin was too far away from where Julia was for her to want to bother to come there. Somehow, the noisy dancing didn't seem as if it would appeal to Julia anyway. So she must act on her idea quickly. And with the plan resolved in her mind, Susie finally fell asleep.

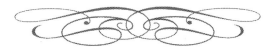

Chapter Six

Taffy's Secret Revealed

The very next day after Julia's emotional visit with Susie, Julia made a decision. She had barely slept at all, her mind in a whirl with the revelation that little Taffy was her very own niece! Somehow, she must figure out a way to stay longer at the Davis plantation. It was just too unbearably heartbreaking to have to leave now, knowing she might never see Taffy again. She only wanted a little more time—just a little more time. If her decision turned out the way she hoped, she might actually have some control over staying longer. Just mouthing those words—*decisions* and *control*—was frightening and strange to her. But she decided to try.

That afternoon, Melinda and Louise came flouncing into the sewing room for their last fitting. The beautiful new clothes were hanging up, almost finished now except for that final adjustment that would make them a perfect custom fit. Julia still had some hand sewing and trimming to complete as well.

The girls tried on each outfit, and Julia took a skillful tuck here, a tuck there, and marked the hems and cuffs. For that brief hour, the girls forgot Julia was a slave. They were relying on her talent and skill, and the atmosphere was one that produced a natural, give—and-take conversation. They were completely unaware of their changed attitude, but Julia was very conscious of the difference. In the tiny world of a sewing room, Julia was on equal terms with her white slave owners. In this one isolated situation, they were dependent on her decisions and ability.

Melinda tried on the deep red velvet party gown next. While she stood before the long mirror, Julia nipped in the waistline just a little tighter with pins.

"Melinda, you will be the envy of all the girls at school when you wear that beautiful gown!" said Louise.

Melinda's pale complexion and light brown hair seemed to take on a new glow reflected from the rich color of the velvet. Melinda twirled around with pleasure, admiring herself in the mirror.

"Why don't you call your mother in to see how this looks, Melinda? You still have to decide whether you want any lace at the neckline." asked Julia.

"I like it just the way it is. It looks more grown-up this way," replied Melinda.

"Well, Mrs. Davis should see how they look, now, before they are completely finished," said Julia, speaking firmly.

"I'll go get her," said Louise, still wearing her almost completed new suit of pale blue-gray flannel.

Mrs. Davis was delighted with all the clothes, but she and Melinda disagreed about adding lace ruffles at the low neckline of the velvet dress.

"What do you think, Julia?" asked Louise.

"I think it is more elegant with no trimming at the neck," said Julia, surprised at herself for speaking right up. Then she took a deep breath and said, "Mrs. Davis, there is so much fabric left over from Louise's blue flannel suit, would you like me to make something for you while I'm still here?"

"Why, I've been so busy getting settled in, I haven't even thought of any new clothes for myself lately," replied Mrs. Davis. "But, yes, now that I think of it, I could probably use some new outfits. But I don't care for that pale blue-gray for myself. I'll go shopping this week, while you finish up the girls' clothes. And by next week, you can start on mine. I might as well have a new afternoon gown while you're still here, too."

Julia's heart beat faster. She had accomplished what she wanted—more time to spend here, working in the sewing room. Now she would have the chance to accomplish something she wanted very much to do.

The next day when the family was out visiting and shopping, she called Taffy up to the sewing room. Taffy had not seen the new clothes in their near completion, and she looked at each outfit in wide-eyed wonder. Just as her mother had done, Julia had created these wonderful clothes out of folded piles of cloth. Looking at them made her long for her mother again.

Julia sensed Taffy's reflective sadness. "Come here, Taffy, and look at the fabric in this trunk of mine. There's lots of different printed cotton left over from dresses I have made, enough to make a brand-new dress for you. Which one would you like to choose for yourself?"

"Was one of these for Miss Louise?

"Yes, I did make her one cotton dress—the lavender print."

"I'd like that color, too," said Taffy, running her hand over the soft cotton fabric.

"Fine. Now let me take a few measurements on you, and I will begin to cut it out. I can even make a fluffy, white petticoat to wear under it, as there's plenty of that here, too. Here's a box of trimmings and lace you can look through, and choose whatever you think would look best with this dress. This dress will be exactly as you want it to be, with no one else's ideas at all. Does that please you?"

"Oh, yes. My mama made me a blue cotton dress, but it's getting too small for me now. But I still like it better than Melinda's old dresses."

"Of course you do. You bring me that blue dress, and I'll see if I can let it out to make it last you awhile longer," said Julia, giving Taffy a hug and kiss before she ran downstairs to the kitchen.

Later that afternoon, Mrs. Davis came to the sewing room. "I'm afraid I got carried away when I saw all those wonderful new fabrics they just received at the store. I've selected fabric for a new skirt and matching jacket and also mauve taffeta for an afternoon dress and jacket. But I don't suppose you will mind staying here longer."

There was something about the combination of Julia's talent and the professional atmosphere she somehow created in the sewing room that made even Mrs. Davis unconsciously treat her with the polite courtesy she extended to her own friends.

"I didn't know how much fabric you would need, so I just had Mr. Wilson cut me off plenty of both. Whatever is left over, you can keep for yourself," said Mrs. Davis in a sudden glow of pleasure.

After Mrs. Davis had left the room, Julia unfolded the expensive cloth and measured the length and width of it all. Indeed, Mrs. Davis had bought entirely too much! Since she did not know anything about sewing, the amount had been just a wild guess on her part. Typically, Mrs. Davis was never concerned about such practical details anyway—not so long as the expected results pleased her. *Best of all*, Julia thought, *she'll have no idea how long it should take me to complete these outfits. And as long as they come out to perfection, I can stay here and take as long as I please.* Julia could hardly wait to tell Susie the good news.

That evening, as Julia left the kitchen, Susie whispered to her, "I'll be coming over tonight after Taffy falls asleep so we can talk. I have some special things to talk over with you."

The first thing Julia said when Susie arrived was, "I'm surprised, Susie. I'm going to be able to stay here longer than I expected. I'm pleased to say I figured out how to do it, and my plan worked out! Mrs. Davis is having me make clothes for her now, and none of them have any idea how long anything takes, so that means I can spend some time sewing for Taffy. There is so much fabric available now that, if I have the time, I'll try to sneak in making a new dress for you, too, Susie. I'd really like to be able to do that for you, now we are such good friends and we share our love for Taffy."

"Don't fret, Julia, if you don't have time to sew for me."

First, Susie checked that the door was locked and the shutter closed. Then Susie sat down on the bed, patting the space beside her. "We have more important things to discuss than whether I have a new dress to wear. I may be needing something warmer than a cotton dress before long anyway."

"Do you know about the Underground Railroad, Julia?" Susie said in a serious whisper.

"I've heard about it, yes. But I don't know anyone involved, so I've never heard any details of how well it works out."

"Well, I have a good friend named Sam who comes by here once a week with supplies he delivers to several plantations. Sam learned to read from Della and William, too. He's one of the organizers of the Underground in this county. Sam wants Taffy and me to join the next group of runaway slaves. He'll be going, too, this time. He says that, if war comes soon between the states, the Underground won't work any more. Right now, he has good contacts and maps to get us safely all the way to the North. The group has to be kept small for safety—about eight or nine is all he wants to leave together. But I think he would agree to take one more when he hears that you are Della's sister. I want your permission to tell him about you—that is, if you are interested in escaping with us. Oh, Julia, this is your chance, too! You will come with us, won't you?"

"I don't know what to say, Susie. Just listening to you frightens me. I don't know if I could get up the courage to run away, and I'm afraid to depend on people."

"Sam will have it all carefully planned. He is very cautious. All you'll have to do on your own is sneak out at night when Sam gets the message to you. After we all meet somewhere, you won't be alone at all."

"But I don't know anyone over there I can trust with secret messages. I just don't know anyone really."

"You can leave all that to Sam. He has contacts all over the county, and he knows exactly who can be trusted. You have to believe that, Julia."

"I don't think I dare do it, Susie. I'm so afraid I might be captured, and then what would happen to me? I'd rather be shot than end up as a field slave. And I've never had to live in a slave-row shack."

"Julia, what do you think Della would have done? She was always telling me to believe that things would work out for the best and that I should believe that someday I would be free. I never thought that way until I came here and Della looked out for me. I think she would want you to try to escape if a good chance came up."

"I'll think about it, Susie. I promise I will."

"Think hard and fast then, because the last time I saw Sam at the swamp dance, he said, if we go at all, it has to be soon now. We have to get going before winter sets in up North."

"You're right about Della; she was more hopeful than I was. But she was older, too. I was only sixteen when we were separated, and it just tore me apart. I think she probably handled it better and was much stronger than I could ever hope to be. She was dedicated to teaching other slaves to read, too, just like our Mistress MacGregor. But look what happened to her in spite of her courage. She's lost everything!"

Susie took Julia's hand in hers. "Julia, maybe you should try to escape for Taffy's sake. She will definitely be going with me, and I will always take good care of her. She's like a sister to me. But if you go, too, then she'll have a real blood relative with her in Canada. There's something else to think of too. How do you know that Della might not have already escaped and that you might all three get together someday?"

"In my wildest dreams, I cannot imagine such a miracle could happen to us," said Julia sadly.

"Listen to me now, Julia, because I have something else to tell you. I was so caught up in your own story the other night that I didn't get around to mention that Sam is *almost* certain that he knows where Della is! What do you think of that?"

"Della is somewhere nearby then? How does he know?"

"He has contacts at other plantations all over the county. These slaves are all involved in the Underground Railroad, so they go to other swamp dances to get news and pass on information. It means they must spend most of the night just walking there and getting back before dawn, but that's how they do it. Sam has a new contact now—his name is George—who recently described a new cook at a plantation way across the river. Later, he found out her name is Della. The house slaves there all live in a wing of the main house, so it's difficult to get secret messages through. So far, she has never gone to a swamp dance or a Sunday meeting. But someday, there'll be a way to get through to her."

"Oh, Susie, maybe she can escape with us too!"

"Sam says there's no possible way for her to do that; she's too far away to meet up with us in time. But you see what could happen. Someday she might escape with a group starting out from over there."

"What kind of place is it? Is she safe there?"

"Sam says it's a very large plantation that is run very well, and she's a cook there. The contact through George said they do a lot of fancy entertaining over there. So they would value Della and want to keep her, wouldn't they? I just hope she doesn't teach anyone to read over there."

Julia looked at the window nervously, thinking of her braver sister, now nearby. "Oh, I hope not. Della was always braver than I could ever be. To think she is somewhere around this area. That thought does give me comfort, even if we can't get a message to her yet."

Julia had so much on her mind that she awoke before the sun came up. She was eager to get to the sewing room and begin work on her own personal sewing plans, but she didn't dare go into the house and up the stairs that early in the morning. Instead, she dressed and went for a walk through the pine grove. The birds were just beginning to awake, but no sunlight filtered through the dark pines as yet. It was cool and damp. Julia's sewing projects whirled around in her mind, but she was also thinking hard and fast about the escape plans Susie had talked about. She knew she had to decide soon, or Sam might choose someone else in her place. Susie had said that eight or nine, ten at the most, was the limit for the safety of the runaway group.

She was afraid to go, but how could she not go? She had figured out a way to stay here a little longer just so she could be near Taffy. Now Taffy would soon be leaving. And if she had the courage to go, she would be with Taffy all the time—hopefully, for all the long trip North and into a new life as a free woman.

I have to get up the courage to go, she silently kept whispering over and over to herself as she walked along.

"I must try to imagine what it would be like to be a free worker—to be paid for my sewing all day and then go home to my very own place and to be able to come and go as I please."

She considered the difference. Anything she did for herself now had to be sneaked in—time "stolen" from her slave masters. Here she was now, planning to sneak in time to sew for her own niece, using time and materials that belonged to other people. Was it really stealing? Wasn't that all part of being a slave—to steal, to sneak, to hide, to pretend, to fake anything for a small advantage, to play dumb if that served one's safety and health better? At least, the skills she'd learned in her unusual childhood with Mistress MacGregor had spared her some of that. As long as she could spend her days making beautiful clothes, she could stand the rest of the ugliness of being in bondage.

Julia's thoughts were in such turmoil that she absentmindedly walked and walked until finally the wide meadow opened before her. The rising sun cast long shadows as it glittered through the tall pines. A mellow glow of pink and golden light flooded across the field, and the sight of it gave courage to her faint heart.

"My heart and soul are still my own; I will listen to my heart. I hear what it is saying. It tells me to go—to escape and be with Taffy forever," she declared in a loud whisper. With this decision fixed in her mind, Julia felt a surge of strength flooding through her. She could hardly wait to get back and start to work.

"I must work extra hard and fast now," she softly told herself. "I have to complete Mrs. Davis's clothes before I can leave here. What if they decide to escape before I finish everything? Would I be able to leave from this place just as well?

But I need to return to pack up some heavier shoes and warmer clothes that are back at the other plantation. What about Taffy and Susie? They should have warmer clothes, too, not just those cotton dresses. I must find time to do that, too, as well as make the lavender dress for Taffy.

"Freedom clothes! That's what they'll be. That's what I must make for all three of us!" she said in a loud whisper.

Julia broke into a run, and she didn't stop until she was at the kitchen door.

As soon as she softly closed the sewing room door behind her, Julia unfolded the blue-gray flannel and measured it once again. It was a cold-weather fabric for Judith to wear in the North. Judith had said the leftovers were for her to keep for herself. She had thought little about it at the time, but now she knew exactly what she hoped to cut from it.

There was just barely enough. But Taffy was still so small that hers would take less, and with clever cutting and piecing, she could manage to make three warm, flannel skirts out of it.

The idea made her laugh to herself. *Imagine, making escape outfits out of such expensive and pale-colored fabric!*

We'll be the most stylish slaves that ever escaped to freedom. Julia giggled to herself.

The fabric for Mrs. Davis's new suit was a bright pink. That would not do for people on the run and in hiding. What about all that extra taffeta? That wasn't appropriate, either. She measured it, anyway. When she saw how much extra there was, she had another idea for that.

Whoever sold me all this mauve taffeta must have thought I wanted gowns made for her entire family! Well, both Susie and Taffy go by the last name of Davis, so they shall have mauve taffeta skirts! They can be stitched up fast, with little detail. They will be light to pack. And when they reach freedom, they will have mauve taffeta skirts to celebrate in! I might even have time to make one for myself.

Julia plotted out her time by the hours and by the days. Mrs. Davis and the girls rarely dropped in during the first part of the morning or in the early afternoon. She could quickly cover up her own clothes with a large piece of cloth. *And I'll do some hand sewing at night by candlelight in the cabin*, she decided. *That will speed things up.*

With her plans all figured out, Julia got right to work on the large table and began to cut out all the slippery mauve taffeta first.

�֍ �֍ ✗

Susie could hardly wait to tell Sam the news that Julia was Della's younger sister, making her Taffy's aunt! When he came around to the back hitching post, Susie ran outside to tell him all about it.

"And now she wants to escape with us, Sam. She's terribly afraid, but I told her you would figure it all out. And you will let her come, won't you?"

"Taffy's real aunt? And Della's sister? We can't leave someone as special as that behind. Where is she? I'd like to meet her," said Sam.

Susie ran up to the sewing room and knocked on the door.

"Julia, come down to the kitchen and meet Sam. He can only stay a few minutes."

The three of them sat down at the kitchen table and talked about the plans. Only Miss Sarah was at home, so they could talk easily while they ate the cookies Susie placed on the table.

First, Sam told Julia how much Della and William had meant to him. "I wish we could figure out a way for Della to escape with us," he added. "But she would have to cross the river first, and it would just take too much time. We'll figure out a way, somehow, to let her know that we have all escaped. I don't know how or when, but we'll think of some way, eventually."

Meeting Sam was the best thing that could happen to Julia. She could see firsthand how reliable he was, and that helped to calm her fears about making the escape.

"I'm so afraid I'll be caught before I meet up with the rest of you. I intend to try, but I'm terrified."

"Julia, there isn't much danger in the part you have to do alone. There's more danger later, after we get going and the slave masters realize there has been an escape. But then it's not your problem to solve and worry about. We'll all be together, and it will be up to me and a few others to see that we get away safely. All you'll have to do alone is leave in the middle of the night and meet up with us. Now, I'll have a plan all worked out, and it will probably be like this. I have a good contact now at the place where you are, and his name is John. Do you happen to know him?"

"Sam, I stay by myself, and I don't know anyone."

"Well, John takes care of the horses over there, and he drives the family carriage. You must have seen him around?"

"Oh, yes, I have seen him then driving the carriage. In fact, he is the one who drove me over here!"

"Good. You can trust any message you get from John. But if he cannot speak to you directly, in secret, he might need a secret word or two that he uses as a signal in your presence. Let's see, I'll decide right now. That way, you'll know it, in case you leave before I get back here again. This will be it: 'The rain clouds look like we'll have thunder tonight.' That way, he can say 'tonight,' or, 'tomorrow night,' or even, 'two nights from now.'

"Now, here's what you must do to make this work. Go for regular walks in the evening as soon as you return there. Walk by the stables; he lives above them, so he'll be there. Never speak to him. Don't stop. Just walk by. I'll tell him what you look like. Then you will know when to leave.

"Now, the next part is finding us. Do you know where the swamp dance cabin is? The one we go to?"

"Goodness no. I've never been to a swamp dance!"

"It's easy to find from where you are. There's a path through the woods that starts right behind the smokehouse. Just keep walking until you get to a little plank over the brook. Well, you know what is a good idea?" Sam's face lit up and smiling, "Why don't you come to the swamp dance tomorrow night with Susie and Taffy, and then we can show you exactly where you go to meet us. Then, you'll feel better about it, because you will have walked the area ahead of time with us. I better get going. See you all tomorrow night!"

"And I have to get upstairs and keep sewing," Julia said quickly. "I still have a lot of work to do before we leave!"

"And I want to make another big batch of cookies to give to Aunt Crissy to hand out," added Susie.

"By the way, where is Taffy?" asked Sam as he walked out to his wagon.

"Taffy is in the library dusting, you know? No one is around today, and there's little to do, so I said she could stay there until I call her," replied Susie.

✄ ✄ ✄

Sam waved good-bye and started the horse around. He headed toward the front and down the front driveway. Making these deliveries was the most pleasant task he did as a slave. Just driving along with time to think quietly was special enough. But his friendship with Susie, and before that, with Della and William, was the best part of all. He still could hardly believe the news he had heard on today's visit—that the visiting seamstress had turned out to be Della's long-lost sister! She didn't actually look that much like Della, but there was a strong resemblance in the way she spoke. It was hard to describe. More like an educated white lady? He wondered if Mrs. Davis ever noticed it. *Probably not*, he thought. "*She seems to waft in and out, preoccupied with her social affairs.*

Good thing she is, he went on thinking, *with her house slaves all involved in their own projects—Julia upstairs sewing for Susie and Taffy, Susie baking for the field slaves, and Taffy in the master's library reading his books!*

The Davis's was a very loosely managed cotton plantation, Sam knew. From his many underground contacts, he knew that Master Davis was far more involved in the state politics than he was in growing cotton or in keeping an eye on his slaves. All in all, slaves at the Davis place had a fairly easy time of it.

Except for Della and William, he reminded himself. *That was one time when Master Davis had showed he could be just as cruel as any other slave owner—to separate parents from their own children. I hope Susie keeps her mind on Taffy in the library, wrapped up in reading.*

Just as he was thinking these last thoughts, a carriage rounded the bend, coming his way. It was Master Davis, returning from another of his political meetings!

Sam took in a sharp breath and forced himself not to look back toward the house. So peaceful looking compared to his own nervous feelings.

With the library windows open, however, Taffy heard the carriage rolling over the gravel driveway. She carefully placed her book on the shelf in its same place, grabbed her feather duster, and left the room. Susie was right there, coming for her.

"Good girl. You had your ears open while you're reading. Run upstairs to Julia. She has your lavender dress ready for you to try on now."

That night, Susie let Taffy stay up and go along with her to Julia's cabin.

"Julia has almost finished the clothes she is making for us now. She's been working on them every night in the cabin. She's ready to have us try them on. I haven't told you this, Taffy, but she's making you something else besides that lavender dress."

Susie brought half a pecan pie along to Julia's.

"I thought we'd celebrate your getting these clothes finished, Julia."

Taffy looked around the room with interest. She had never seen these clothes in the upstairs sewing room! Lying on the bed were three blue-gray skirts, one obviously for her! The lavender dress was draped over a bench.

"It's all finished, Taffy. You can take it back with you and wear it," said Julia.

Taffy held the dress up to her body. Something slid onto the floor.

"It has a petticoat, too!" she said happily.

"Thank you, Julia. It's my very best dress forever. Susie, can I wear it to the swamp dance tomorrow night? We're going, aren't we?"

"Why, yes, we can go. Julia, you must come, too. Remember what Sam said, about showing you the path that goes from the swamp cabin back to the place you came from? Besides, you need to get away from all this night sewing for a change."

"I'd rather stay here and sew, Susie. Sam said the path is easy to find anyway."

"You'll feel much better having walked it a ways. Besides, you'll have a good time. Even just sitting there watching is fun. You don't have to dance if you don't want to. Julia, please come with us!"

"All right, I'll come along. I don't know what there is about you, but you do get me to do things I wouldn't think about on my own!"

Susie and Julia had previously agreed that they would not talk about the escape plans in front of Taffy. She might be too full of worrisome questions. They would wait to tell her close to the time set for leaving.

Julia had the girls try on their gray skirts so she could mark the hems and see how tight the waists should be. The long skirts were fairly narrow, but Julia had made slits in the back seam for easy walking. Each skirt had a deep pocket on one side.

The mauve taffeta skirts were still a secret from both Susie and Taffy. She hoped she could finish them, too, but they were not needed along the way, anyway. They were just a special celebration surprise, and she could mark their hems and adjust their waistbands according to the gray skirts. Julia had enough mauve taffeta to make one for herself, too.

✖ ✖ ✖

The swamp dance was in full swing when the three girls arrived. Susie found a plank long enough for the three of them, in the same corner near the musicians.

The same two boys were also in the corner, keeping time with their own handmade instruments. The taller boy was totally into keeping the beat on his drum. The smaller, younger boy had a different instrument tonight. Instead of his mule jaw and piece of iron, he was blowing through a hand-carved wooden instrument that had little holes.

Taffy looked at it with interest. It looked just like the ones she had watched her daddy make in the carpentry shop. When the boy stopped playing, she asked him where he had gotten his instrument.

"There was a slave working at the plantation where I live for a while, making furniture. Sometimes I used to go watch him. He showed me how to do some things, and then he made this for me."

"Can I try to blow through it?" asked Taffy.

The boy handed the instrument to her. Taffy tried, but nothing but air came out.

She handed it back. "Here. Take good care of it. I think I know who made it—my daddy!"

"Did he make one for you, too, then?"

"No, I guess I was too little. And now he's gone away."

The boy thought for a moment, and then he said, "Well, you can keep this one, if your father made it, and he's gone now."

"You keep it. He made it just for you. I have other things he made just for me."

After a while, Sam appeared and went outside with Julia and Susie. Taffy stayed beside the two boys, watching the dancing. Sam led Susie and Julie behind the cabin and showed Julia a fallen log where the path began, and then they walked along it so he could point out the turn to make at the plank across the brook. On the way back again, a very tall figure loomed up, heading their way along the path. It was George!

"I was looking for you, Sam. I have some information to pass on, and I also have some news about that new cook named Della."

Sam introduced George to Julia and explained that she was Della's younger sister and what a strange coincidence it had been for them all to meet.

Julia could hardly see what George looked like in the dark, but she walked along beside him, asking him questions about Della. George was certain now that it must be the same Della, all right. But they still had no way to directly contact her. George promised, however, that they would keep trying.

"Are you going to stay at the dance awhile, George?" asked Sam when they reached the cabin, the music and lights enticing them in.

"No, I have a long walk tonight and another stop to make. Well, I'll come in for just one dance, if it's not too fast and Miss Julia will be my partner?"

Julia had no desire to get out on that hard-packed dirt floor with all those whirling, dust-raising, stamping dancers, but how could she refuse this very kindly man who was trying to contact her sister? So she politely said yes.

Julia hardly knew how to dance at all, but this time, the fiddlers started up a slower melody, and George gently twirled her around and around. Finally, they both sat down on the sidelines together and continued talking for a long time.

"I thought George had to leave right away," commented Sam.

"Well, he seems to have forgotten he said that." Susie laughed as she glanced over her shoulder at George and her new dear friend sitting there, both wholly absorbed in whatever they were discussing.

On the way home, Sam walking with them, Julia asked him questions about George.

"Is he going to escape with us, do you think?"

"He isn't one of our group that I know about," replied Sam.

Taffy was now fast asleep, draped over Sam's back, so he and Julia and Susie could talk about the escape plans.

"We can't wait much longer now—maybe another two weeks, that's all. Don't try to hide away any bundles of clothes yet, but you can be thinking about it. One good idea is to cut up your quilt into two sections, so you each carry half. But cover it over with some burlap so it won't be so noticeable. The day or two before, gather any warm clothes you can and make up your bundles. The last day, add whatever food you can safely take. Then hide the bundles outside the cabin—not deep, just scoop a hollow and cover them with dirt and leaves. That's just in case any search parties come by at night; there will be no clues inside of an escape. Remember, it's better to leave with less than to be found out, so be cautious. Now, when are you returning to your own place, Julia?"

"Any time now. I've almost finished Mrs. Davis's clothes, and my own personal projects are done. I need to get back and put together some warm clothes I have over there."

❁ ❁ ❁

The very next day, Julia had a chance to speak to Mrs. Davis and tell her that her clothes would be finished by the afternoon. "Fine, then I'll have the carriage take you back tomorrow." Slaves were usually transported in the farm wagons, but there was something about Julia's dignity that made Mrs. Davis unconsciously suggest the family carriage.

Julia spent the rest of the afternoon packing away her personal sewing equipment—her scissors, needles, thimble, pins, measuring tape, and son on. Any leftover fabric was already folded away in her small trunk. The three mauve taffeta skirts were in there, too. She had decided to keep the mauve skirts a secret from Susie and Taffy. They would have enough to carry, since they would be adding food, and Julia would not have that opportunity.

Julia wished she could have made blouses to wear with the skirts, but there was not enough extra time for anything so detailed. But she had taken scraps of the red velvet and fashioned three red bows, hand sewing all the edges at night in the cabin.

Someday we'll buy our own blouses, and then we can attach the bows to the neck, she mused to herself.

After everything was organized, she sat down for a few minutes and just looked around the sewing room. It was no better than any sewing room in any plantation she had worked in, but how different all the memories were in this particular room! In this place, she had come to feel the sense of what freedom might be like, of making friends, of doing things for one's own family. Susie, Sam, and her own dear Taffy—she could not bear to lose them. And terrified though she still was, she knew her resolve to escape was stronger than ever.

Julia went down to the kitchen and asked Taffy if she would like to see Mrs. Davis's outfits before they left the sewing room. Taffy looked them over, taking note of all the details.

The pink suit jacket had designs of gray silk braid on the front, and three rows of braid lined the bottom of the skirt. The mauve taffeta gown had a matching fitted jacket with black satin piping and a white lace ruffle at the neck.

"I wish you could stay here, Julia," Taffy said wistfully.

"We won't really say good-bye, Taffy, dear. Perhaps we'll be together again sooner than we know. Come, sit on my lap for a while, and we'll just relax together. Then I must go to the cabin and get ready to leave. As it turns out, I'll be leaving tomorrow."

Taffy gladly snuggled up against Julia. And for a long while, the two of them sat together in silence, each gathering strength and comfort from the other.

❈ ❈ ❈

Later that week, there was a picnic party at a neighboring plantation. The family carriage was harnessed up, and the entire family, including Aunt Sarah, set off for the afternoon and into the early evening. There was nothing to do in the kitchen, so Susie told Taffy she might use this time to "dust the library." With everyone in and out the past weeks, Taffy had not been able to read in the library. Happily, she hurried off at once, feather duster in hand.

As usual, as soon as she closed the library door behind her, the mellow room became her own private retreat. There were no books on the shelves just for children, but she didn't care. There were books of poetry that had a rhythm that made them easy to follow along. Today, Taffy selected a small book of nature poems that were her favorite. She curled up in the leather chair and became totally engrossed in reading. The hours ticked by on the grandfather clock in the corner.

Later in the afternoon, the sun disappeared behind fast-moving clouds that piled up swiftly. Way off in the distance there was the low rumble of thunder. Taffy did not notice when the first raindrops began to fall. After a while, the rain was heavier, and the thunder grew louder. Taffy got up and closed the long window so the rain wouldn't come in. Then she returned to her book. Lost in the rhythms of "The Lady of Shalott," she didn't hear the carriage roll up the driveway to the front door, much earlier than planned.

She didn't hear the Davises get out and scurry inside. Master Davis, Aunt Sarah, and Melinda went straight up the stairs to change their wet clothes, but Louise headed for the kitchen. Mrs. Davis was already standing there, informing Susie that they wouldn't need a thing to eat later except maybe a cup of tea and some cookies.

"Oh, excuse me," said Louise. "I was looking for Taffy, as I have something for her from the party. Is she around?"

Susie stammered and replied, "Uh, She's in the library, dusting."

With Mrs. Davis standing right there, she was afraid to lie and say that Taffy might be in their cabin, as Taffy was supposed to stay with Susie until the end of the day, and doing useful tasks. The kitchen was obviously well tided. She brushed her hands nervously over her apron.

In a rush of words, she quickly added, "Miss Louise I'll go get her. She should be back in the kitchen now anyway. Wait right here while I go get her."

Susie started for the door to the dining room, but Louise was too quick for her. "Never mind, Susie. I'll find her myself."

Mrs. Davis continued telling Susie what the plans for the coming week were. But Susie, now unable to leave, was too distraught to even hear what she was saying. Oh, why hadn't she just said Taffy was in the cabin or down at slave row. How stupid of her! Hopefully, Taffy would hear Louise's approaching footsteps.

But Louise was in a playful mood, and she tiptoed up to the library door and then bounced in, saying, "Surprise, Taffy, I have something special for you—a big piece of chocolate cake from the picnic today. The storm sent us indoors over there, but we all decided we'd come home since we were all soaking wet. I never saw a storm come up so fast. Taffy, what are you doing in that chair with a book? You're reading it! You can read, can't you?"

Taffy had slammed the book shut so fast that it slid off her lap onto the floor. She jumped out of the chair and grabbed her duster. But it was too late! Louise had seen her reading! "No, no, Miss Louise. I can't read. I was just scared of the thunder and lightning, so I hid in the chair with the book I was dusting and looked at the pictures."

Taffy reached down to pick up the book. But as she'd been with Susie, Louise was too quick for her.

"Oh, let's see what it is. Hmmm, I don't see any pictures in this book at all. Hmmm, you must read very well indeed to read a book like this. Imagine that, a little slave child who can read the master's own books. What do you know? This is mighty interesting."

Taffy could see she had been found out for certain. There was no use denying the obvious truth. She began to sob and shake with fright. "Please, Miss Louise, don't tell on me. I'll never look at a book again. I can hardly read anything. I just like to pretend I can."

"Hush, Taffy," Louise replied. "You can't fool me. You were just as engrossed as could be in this book. I can tell when someone is reading."

Footsteps were heard outside the door, and in came Melinda. "Louise, where have you been? You're still in your wet clothes. What's going on in here? Why is Taffy crying?"

Louise answered, quick as a wink. "Oh, Taffy feels badly that I'm leaving so soon, and I just gave her a piece of cake from the party. I guess no one ever brought her anything like that before, so it made her all teary eyed. She was dusting the library when I came in."

"Well, I'll talk to you later, Taffy. Come on, Melinda. Come upstairs with me while I change my wet clothes, and we'll gossip about the party. I know you had your eyes on that handsome young man from Atlanta who was there."

As the two girls went up the stairs together, Melinda scolded her cousin. "You shouldn't be so friendly with our slaves. You'd think the way you behave that Taffy was another cousin in this family, when she's only a little pickaninny slave here."

Louise made no comment but continued to distract Melinda from the subject by gaily referring to the events of the party.

✂ ✂ ✂

That night, Taffy tearfully told Susie what had happened. Taffy had been so frightened that she had not heard Louise's last remarks to Melinda, covering up for her.

"Will I be punished now, and sold, like my mama and daddy?"

"Hush, hush, Taffy. Miss Louise is not a Southern lady. We'll just have to hope she is a real Northerner and doesn't think people should have slaves at all. And she's going home soon. I don't think she'll bother to say a word about it."

"I shut the window because the rain was coming in. That's why I didn't hear them come up the driveway."

"I know, I know. I'm not blaming you. They weren't supposed to return until much later. That's why I didn't come and get you. I thought we had plenty of time left."

Taffy finally fell asleep, exhausted from her frightening experience. Susie stayed awake a long time with her own worries, however.

Sam will be so upset with me, she thought. *He'll think it's my fault more than Taffy's. He never liked this idea, anyway. I guess he was right. I never should have let her do it.*

And what if Louise was not a real Northerner at all and was a spy? Still, she had seemed to really take a liking to Taffy.

What if Taffy is sold and sent away? My heart will break, and I will die.

The thought of it was too unbearable to even imagine.

Finally, Susie fell into a restless sleep, silently praying that Louise would keep this a secret.

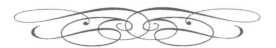

Chapter Seven

The Escape

All that last week of Louise's visit, Taffy and Susie went about their kitchen work with a nagging fear. Their fear of being found out that they could read made them quiet and tense. The cheerful atmosphere they usually created in the kitchen was gone.

"I don't like feeling scared all the time, Susie."

"Neither do I, Taffy, but it's part of growing up a slave. You just have to accept it and then try to forget about it when you can." "Growing up a slave." Taffy repeated the words to herself. "Growing up a slave." What did that really mean?

The word *slave* had never had any personal meaning to her. Until this summer, she had not even been aware that she was a slave. Then her mother and father were slaves, too! And Susie, and Sam. And Aunt Crissy and all the others down at slave row—were they the same kind of slaves? Where did the difference begin or end? These disturbing thoughts rattled around in her head with no answers.

All her young life, so far, Taffy had been protected from thinking these thoughts. Her mother and father had seen to that. She had been protected by their love and their intelligence. How had they managed to keep Taffy from being conscious of being a slave when they were slaves themselves? Taffy was still too young to ponder these thoughts. All she knew and understood was what she observed.

Every morning, her mother had dressed in clean cotton dresses and pinafores and had gone to the "big house" to cook and sew. Big Sally had been considered the head cook, but as her health had begun to fail, Della had taken over more of the special dishes, always insisting that Sally sit down awhile and "rest her bones." When Susie had arrived, a very frightened twelve-year-old, Della had immediately begun to teach her the skills of fine cooking. Somehow, Taffy's mother had known far more about elegant dishes and desserts than Big Sally had. Together, the three slaves had run a very professional kitchen. And it had been a cheerful one too—with no squabbling—a kitchen that was the envy of all the plantations in the county.

Several times a year, Della had spent her days upstairs in the sewing room, creating magic out of folded piles of fabric. Taffy had always loved to hang around when her mother was cutting out the fabric. Her mother had let her collect assorted scraps in a box and had given her a small scissors to cut them up in any way she pleased.

Her father had created his own magic. Every day, he went out behind the smokehouse to a carpentry shop shed, where he kept all the tools and lumber for making repairs on the plantation. But, besides repair work, he also could build furniture of his own design. This skill was also the envy of other plantation owners, and thus, he had, at times, been sent out to neighboring plantations to do special projects for other slave owners. In his spare time, her father had made wood toys for Taffy and other slave children. He could sing, too, and he had made wooden instruments that were used at the swamp dances.

The crude shacks for the field slaves down at slave row were not as nice as the cabin where she lived, but Taffy had never paid any attention to that. The slaves who lived there were friendly and kind to her, and there were other children to play with. She had never seen a slave whipped on this plantation. It was not allowed. Any white overseer of the cotton fields who tried that was immediately fired. Taffy was only vaguely aware that her own living conditions were better than those at slave row, but she had not thought about it.

However, now there was a new awareness that was awakening in her mind—Master and Mistress Davis and their two children were different. They were not the people she would run to in times of trouble. They were, in fact, the ones who were causing her fear. No indeed, the people she knew down at slave row were the ones she could go to for help or comfort. But Susie said that some of them could not be trusted either. It was all confusing and hard to understand—especially that awful word, *sold*. That was what had taken her parents away from her.

Now there was a new feeling on top of this vague, troubled awareness, and that was just plain fear. She had started to become accustomed to waking up feeling scared, and going to bed feeling scared.

Still, nothing bad was happening. Everything went along exactly in the same routine. Perhaps Miss Louise had not mentioned the incident in the library after all? Not even to Melinda? The two of them were always whispering and laughing together as if they had very important secrets to share. Melinda never whispered or laughed with Taffy. Neither did Miss Louise, but she still seemed so friendly and kind to Taffy, and she had not appeared angry that day in the library. Taffy couldn't help liking her.

"I wish I could hug Miss Louise good-bye," she said wistfully.

"Well, you get any such notion right out of your head. Even though Miss Louise did show special kindness to you once in a while, you have to remember she's a white woman, and you are just a slave to her." Susie's voice was unusually sharp.

Susie was much more frightened than she wanted to let on to Taffy. In spite of being so skilled and valuable, Taffy's parents had been quickly sold, leaving their only child an orphan, just because they could read. In the plantation owners' eyes, reading was, for a slave, a worse sin than stealing or lying. What if Master Davis did learn about *their* secret sin from Miss Louise? What would become of them then? Would they both be sold and separated forever? Susie didn't know who she was more terrified for—herself or poor little Taffy. So far, she had managed to give Taffy some continuity of love and protection. But without Susie, the little girl would be totally alone. Thinking back to her own lonely childhood, without either of her parents in her memory, the thought of Taffy suffering the same fate was more than Susie could bear to dwell upon.

Still, the week dragged slowly by, and nothing happened. The two cousins were in and out all week long, shopping and visiting. The twelve-year-old son had already left for his boarding school. Master Davis was in and out on political matters and concerns about the possibility of a war. Mrs. Davis was also in and out with her own social affairs. Julia was gone, but the mauve taffeta outfit, and the pink suit were now being worn and admired.

As Susie watched Mrs. Davis get into the carriage one day, dressed in the pink outfit, she sighed to herself. *Della would have been the one to make such a beautiful skirt and jacket,* she remembered, *and we would have peeked out the window together to admire it. I guess I'm just going to miss her for the rest of my life.*

✼ ✼ ✼

Sam came by one day, but he could not even stay long enough for a treat from the kitchen. Susie walked out to the wagon as he unloaded supplies. Sam told her in a low voice, "My friend has made the contact with the stable man where Julia is. He knows just what to do. We'll just hope that Julia will have the courage to make a try for the escape. It won't be long now. I'll probably only be coming by just one more time, and I'll have exact details then."

Finally, it was the day before Miss Louise was to take the train north. Susie had instructions to have breakfast ready especially early, before Miss Louise and the entire family set out on the long carriage ride to the railroad station. Miss Louise did not appear in the kitchen to say good-bye. Taffy could not shake off a feeling of deep sadness over this attractive, young white girl leaving.

Taffy figured out why she felt so sad. "Susie, saying good-bye is sad, but not saying good-bye at all is even sadder."

That night, Susie and Taffy ate their leftovers in silence. The fear of being found out was still with them, but with Miss Louise leaving the next morning, there was hope that, after all, she had told no one about finding Taffy reading in the library.

Suddenly, a knock sounded against the door. They both looked at each other in sheer terror. Was this the awful moment they had dreaded? Taffy grabbed Susie around her waist and clung to her as she tiptoed to the locked door.

"Who is it?"

"It's me, Louise. Please, open the door quickly."

Susie undid the wood hinge and opened the door just a crack and peeked out. It really was Miss Louise, her face almost covered with a black shawl. But white folks never came calling on slaves unless there was trouble afoot!

"Let me in, quick," whispered Louise.

But Susie just stood there, paralyzed with fear.

Louise gave the door a hard push and entered the room, closing and bolting the door behind her.

"I can't be gone long, or Melinda will notice," she whispered, taking off the black shawl and putting it on the bed.

"No one saw me head out here, and if anyone did and questions me, I'll just say I needed some cool night air. And if anyone sees me actually coming and going from here, I'll say I wanted to say good-bye and tell you how much I liked your wonderful cooking—which I truly did, and I do thank you. After all, I'm not a Southern lady. I can say what I please to you as equal friends."

Louise's sharp eyes glanced about the room, and she noticed a book lying at the foot of the bed. Taffy had not remembered to hide it when the knock on the door had sounded.

"Don't worry about me." She laughed nervously, "I didn't come here to spy on your reading habits. I came to help you escape from this miserable slavery."

"Come, sit here on the bed with me, so we can whisper together. I don't want to talk near the window, just in case."

She gently pushed the two girls, still clinging to each other.

"Now, here's the story. I haven't just been giggling and whispering about gossip while I've been visiting here. I've been doing a lot of snooping for my friends up North who hate slavery, and who are helping run the Underground Railroad. Do you know what that is?"

"Oh, yes, I do," whispered Susie. "My friend Sam who makes regular stops here with kitchen supplies tells me all about it."

"Good, then I don't have to waste time explaining it. But there are other things you should know. First, it is now likely there will be a war between the North and the South over slavery. Once the war begins, it will be harder than ever—maybe impossible—to keep the Underground Railroad going."

Louise bent forward and whispered even more softly, "Also, there's talk going around that slaves in this county are secretly learning to read, and there's going to be a search party to check all the slave quarters for any hidden books. There are more slaves who can read than you can imagine; but they are all so scared, they don't even dare tell each other. But it's happening just the same, and I tell you, if I had to stay down South, I'd be secretly teaching slaves to read, too. Sometimes it's the white women who are secretly teaching their own slaves to read, because they know in their hearts that it is shameful to keep fellow humans in bondage. Plus, if war comes soon, which many think it will, slavery may be ended legally, and they figure their slaves might as well start out knowing how to read."

Susie started to say something, but Louise hurried on. "Wait, let me finish. You must bury your book right away so no one can prove that you can read. You both will always be under suspicion anyway because of Taffy's mother and father teaching other slaves to read. Yes, I know all about that. They are heroes to many slaves. I also know that Mrs. Davis begged Mr. Davis not to sell and separate you as a family, but he was convinced he had to set a hard example to other slaves here and in the area. Melinda brought it all up. She wondered if it was possible that Taffy could also read, but I told her you were just too stupid a child to learn anything so difficult!"

Susie and Taffy listened with rapt attention, their eyes never leaving Louise's face.

"I think you should both take advantage of the Underground Railroad and flee north to Canada where you'll be free. Now, I know someone who can contact you about a runaway group. It has to be soon, or winter will be setting in up North. You should begin to get ready. Gather up any warm clothes you can. And be sure to wear shoes—boots would be better. It's a long, long way, and it will be colder as you move north. But don't steal any clothes from the house much ahead of time—it isn't worth being caught, so be careful. Families along the way can give you clothes. Susie, you do understand everything I'm telling you, don't you?"

"Yes, I do; you see, my friend Sam is already a leader in the Underground Railroad, and he wants us to leave with him on the next escape being planned."

"Oh, that is fine, then. I recall, now, I have heard about Sam. I did not happen to have direct contact with him, but my new and better list of stops along the way will be available to him and others to use. I've worked hard to get as much good information and help organized as I possibly can. It's not easy to plan these escapes. It's not easy to know who to trust. But there are many loyal folks involved in it, all the way North, who want to help you."

"Are the people you have contacted from the neighboring plantations?" Susie asked her.

"Mostly, but at the last picnic, I contacted someone from a plantation way across the river. They are working on an escape plan over there, too."

Louise rose to leave, wrapping the shawl around her shoulders and over her head. Then she stooped down and gave Taffy a hug and a kiss. "Don't worry, my dear; just get out of here while you still can, and you will grow up a free woman. God bless you both."

Louise pulled the black shawl well over her face again and disappeared out into the darkness.

"Do you really think we should run away, Susie?"

"Yes, I think we better go if we get the chance to do it. Your mama and daddy knew about the Underground Railroad, but they didn't get the chance to escape. Or you might be already living in Canada. I think they would want you to be brave and do it. I think they would say, 'Go, Taffy. Run away as fast as you can and keep up your courage!'"

Susie's brave words calmed Taffy's fears so she was able to fall asleep, but first, she and Susie crept outside and buried the little box with the book and papers inside. They covered the top of the hole over with pine needles so no one could notice the ground had been disturbed. Then they silently went back inside and crawled into bed.

"Can we dig it up and take it with us when we leave?"

"We will if we have time. I promise you that."

"What about Julia? Can she run away with us, too?"

"We hope she can. She already knows about Sam's plans. Get to sleep now. We can't do anything to help Julia, and fretting about it won't help. We need to get all the rest we can, because there won't be much of that once we get away."

Taffy fell fast asleep after that, but Susie remained wide-awake, thinking of everything Louise had said. She had briefly mentioned another group planning to escape from a plantation somewhere across the river. Could that include where Della now lived? Could it be possible that Della would try to escape, too? Della always believed in being hopeful, no matter how impossible a situation appeared. Could the impossible happen? Could Della make it to Canada? Was it possible that, someday, Taffy, Susie, Sam, and Julia would get there and be able to find her? Would Taffy's father get there, too? What kind of dream was she concocting, anyway? In all that vast land, could such a miracle really happen?

✄ ✄ ✄

Three days after Louise left, Sam came by in the wagon with flour, sugar, and grains. He was nervous and would not stay long enough even to have a piece of warm peach pie.

"Wrap it up, and I'll enjoy it on the way back. Walk out to the wagon with me, so we can talk outside the house."

Standing by the wagon, fussing with the harness, he whispered to Susie, "It's all set for the third night from today. There will be no moon then. That's what we waited for. Now, listen carefully. This is what you do: Get your bundles ready and find a hiding place for them outside the cabin, just as I told you before. There is a chance that search parties could be around any night now. Collect any food you can that will keep awhile and hide it outside too.

Now, here's a very important part. The night we leave, you must get ready for bed as usual—meaning you have your nightclothes on, just exactly as you would do any night. This is in case any search party comes by and inspects your cabin. Nothing can look unusual. They usually are done searching before midnight.

You don't need to worry about missing the signal to get up and leave—it will be past midnight. But you do have to worry about falling asleep and missing it that way!"

"Oh, Sam, you know we'll never be able to fall asleep that night!"

"I guess you're right. I certainly couldn't. Now, here's the signal to get up and leave. You will hear an owl hoot three times and then a short silence. Then the owl will hoot again three times. Do you have that in your head?"

"Yes, Sam, I do," replied Susie, trying to look calm. But her heart was pounding, and she felt terrified.

"Good. I know you can do it. Susie, you have to be able to do it. I won't go if you don't show up, and Taffy with you. But this is a good time for it, as we have a new and better list of secret stops along the way. And it comes through the visitor you had here, Louise. I never happened to meet her, but she made other contacts while she was here and was extremely helpful."

There was something about Susie, standing there, looking so serious and capable but also so young and fragile—it made Sam's heart ache for her. He knew it would take all her courage to accomplish this first and dangerous part of the escape.

"You can do it, Susie. The plans are very carefully worked out. After that second time the owl hoots, that's when you get up and get dressed. It means that a slave I have contacted has been sneaking around in the pine grove behind your cabin and knows there is no search party anywhere nearby. Now, you dig up your bundles and get going, down through the pine grove, down to the swamp dance area. No moon, so it will be very black, but you know the way very well. You know the plank crossing over that brook? Don't cross over; instead, you take a right into the large forest that comes out at the wide field."

"I know, Sam. I know all that way, night or day."

"Stop and rest a few minutes at the opening to that big field. Listen carefully. If you don't hear any sound, you make a run for it, across that field. It will be pitch-black out there with no moon. But your eyes will have adjusted to the night by then. Try to run in a straight line toward the tallest tree you see in the middle of the forest across that field. That should put you in the right area where there is a big fallen log. If you don't see the log, don't panic. Just go into the woods—about twenty-five steps, anyway—and just stand there and wait.

"You just wait there until the owl hoots three times and three times again. Now it's your turn. You hoot back, in exactly the same way. Then you wait again, and we'll find you. No calling out loud, no matter what happens. You understand?"

"Yes, Sam, I understand," she said, nervously patting her apron skirt.

"There's going to be eight of us, I think, in this runaway group, and we don't want to spoil it for anyone."

"But what if you don't find us?"

"You can wait almost all the rest of the night. If needed, we'll have to make the owl signal more than one time. If no one ever shows up, you have to get back to your cabin before daylight. But you would have plenty of time for that. But we will make it. You have to believe we will make it, Susie."

❈   ❈   ❈

Taffy and Susie were terrified of each step of the plan;

yet they knew they would not back out. Those last two days, the big kitchen had never seemed so appealing and safe. The kitchen was the one place where they felt they had some control over their lowly status in life. After all, they were the ones who cooked all the meals for the family. They were the ones who made it possible for Mrs. Davis to smile and accept compliments for her lovely tea parties. Working in the kitchen, Susie especially felt confident and happy.

The rest of the time, she tended to sink into a more melancholy state of mind. Taffy's spirit was naturally more cheerful because of her happy childhood with her own mother and father. That was an advantage Susie had never had. Working in the kitchen with Della and Big Sally had been Susie's happiest years as a slave. It was hard for her to leave this place and this routine that seemed so safe, so secure.

I must remember, she kept repeating to herself, over and over, *that nothin' is secure or safe for a slave. So I might as well have the courage to try to escape to freedom. Freedom!*

The strange word rang out in her head.

What will it be like to be free? She couldn't even imagine what it would be like. She knew that freedom did not guarantee safety and security, either. But the word still rang out in her head with an irresistible calling.

Those last two days, Susie took what she dared from the pantry. There was a slab of smoked ham leftover that the family would never miss. Mrs. Davis had never been interested enough in meal planning to keep close track of the details, as long as the cooks produced their high-quality results.

There was a closet near the kitchen where the family kept some off-season jackets and scarves. It was not cold enough yet for anyone to need them, so taking a few things would not be noticed. Way in the back, Susie even found a pair of boots that would fit her and pair of the boy's that fit Taffy.

The night before they were to leave, Susie took a pair of scissors back to the cabin and cut their quilt in half.

"We'll each have half a quilt to wrap things in. Then we'll cut up an old gray dress to wrap over the quilts. It won't be so colorful, and it will keep our quilt cleaner. Someday, we'll sew our quilt back together again, Taffy, and that will be a happy day!"

"What about our book? When are we going to dig it up so we can pack it?"

"Not until tomorrow night when we leave. Tonight, we're going to dig a bigger hole. I found a soft place right up against the back of the cabin where we can hide the boots, the jacket, and the food and cover it over with leaves and a few loose branches I found."

Susie was very nervous until it was dark, worrying that a search party might come along to inspect the cabin. One way or another, it all seemed very risky to her.

Maybe I should have waited until tomorrow to take the jackets and things. Well, it's too late now. We just have to go out and bury them.

Finally, Susie and Taffy had accomplished their hiding task, and were safely in bed. If a search party came now, they were certain there was not a clue anyone could find. But no one came, and they fell asleep. It would be their last night in their secure little cabin—their last night in a real bed for many nights to come.

The last day in the kitchen, Susie roasted a large turkey for the evening meal.

To herself, she admitted, *How strange it is. I'm still thinking about them and their meals—that roasting a turkey will leave them with several days of good leftovers!* She also knew she could take a few slices for their food bundle. With that in mind, she had Taffy make a double batch of apple raisin bars sprinkled with nuts.

Finally, the workday ended, and the kitchen was cleaned up for the night, for the last time. Taffy dashed out quickly and ran to the cabin. But Susie lingered for one last look around and for the memories of good times shared there with Big Sally and Della, the closest person to a loving relative she had ever known.

She and Taffy had already eaten a substantial meal in the kitchen, so there was nothing left to do but shut the door behind her and go to the cabin.

Again, they went out to the hiding place, this time hiding the package of turkey slices.

"Let's just hope no wild animals can sniff out that turkey and ham," said Susie, as they heaped more dirt, leaves, and two branches over the hole.

Following Sam's plan exactly, they prepared for bed as usual. The clothes they would normally wear the next day in the kitchen were hanging neatly on hooks in the corner of the room. The gray, homespun dresses they would wear tonight were also hanging in the corner. The dress Julia had made for Taffy of lavender cotton was in the hidden bundle. Her outgrown blue dress they would have to leave behind.

The dark hours dragged by slowly. No footsteps were heard, and no search party came by. It was getting harder and harder not to doze off. Finally, off in the distance, they heard an owl hoot three times, very softly.

"It's a good thing we didn't fall asleep, Taffy, or we never would have heard that owl hoot," whispered Susie.

In a short while, they heard the owl hoot three times again, this time a little louder and closer.

"That *must* be the signal," whispered Susie. Certainly a real owl would not hoot in exactly that same pattern, she hoped nervously. Her heart pounding and her throat dry, she got out of bed and dressed in the gray dress. Taffy took a few more minutes to lie in bed.

The weather was still warm, and they did not need anything more than the dresses to wear. The few other clothes they had were packed in the hidden bundles.

"Here we go; there's nothing else we can do in here," whispered Susie. In the pitch-blackness of the moonless night, she had no desire to linger for one last look at her cozy, little cabin.

They crept silently out the door, closing it softly behind them. They heard no unusual sounds in the black night—only the soft hissing of the night breeze through the tall pines and the whir of crickets. The hole around back had not been disturbed, and they quickly uncovered the two bundles wrapped up in the gray fabric.

"I think we can take time to dig up the book, Taffy," Susie whispered. Susie dusted off the book and tucked it into her bundle, but she didn't the box and papers and pencil. Those she carried over to a hollow spot and covered it over with leaves.

It's just as well no one ever finds out we were reading and writing, thought Susie, *in case we are captured.*

Even in the dark, it was not hard to find the familiar path through the pine grove that led down to the swamp crossing. The only thing that slowed them up were soggy places from the heavy rain the past week. Finally, they were standing at the edge of the wide field. Their eyes had adjusted to the black night, so they could make out the silhouetted edges of the deep woods on the far side of the field. Across that open expanse, it looked fearfully far away.

For the first time, Susie thought of the unseen hollows and bumps in that wide field.

"It's good we are wearing our light, familiar shoes," she whispered. "We can't take time to look down at our feet for every hole or puddle. Once we start to run across, we have to keep going as fast as we can. Do you see that tallest tree, Taffy? We'll keep that in sight as we run. That should help us stay in a straight line, as Sam told us to do. We don't want to end up running in circles. All right, off we go!

"Go ahead of me, Taffy," she whispered, and she gave her a pat on the back. *I don't want Taffy falling down behind me where I can't see her,* thought Susie.

Susie tripped once over a rough spot, but she managed to catch herself and keep going without tumbling. Taffy, so small and light, seemed to be flying across the field ahead of her!

It seemed forever to Susie before they reached the protection of the woods. Gasping for breath and just from the fright of it all, they stood still for a while.

"Where's the fallen log, Susie? I don't see it," gasped Taffy in whispers.

"Let's take ten steps to the left. If we don't find it, we'll take ten steps back, and then we'll take ten steps to the right. Then we'll return if there's no log. Then we'll go our twenty-five steps into the woods from here. I really thought we ran in a straight line. I could see the highest tree right in front of me all the time," Susie gasped.

Ten steps to the left produced no fallen log. Ten steps to the right, and they almost fell over it.

"Now, twenty-five steps back into the woods," Susie whispered thankfully. Her heart was still pounding from the run.

Deeper in the woods, they waited what seemed an endlessly long time. Strange rustling sounds frightened them, but nothing happened; no one appeared. Thirty minutes? An hour? Maybe it was only about fifteen minutes but just seemed endless. Finally, they heard an owl hoot softly, three times in a row.

Then there was silence.

Taffy and Susie now hardly breathed at all, waiting.

It seemed the longest silence in the world.

Then the owl hooted again! Three times in a row.

The girls hooted back, just as they had been told. They waited again, in the black silence.

All of a sudden, there was the sound of crunching twigs, coming closer. Taffy and Susie stood still, clinging to each other, frozen in fear. In another few minutes a dark form appeared.

And it was Sam!

"Good work. You made it!" he whispered, giving each of them a quick hug.

"The rest of the group made it, too. They are all waiting down the trail aways. Follow me, single file, and don't speak one word to anyone. Once we meet up with them, we're really on our way."

After they had walked about twenty minutes, Sam stopped and made the hooting sound, three times in a row, and then again. Off in the distance, the same sound was repeated.

"That means it's all clear with them. No search parties around as far as we can tell. Remember now, no talking to the others when we meet up. We start right in walking, and there's no stopping the rest of the night. If you have to go to the outhouse, now's the time to do it."

Susie and Taffy made a quick trip behind some trees, and then they were off again.

Sam made one more remark before they reached the group. "Come dawn, we'll rest for a while, but not for long. Once we get beyond the plantation lowlands and hit the higher forests, we can take a longer rest. By then, we'll be many hours ahead of any search party organized just to hunt for us. But we still have to be on guard for other agents and search parties, all along the way, except in the real wilderness areas. Before we reach the first stop on the railroad, it amounts to walking both day and night."

After a few more steps, they met up with the others. Susie and Taffy could only make out vague shapes in the darkness. No one spoke a word. The black forms shifted about and became a single line, spaced out. Susie noticed that some of the forms were tall, but two seemed to be wearing skirts, and one was short and thin as a pencil. Susie, Taffy, and Sam were at the end of the silent line.

It was Sam's preassigned duty to hang back once in a while and listen for the sounds of any suspicious noises following them. Then he would catch up again.

All the rest of the black night, they kept up the steady and silent pace.

Taffy was beginning to feel she could not put one foot in front of the other one more time without falling down in exhaustion. A chilly ground fog was swirling around them, and she could barely make out Susie in front of her. Sometimes she turned around and could see no sign of Sam at all. She wanted to call out to Susie or Sam, but she kept her promise not to say one word, ever, while they were walking along.

All of a sudden, Susie stopped walking, and Taffy caught up with her. The tallest man, at the front of the line, had stopped. And now everyone was almost bunched together. He pointed in silence to the left of the trail. There was a slight clearing in the tangle of bushes, and more swirls of damp fog were rising from that direction. Everyone scrambled down a steep embankment to a deep hollow and a narrow stream bordered with rocks. Sam, close behind Taffy, guided them to a flat ledge. The others seemed to disappear like ghosts into the fog. Sam silently indicated with his hands that they should sit down on the flat ledge.

Once all three were huddled close together on the ledge, Sam spoke in whispers to them. "It's almost morning. I can already sense a difference in the darkness. We plan to rest here a few hours and then start up again. It's going to be deep wilderness ahead, so we can dare to walk right through the day in this section. So get something out to eat and try to stretch out on this flat rock and take a nap."

Susie and Taffy did not need to be told twice to open up the food packages. Sam ate with them and whispered, "The plan is to keep in sections of three, in case we have to suddenly hide. There are eight of us altogether. We are one section of three; and there's two other sections."

When they had finished eating, Sam whispered again, "Before you fall asleep, I have a surprise for you. I'll be right back with someone."

Streaks of pale light were sifting down through the trees and mixing with the rising fog. Sam disappeared into the gray light and soon returned with not one, but two shadowy forms, dressed in long skirts. He guided them over to the flat ledge where Susie and Taffy were huddled together.

For the first time, they could see for certain that there were two other females in their runaway group of eight. One was a short, plump woman, perhaps in her forties. But the other one was slim and tall.

"Julia!" Taffy cried aloud, forgetting she was not supposed to ever speak above a whisper on the trip.

Julia reached out and took Taffy in her arms and hugged her closely.

"Yes, my dear one, it's really me. Don't speak. Don't say a word out loud," Julia whispered. "But it's really me. I made it. I really did it! I was so scared I thought I would just drop dead with fright before I got there. Now we are all together again, I'm not afraid anymore. I can keep going for weeks, months now!"

Julia held onto Taffy as if she would never let her go.

Susie handed Julia and the other woman the parcel of food. But Julia said, "No, no, keep it. Clara has food with her she wants to share, too."

In whispers, as they crouched together on the flat ledge, Julia managed to tell the details of the first part of her solitary escape.

"Just as Sam told me to do, I walked by the stable every night. One evening, the stable man mentioned the rain clouds making thunder the very next night! I was terrified! I hurried back to my room and fixed up my bundle and hid it under my bed. There was no way I could take any food. I couldn't imagine how I would slip out of that big house without tripping over something in the dark, but I did it. I made it all the way behind the smokehouse without even waking the dogs and starting them barking. At least, you two were together, but I was all alone. I can hardly believe I did it. But I thought of you, Taffy, and I just kept going, putting one foot in front of the other. I couldn't see just where I was putting my feet, either, but at least there was a definite path to follow."

"All of a sudden, though, the ground became soggy, and I knew I'd never see real puddles. That slowed me down, and I was getting more scared with every step. And then, you won't believe what happened! I heard a voice whisper my name! I thought I would die of fright right on the spot! But the voice quickly added, 'Julia, don't be scared. It's me—George!'

"Then I heard crunching sounds, and the next minute, he was right there beside me! And you know what he did? He just picked me up and carried me over all the puddles until we got to dry ground again! He told me that he was thinking of me having to cross that low place. After all the rain we had, he was afraid I would stumble into a wet hole in the dark. So he left the group and walked back to find me. Oh, you can't imagine how thankful I was he thought of me! He had never mentioned to me at the swamp dance that he was even considering being a runaway. But he said he didn't make up his mind until the day before the group left."

For the first time, the other woman whispered, "I was already at the meeting place ahead of Julia, although those puddles slowed me down, too, even though I had boots on. I went right into one puddle over my ankles. I couldn't believe my eyes when George appeared with Julia! I knew her! We were both at the same plantation. But Julia lived inside the big house, and I lived behind the smokehouse, where I worked. Neither one of us knew that the other was planning to escape by the Underground Railroad. Actually, I didn't know I was going until the last few days. There was a slave in the smokehouse who was going, and then he changed his mind and decided to wait until another time. He told me I should take his place. I had only seen Julia a few times when I took things over to the kitchen. But when she came up to me, we just hugged as if we were close friends, and we cried on each other's shoulders for a long time."

"Can Julia stay here with us while we take a nap?" asked Taffy.

Sam thought a moment, and then he whispered back, "Yes, both Julia and Clara can this time. We are all well hidden down here. Just be sure you remain very quiet, Taffy."

But as soon as Julia cradled Taffy into her arms, she fell fast asleep.

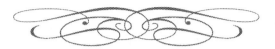

Chapter Eight

The Underground Railroad Journey

Once the surprise and joy of discovering that Julia was one of the eight runaways had subsided, the weary journey began to blur in Taffy's mind as they trudged on and on and on.

There had been another surprise, however, that foggy morning when they climbed back up the banks of the ravine. For the first time, she saw her young musician friend from the swamp dances! Taffy stared at him, wide-eyed. It was Tom!

"I didn't know you were going to escape, too!"

"I didn't know you were, either!"

"Did you bring your flute with you?"

"Sure did. That's the one thing I wanted most to keep with me."

Taffy ran to Sam, trying hard to whisper, "Sam, you never said Tom was coming, too!"

"We didn't know for sure until the last few days just who was coming, Taffy. George didn't decide until the end, and Clara was a switch with someone else. John, the stable man always wanted to come, as long as I promised that Tom could come with him. At first I thought he was too young to keep up. But two other slaves later backed out, so I gave them the chance after all. John convinced me that young Tom is very strong in spite of being so thin. He's had to work hard caring for horses, and he's got long legs."

"Will he have to be carried sometimes, like me?"

"Perhaps not. He's almost as tall as I am."

"Well, I won't have to be carried either," said Taffy bravely.

It was slower walking as they began to climb higher and higher into the mountainous wilderness. Because they were safe now from search parties, they made the most of it by walking night and day with short stops for rest and food. They must be reaching Canada and freedom soon, thought Taffy, as she wearily plodded along, trying hard to keep up.

The fact was that they had not even reached the first official railroad stop! There was plenty of fresh stream water to drink, but their combined food supply was now becoming dangerously low.

Sam no longer had to fall back to keep watch. This meant he could carry Taffy for longer stretches at a time. But Tom just kept plodding along at a fast pace on his long and spindly legs!

"Come on, Taffy. Climb aboard the special railroad express!" said Sam cheerily.

"I can walk," replied Taffy as she stumbled along, on the verge of falling down.

"You're light as a feather on my back, Taffy! Up you go! It's better for all of us for you to be carried than to hold us back from our fast pace, you know."

Taffy was far too exhausted to resist. They were still climbing uphill. Once secure on Sam's back, Taffy fell fast asleep in welcome relief from trudging on, tired and hungry.

Days, nights, rest stops. Streams to wash in. Tiny bites of food to nibble on, as hungry after eating as before. Walk on, be carried, walk, be carried, rest, eat, sleep while being carried, Oh, blessed sleep.

It all became one exhausting blur to her. Worst of all, at least to Taffy, was keeping the silence. Even on the stops for rest and eating, only brief whispers were allowed. At least when they stopped, she had a chance to be close to Julia which she found very comforting, for Julia would hold her close and massage her back so she would quickly fall asleep for the short period they had for resting.

One morning after a rest stop, George and Sam decided to change positions. That meant Sam was at the front of the line, with Taffy behind him and Susie following her. Susie longed to walk beside Taffy and put her arm around her, but the rule was single file. The middle trio was Clara, young Tom, and John the stable man. Both Tom and John went by the last name of Taylor, which of course, was the last name of their white master. Then came Julia, and at the end of the line was tall, distinguished-looking George. George said that John had the right idea when he'd said he would never speak his white master's last name again as his own, and when he reached freedom, he would take a brand-new name for himself.

Taffy managed to keep up the pace all morning. But after the next rest stop, she began to fall back again. Twice, Susie caught up with her and patted her lovingly on the back. Taffy felt disgusted with herself for falling behind, but her legs would hardly move without trembling. Didn't her friend Tom ever fall behind? He seemed to just float along on those long, skinny legs. But at least no one ever made fun of her or called her "baby."

"All right, Taffy, here we go. Time to ride the express train north. Tickets, please. Have your tickets ready."

That meant Taffy was supposed to hand Sam a pebble, a twig, or a leaf. Sam made it seem like a game, and once she was scooped up and hanging on, her head slumped over his neck, she fell fast asleep in a few minutes.

That's where she was, sound asleep, when all of a sudden, Sam stopped quickly, and everyone crowded around them. Taffy opened her eyes to discover it was already late in the day—so late that the sky was already deep in shades of rose and violet. They were standing on the edge of a high bluff, overlooking a broad valley below. A pale, crescent moon hung low in the darkening sky. Mist and shadows blurred the edges of the cleared valley where it met the forested hills. Three log cabins and a barn were clustered in the center of the clearing, and smoke was rising out of the chimneys.

Sam set Taffy down on the flat ledge, took a piece of paper out of his pocket, and looked at it.

"This has to be it—our first railroad stop!"

"And it's thanks to Louise, because she's the one who secretly handed out these newest maps," Susie whispered in Taffy's ear.

Taffy blinked hard and looked down at the beautiful valley. Ever afterward, she would say it was the most beautiful sight she had ever seen. John volunteered to go ahead and make certain it really was a railroad stop and that it was safe for all of them to climb down the hillside and cross the open fields below.

Silently, they all watched as John finally made his way to the door of the largest cabin. The door opened, and John entered. They all waited breathlessly for what seemed endless minutes. Then the door opened, and a soft light glowed from within as the door was opened wide. John and two other figures stood outside and waved and beckoned to them to come down!

As they crossed the field to the first cabin, the two other cabin doors opened, and several people came running out and waited for them. The weary travelers were so used to whispering, they still did so. But the people just laughed out loud and said to them, "You don't need to whisper while you are here with us! This is pioneer wilderness country. There's no other settlement for fifty miles, and none of us are interested in keeping folks in slavery. We want free opportunity in the new lands opening up for folks who want to work hard and be independent!"

These were white people talking! At first Taffy didn't know what to make of them, and she began to feel that tight, resentful feeling she had begun to develop over the summer back at the plantation. But it was impossible to feel that way for long among these kind and cheerful people, and she was soon caught up in the comfort and merriment they offered.

Everyone talked at once and fussed over them. Finally, all the practical decisions had been worked out. They knew where to go to find the outhouse, where to get washed up outside, and how they would all be divided up for sleeping arrangements that night. But first, they would have a hot meal, with the pioneers waiting on them. They sat down at a long, rough wood table in front of a roaring fire in the fireplace and were handed steaming bowls of thick soup filled with chunks of meat and vegetables. Then big hunks of crusty bread were passed around with butter and jam to spread on it.

After that, there were mugs of something hot and spicy to drink and chunky bars of something sweet to go with it.

There were several children in the pioneer group of families. But they were too shy to join in and just hung back in the shadows and watched.

When the pioneer men and women realized how long the group had been walking with no real rest or hot food, they insisted that one night in their valley was not enough to give them strength to go on.

"You must stay here two nights. Once you get farther north, you will never again be as safe as you are right here in this wilderness."

The men in the runaway party were led to the next two cabins and divided up there, but Clara, Julia, Susie, and Taffy were to stay at the first and largest cabin. Warm quilts were brought out, and they wrapped themselves up and soon fell into a deep sleep in front of the banked fire.

The next morning, everyone was given bowls of hot oatmeal in the separate cabins. The former slave men insisted they wanted to be helpful, so they helped the pioneers clear some land and mend a section of fence behind the barn. But the women pioneers would not let the women slaves do anything except rest and take a hot bath in a wooden tub set up in front of a once-again roaring fire.

Taffy and Tom were finally spoken to by the white children and invited to play outside. Soon Taffy and Tom were running and yelling as they played crack the whip and other games, as if they had never been so tired that their legs trembled with every step forward.

That night, once again, they all piled into the large cabin and shared a meal of roasted goose with stuffing and vegetables.

Everyone was relaxed and talked and laughed as if they all had known each other for years. The pioneers said this was the very first group of runaway slaves they had taken in, as the map was new. About a month ago, a small party had come into the valley and asked them if they would be willing to be part of the Underground Railroad. With more slaves trying to escape and the possibility of war closer each month, there needed to be more isolated routes for the railroad to operate.

As they continued heading north, there would be more and more white people who were opposed to slavery, even though their states were considered "border states"—meaning they could go one way or the other if it finally came down to a real separation of the country, North and South, and eventually, an outright civil war. The problem was, however, that though there would be more people willing to help the slaves in their flight for freedom, there would not be this wilderness area where no search parties ever bothered to go.

Once again, Susie, Clara, Julia, and Taffy gratefully wrapped themselves in the quilts and slept soundly in front of the fire. Taffy thought how wonderful it would be to stay in this beautiful valley forever.

Before she fell asleep, she whispered to Julia, lying next to her, "Is this what freedom is going to be like?"

"I hope so, Taffy. I do hope so.

❈ ❈ ❈

The next morning, they had another hearty breakfast, and hefty parcels of food were packed up for them. It was hard to say good-bye to the kind people in the secret valley. There were handshakes, hugs, tears, and cheerful wishes all around. The eight runaways made their way across the open field and up the hill. When they reached the bluff where they had first sighted the valley, they all waved a final good-bye to the tiny figures waving from the front of the large cabin.

The attitude of the eight runaways changed after their stay in the secret valley. The experience had affected each one of them deeply. It wasn't something they knew how to express or even acknowledge—it was just a feeling. But it changed them as a group. They became more open and trusting of each other. Each one also felt more optimistic that they would be successful in their attempt to escape to freedom.

Of course, they had started out with the common goal to escape from slavery. Still, basically, each slave had been a loner. Being part of a small trusting group was not part of a slave's experience. The only group event that came close was their church meeting, but that was a large assortment of slaves from different plantations. That was the closest they could get to a sense of belonging and sharing of misery. For undeniably, each slave had his or her own personal and tragic story.

At the first long rest stop after leaving the pioneers, the eight of them were more inclined to stay together. It was safe since they were still in the wilderness of high country, but they also had their recent good experience to share. Once again, they were in a deep secluded valley. But this one was smaller, and no settlers' cabins were to be seen. They dared to build a campfire, and for a long time, they sat around it and talked about their two nights in the other valley.

No one, except Julia in her youth, had ever had such an experience before with white people. And not even in Julia's unique situation had she actually been waited on before! There they all were, the first meal there, sitting at a long table, with all the white folks scurrying around, filling their bowls a second time, passing bread, all the while laughing and talking as if this was a pleasure for them to do! The second night's big meal had been even more amazing. This time they'd all managed to crowd together at the long table—the white folks and themselves—but it was still the pioneers who had done the jumping up and waiting on them!

Sitting beside each other by the campfire, Taffy and Tom talked together about their own experiences. Neither one had ever played with white children before, but it had all seemed as natural as playing down at slave row.

"Where did you and the boys go after we went inside?"

"We went around back to watch the men help build a fence. Then Carl asked me to show his father my wooden flute, and his father looked it over very carefully and wrote something down on a piece of paper. He said he was going to try to make one like it for Carl. Carl did pretty good getting sounds out of it.

"After that, his mother made me take a hot bath, and she got out some of Carl's clothes and said I should keep them. And she said she planned to throw mine in the fire, including my shoes. She said the reason I had a blister on my foot was because my shoes were too small, so she made me soak my feet and then she put some gooey stuff on the blister and covered it over. And you know, yesterday and now, I don't feel it at all!"

"I didn't know your foot hurt you, Tom. You never said anything about it."

"I was afraid to. I was afraid if I couldn't keep up, or if I complained, they might make me head back, alone."

"Sam would never do that! He would have carried you instead, and he's the one in charge."

"Yeah. I guess John would have, too. But he's not all that strong, and he's wanted to escape for as long as I can remember. He always took good care of me back at the stable, ever since I lost my mother.

"You were inside for a long time in the afternoon. What were you doing?" Tom asked Taffy.

"Oh, Jane and I went up the ladder to the loft where she slept, and we played with her two rag dolls. She had different clothes to dress them in. She even said I could keep one of the dolls, but Susie wouldn't let me. She said we had too much to carry already. But you know what her mother did? She made me a tiny rag doll out of scraps of cloth, and she embroidered a little face on it. Then she left a hole in the back and said, when I got to Canada, I should just stuff the doll with beans or anything I could find and sew it up—you know, like the bean bag we played with there, to toss around and try to catch!"

The next few days, there was rough walking, up and down hills. At last they came to another pioneer settlement, and once again there was hot food, warm quilts by a roaring fire, and a hot bath in a wooden tub. There were no small children in this group—the youngest being about Susie's age. Taffy and Tom spent the leisurely time together, and Taffy was finally able to get some sounds out of Tom's wooden flute. But the sounds were nothing like the real melodies that Tom could play so easily.

"Did my daddy ever get to hear you play on it?"

"Yeah, he did, because he was at our plantation building things for quite a while. He said I should practice every chance I got and I'd be a real musician someday."

That Tom had known her own daddy made their friendship all the more meaningful to Taffy.

When they left this pioneer group of three families, they were warned, "You must stay on guard; settlements will soon be closer together. But the good part of that is that you will have rest stops more often."

They all bid each other a warm farewell, and once again, the eight runaways trudged off into the woods.

Once again, the weary journey began to blur for Taffy. Sometimes her legs trembled so much they almost collapsed under her. But just when she didn't think she could walk another step without crying, Sam or George would carry her, and she would fall fast asleep. When George carried her on his tall back, he softly hummed tunes as they jogged along. Even the railroad station stops blurred for her. She was so tired she was only vaguely aware of the kind faces and helping hands. After the hot food, all she wanted to do was curl up inside those puffy quilts that were always offered and go to sleep by the warm fire and sleep, sleep, sleep.

Then one day, the routine changed. For several hours, they hid beside a river, until, upon a certain signal, they met up with several white men who had four small boats. In the dark of night, they were rowed down the river. When they reached a rickety wood landing, they got out and were led to a huge, canvas-covered wagon. There was room for all of them to crouch down in the bottom with hay heaped over them. All the rest of the night, they rumbled and bumped along.

Sometime in the morning, the sounds changed. A different kind of sound came from underneath, as if the heavy wagon wheels were bouncing over a rough, uneven planking. Suddenly, a piercing whistle blew and made them all jump. After that, it became smooth and quiet except for a steady swishing sound. How long this went on, they could not judge, as by now they were very weary of being in this cramped position in the bottom of the wagon. But eventually, the whistle blew again, several times. And then the swishing sound stopped, and they bounced over the rough planks again.

They could hear voices close by, all around them, it seemed. And twice, the wagon stopped for them to get out briefly. Then it rolled on again. After a while, the roadbed beneath them settled into a fairly smooth path with occasional ruts and bumps, giving them a smoother ride. At one point along the way, the wagon stopped, and each runaway was given a few minutes to get out, run into the woods they were passing through, and relieve him or herself.

It was almost dark when they were told to climb out of the wagon, stiff and cramped. They found themselves in a large fenced-in barnyard. Quickly, they were guided through a huge cow barn and out back into a clean, attached shed with no windows. Clean hay covered the floor, and a high pile of blankets was stacked nearby. Hot food was later brought out to them, and then they were able to fall asleep, stretched out with plenty of room to toss and turn and get the cramps out of their aching limbs.

The next day, they were once again hidden in the wagon for a long daytime trip. That night, after dark, they arrived at another farm, where they were led up to a loft in a high barn. There was plenty of sweet smelling hay, and Taffy and Tom settled down next to a small window where they could watch a full moon and twinkling stars in a clear sky.

For a long while, no one could get to sleep. Their arms and legs were still too cramped. Sam decided that each person, in turn, could walk up and down the length of the loft. That way, there would be little sound of footsteps overhead, just in case anyone was below. They had been assured, however, that it was very unlikely that any agents would be scouting around in this area.

When it was John's turn to walk up and down, he stopped by the window, looked out, and said, "Next time we see a full moon, Tom, we may be free!"

After he turned and began walking back, Taffy asked Tom, "How old were you when you lost your mama? Was she sold like my mama and daddy were?"

"John told me I was five. John told me what happened when I was older. My mother and some other women slaves found out they were about to be sold to someone who didn't want any children along. One way or another, she knew she would lose me. So she told John she would rather take her chances and run away instead of being sold without me. She knew I was too little to keep up with an escape group, so she told John to look after me. He had always been a good friend to us. John has wanted to escape for years, but he was afraid to do it until he met up with Sam and heard his good plans."

Taffy said, "Maybe you'll find your mama in Canada. That's what I'm hoping to do." Tom gazed at the clouds passing over the pale moon in the vast sky above them.

"It's been a long time now, seven years since she ran away. Tom glanced at 3 bright stars near the moon. He sighed, but went on to say, "But I can read, and that might help me find her. John taught me to read. My mother could read a little, too."

"Sam says that knowing how to read and write will be the most important thing in helping us find our families. I hope we get there soon. My legs get tired so quick I think I will fall down. Tomorrow we have to start walking again, Sam said. Don't you get tired from walking, Tom?"

"Yes, but I don't feel like falling down. Now that my foot sore is gone, I don't mind getting tired and numb. I could even carry you, Taffy, if I had to!"

Taffy looked downcast at that remark. "Tomorrow I'll try to walk all day without having to be carried. I'm not a baby, you know."

"Taffy, I'm a lot taller than you are, and my legs are longer. I'm almost as tall as Sam!"

All that night and the next day, they had a chance to rest and have hot food. At nightfall, they once again began trudging on through hilly woodlands. In spite of her brave remarks, Taffy soon found her legs trembling again and was relieved when Sam told her get on board the special train.

Once again, the long trip became a blur. And added to her discomfort was a recurring cough that increased her deep weariness.

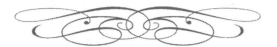

Chapter Nine

Daisy Keeps the Family Secret

The morning after her tenth birthday, Daisy woke up early and hurried down the kitchen stairs to see what was going on. "Where are the runaway slaves?" she asked Aunt Mary. Mary usually stayed home on Sundays, but because the new arrivals were hiding in the cellar, she wanted to be there to help keep guard. She was already busy mixing up a big batter for muffins.

"They're fast asleep down in the cellar. Don't you go snoopin' 'round there now. They need to sleep while they can, without worrying about who's sneakin' around. If any Southern agents come 'round here today, we'll have to wake them fast and help them get into that old dry well, quick as they can. It's Sunday, but still, you never know what those agents will do."

"What about their blankets and things when they hide? Won't the agents see that someone was down there?"

"You think of everything, don't you, honey lamb—just like your family. There's a plan to hide every clue. The minute those agents knock on the front door, everyone inside this house goes into action. I'm closest to the cellar stairs, so I go right down and help them hide in the well.

"Then, whoever answers the door and lets them in, makes certain that they go upstairs first and tries to stall them off as long as possible. That way, by the time they get to snoop in the cellar, everything has been done, and there's not a sign that a living soul was ever down there!"

Daisy listened wide-eyed to Aunt Mary. Whenever Aunt Mary explained something to Daisy, it always seemed very important and very exciting.

"I think I'll stay home from Sunday school today," said Daisy.

Just as she said that, her mother entered the kitchen.

"You are going to Sunday school, Daisy, as usual. Only your father will stay home, just in case there is any trouble or the agents come around in the morning."

After Sunday school and church, Daisy ran home ahead of her family, not stopping to talk to her friends as she usually did.

Breathlessly, she ran into the kitchen and asked, "Are they still in the cellar?"

"Yes, they are, honey lamb. And I hope they are still sleeping. You go outside in the yard and swing for a while and cool down. You can also keep a lookout down the sidewalk. If you see Mr. Carlson coming down the street with any strange men along with him, you run right in and tell me, Daisy," said Aunt Mary.

Daisy sat in her swing pushing her feet into the worn grass just enough to go gently back and forth. After a while, she did notice some people come from around the corner and head down her street. When they got closer, she saw that it was, indeed, Mr. Carlson, the sheriff. And two men were following along right behind him on the narrow sidewalk.

Daisy ran into the kitchen with this news for Aunt Mary.

"Run and tell your mother, child. I think she went upstairs a few minutes ago."

Mrs. Jackson peeked through the curtains at the front of the house. "Yes, it's Mr. Carlson, all right. Imagine, even on Sunday, those agents want to come looking around here. There ought to be a law against it. Well, at least they can never enter alone, without Mr. Carlson escorting them. He's our friend, but he's required to do it."

Mrs. Jackson came right downstairs to open the front door.

"Go get your father, Daisy. I think he's out back."

Daisy ran to the back door and looked around, but her father was nowhere in sight. Perhaps he had decided to walk to the store for something. Daisy ran back to the front door, just as her mother was holding the door open for the three men to enter.

Right away, Mrs. Jackson said, "Follow me, please. I'll show you upstairs first." And she started up the stairs. Daisy followed behind them. They looked into every bedroom and the sewing room.

"Is there a third floor here?" one of them asked.

"Yes, but we are not using it now."

But they insisted on going up the narrow stairs and looking it over. After that, they returned downstairs and went through the parlor, the dining room, and the study. Then they moved on to the kitchen and the spare bedroom off of that where Aunt Mary slept when she happened to stay overnight.

"Do you have a cellar in this house?" one of them asked.

Mrs. Jackson nodded and led them to the cellar door.

Aunt Mary stayed by the table, where she was busy peeling potatoes for a delayed Sunday dinner.

Down the stairs they went, following Mrs. Jackson. Mr. Carlson stayed up in the kitchen. Daisy followed the agents to the cellar. Just as Aunt Mary had said, there was not a single clue in sight!

Still, Daisy found she was breathless with a cold fear. What if some little clue was overlooked in the haste to hide down in the well? But there was the old sea chest, centered over the worn rug, and not a wrinkle in it to indicate any moving of furniture. Three dusty boxes and a dusty oil lamp were on top of the sea chest. Nothing looked as if it had been recently moved at all.

But what if the men wanted to move the old chest? Then what would her mother do? Daisy wondered. She glanced at her mother. Mrs. Jackson was standing very tall and looking very stern.

She spoke up very firmly. "There's nothing else to see down here. Perhaps you want to check the woodshed and the carriage barn out back." And she started up the stairs and held open the kitchen door to the backyard.

Finally, they were gone, with only Mr. Carlson saying, "Thank you."

"Good, they've had their search, at least for today. They can't come back again on the same day, thank goodness," said Aunt Mary, heading down the stairs to move the chest and let the small group out.

Mr. Jackson came in the kitchen door.

"Well, I see we had our elegant Sunday visitors already. Is everything in good order here? I met up with one of my trusted friends, and he doesn't think we should let the runaways leave tonight. He went for a walk earlier this morning, and he saw some strangers scouting along the falls. That's the route they would be taking tonight. He just had a feeling there was something fishy about those men—obviously not from around here."

"Good. Then I'm going to set up the tub in the spare bedroom and help that weary woman have herself a hot soak and a good sleep in a real bed tonight. She is so thin, I don't know how she had the strength for that long walk."

"Mary, that's a good idea. After you get her settled, why don't you go home, have the afternoon with your husband, and then come back later to see about the slaves' supper. The girls and I will take care of our dinner, and we'll bring the slaves some tea and cake in the afternoon—if they are awake. I hope they can just sleep right through now until supper time. And then with another night's rest and all day tomorrow, they should be in good condition to continue moving north."

The family finally gathered together in the dining room for their late Sunday dinner. The main conversation centered on the runaways hiding in their cellar.

"Do you think the agents came by today by coincidence? Or do you think they had some clue that a runaway party was in this area right now?" Daisy's brother Frank wondered.

"There's no way of telling," said Mr. Jackson. "We all try to keep just as closemouthed about this as possible. There's another part of this group over the other end of town. They will wait until tomorrow night, too. The plan is for them all to meet about two miles downriver from the falls. It's heavily overgrown with tangled bushes down there. I doubt the agents could find their way in the dark."

"Why don't the slaves come upstairs and eat with us now?" asked Daisy. She still had not seen one sight of these strange and mysterious visitors to her home.

"They would be too frightened to sit here in the open with us, even with the blinds and curtains shut tight. Besides that, they are not accustomed to sitting down at the same table with white people. And it would make them feel uneasy," replied Mrs. Jackson.

"Aunt Mary will give them a good, hot meal later. It's safer if they eat right downstairs in the cellar, in fact," said her father.

"What they really need now are sturdy and warm clothes for the rest of the trip. After it's dark, Mrs. Hale is coming over here in her carriage and bringing more clothing from our sewing circle. Daisy, you can stay up later tonight and help us with getting the clothes together."

"I'll lead them myself this time, when it's dark tomorrow night. They'll have good directions to the next stop, and Aunt Mary will see that they have plenty of food to carry along. Beyond that, there's nothing more we can do for them," said Mr. Jackson, shaking his head sadly.

"Father, what will become of the Underground Railroad if war between the North and South breaks out?" asked Cornelia.

"It may mean the end of being able to keep it going. On the other hand, the agents will probably return to the South, and we'll at least be rid of them."

Reminded of all the political problems and unrest about the impending war, Mr. Jackson went on to talk about it. The possibility of war was in the news all the time now. "The South could very well break away and form their own separate confederacy."

"You know what Abraham Lincoln had to say about that in one of his debates?" asked Frank, joining in. "He said, 'I believe this government cannot endure permanently half slave and half free. It will become all one thing or all the other.'"

"How horrible if it goes the wrong way," said Cornelia.

"It's the Fugitive Slave Law that makes the whole issue all the worse," said Mr. Jackson. "We defy the law by helping the slaves to escape, and the Southern plantation owners are of course just seething with anger and frustration that so many thousands of slaves have now been hidden and helped in the North. I'm very afraid it will come down to war one of these days."

All the worries about the coming of a civil war were uppermost in Mr. Jackson's mind. He had completely forgotten his birthday promise to Daisy.

"Father, when can I start to work in the candle factory?"

Actually, her father had never expected that Daisy really wanted to do it. "Well, well. So you really want to work for the money to buy that beaded bag? How about next Saturday morning? There will be five ladies working in the packaging and shipping department and I'll have them find something for you to do for a few hours every Saturday morning for a while. How does that sound?"

That week, Mr. Jackson remembered to stop by the store and ask Mr. Draper to hold the bag aside for a few weeks, saying that he would probably pick it up later.

Daisy could hardly wait for the next Saturday to come. She felt very important getting up extra early to set out with her father. They walked to the end of their street, where they waited for the horse-drawn trolley car to come by. The trolley car rumbled down the street. They got off near the candle factory, but first Mr. Jackson had an idea.

"What do you say we have a real breakfast together in a restaurant? I could use something more than those leftover muffins and coffee. This place makes great blueberry pancakes.

"I don't think most factory workers get treated to breakfast in a restaurant before they begin their workday," Daisy's father said, chuckling, as they both poured plenty of maple syrup over their stack of pancakes.

Suddenly, Mr. Jackson looked worried. "Daisy, there's something important I have to talk to you about. I didn't think of it until now; I've had so much else on my mind. There's something you must promise me. You must never tell a single soul at the candle factory that our house is a stop on the Underground Railroad. Most people around here are against slavery, just as we are. But you never know whether someone might, even by accident, say something to the wrong person, not knowing that they are speaking to a Southern agent, for example. Then, too, sometimes the agents can manage to bribe someone for information about a suspicious house— you know, offer them money to find out something. Do you understand what I am saying?"

"Yes, I understand, Father."

"Now, if anyone asks you any questions about this subject, you just say you don't know anything at all about it. You're just a child, and you very well could not know anything. In fact, you did not, until your tenth birthday!"

"I promise, Father," Daisy replied solemnly. "It's our special family secret, isn't it?"

"Yes, you could call it a family secret. But there are other families all over the North, and even into the South, who are part of it. But we never talk about it, not with anyone—not unless we are absolutely certain they are part of the plan to help slaves escape to freedom."

Mr. Jackson escorted Daisy to the packaging room and told the five ladies to find something helpful for Daisy to do until noontime, when he would return for her. Then he left for a meeting with the bank. Daisy's task that morning was to carefully wrap each white candle in tissue paper and then put twelve of them in a box. When she finished with the white ones, she did the same with the blue and yellow candles.

At first the ladies were especially quiet with Daisy around. It was so unusual that the owner of the business would allow his little girl to work there at all that they did not know what to make of her presence. Could this be just a trick so Daisy could report back that they talked too much while they worked? Because, of course, with no one watching them, they did indeed have a good time gossiping all the while they worked!

Daisy was very quiet at first, until she got the knack of wrapping each candle neatly. Then she too joined in the talking. And she told them exactly why she was there—that her father had said she could earn the money for something special she wanted. After that, the ladies relaxed, and soon all were chattering among themselves again.

Eventually, the subject of runaway slaves came up. One of the ladies said, "If there is soon going to be a war between the North and the South over slavery, then there will probably be many more trying to escape before that happens."

"Once war starts, it will be hard to help runaways," commented another worker.

Then the conversation turned to wondering which houses in the town were on this secret Underground Railroad they had all heard about. But no one ever asked Daisy any direct questions, at least not that day.

After that, Daisy went to the factory every Saturday with her father and either trimmed wicks or wrapped candles. Being there, working along with the grown-ups and all the while knowing her special secret about the hiding place in her own house, made Daisy feel much more grown-up than she had ever felt before.

One morning, the ladies mentioned the local sewing circle, wondering if the group was sewing for the escaping slaves. None of these ladies belonged, since the sewing circle met on weekdays when they were working in the factory.

"Your mother belongs to the sewing circle, doesn't she?" one asked her.

"Oh, yes, she does," answered Daisy, while trying to get the corners just right on a candle being wrapped.

"Then I suppose they are sewing clothes for the slaves?"

Daisy was about to absentmindedly reply, "Yes." But something clicked in her mind just in time! Instead, she answered, "I don't know what they sew, except that my mother likes to make clothes for all us girls in the family. When my oldest sister was married last year, my mother made her wedding gown and bridesmaids dresses for Cornelia and me. Most of the time, she fixes over Cornelia's clothes to fit me. But sometimes she makes me something brand-new. Right now, she's making me a brand-new coat with a real fur collar."

Later, Daisy told her mother what she had replied. "That was good thinking, Daisy. You did not lie. You were just discreet—and wise. The question was probably innocently asked, but we never know for certain how other people think in their hearts about these matters. When a human beings life is at stake, we must be extremely cautious." Then her mother opened the blanket chest in her sewing room and showed Daisy the jackets, mittens, caps, trousers, and scarves.

"What about clothes for children? Don't you have anything for them?"

"That's a good question, dear child. But you know, we have not had any children in the runaway groups that come through this way. I suppose they feel that children cannot keep up with such hard traveling. Mostly, they are fairly young men and women."

"If there ever is any girl my age, Mama, I'll give her some of my clothes."

✻ ✻ ✻

At the end of July, Daisy and her father counted her earned money together.

"Daisy, you have earned more than enough to buy that beaded bag. Tomorrow, we'll go downtown to see Mr. Draper, and you can buy it."

"He might not have it any more, Father. Cornelia and I didn't see it in the window last time we walked by."

"Oh, he probably just wanted to change his window display and put it away for a while."

Mr. Jackson, of course, knew very well that the bag was put safely away for Daisy. He was very proud of his youngest child—proud that she had stayed with her plan to work for the bag.

The next day, at the dry goods store, Mr. Drake reached down and took the beaded bag out of the drawer and placed it on the counter. "Is this the bag you mean?" he asked Daisy, knowing full well that it was.

"Yes, this is the very same one—the one with the blues and reds that looks like a star," Daisy replied, running her hand over the glassy beads.

"Fine, I'll wrap it in tissue paper and put it in a box for you." While he was doing this, he said, "You know, these beaded bags are hard to come by. They are made by Indians out around Wisconsin. There is a legend about them. I should have it written down sometime. The legend is that, if the Indian woman making a beaded bag—it takes a long time, you know, selecting the colors and stringing them together in this complicated pattern—well, if she holds loving thoughts of the Great Spirit and goodwill in mind all during the process of making it, then the bag will bring good luck and wishes fulfilled to the person who becomes the owner. And if that person gives the bag to someone else with loving thoughts, the legend of good luck and wishes fulfilled will continue."

"Well, I paid for this myself," Daisy replied. "I don't plan to give it away."

Mr. Drake laughed and tied some string around the box.

"You never know, Daisy. Even if you keep it until you are a grown-up lady, then you might want to give it to your daughter someday." Daisy scratched her head, "Um, Well, maybe, my granddaughter." Then Daisy counted out the exact amount and paid for it.

Sunday morning, she carried the bag proudly to Sunday school.

During the next few days throughout the country the fear of a real war between the Southern states and the Northern states increased. Tension in the air rose everywhere.

"I just hope that Abraham Lincoln is elected president this fall," Mr. Jackson said at the dining room table one night.

"A house divided against itself cannot stand," said Mrs. Jackson, quoting a passage from the Bible that was spoken by many these days.

"If war comes, I'll sign up to go," said Frank.

"And I'll become a nurse," said Cornelia.

"The war will be over before you get trained to be one," said Frank. "But I'm old enough right now to join the army."

"I might want to be a nurse anyway. If there really is a war, there will be wounded soldiers to take care of afterward, too."

"Let's have no more talk about war at the table," said Mrs. Jackson.

"I need to say one more thing relating to it," said Mr. Jackson. "I've decided that, with all these problems relating to the possible breakup of the Union, I must stay right here. I cannot leave to spend a vacation at the seashore this summer. There may be more slaves coming through, too, as the war tension grows. But Mother and you girls can still go and enjoy it. Frank wants to work in the factory this summer, and he and I can take turns coming down for a weekend visit. With Aunt Mary here even part of a day, we'll manage just fine. And if we have slaves in hiding, she can stay longer or overnight if needed."

❀   ❀   ❀

The summer trunks were loaded onto a large wagon pulled by two rented horses. Mr. Jackson went along in the carriage with his wife and daughters to help them get settled into the rented cottage near the bathing beach. Other families with children Daisy's age had come to the seashore too, so Daisy had companions to play in the sand and go dashing into the breaking waves in shallow water with.

The long days by the sea seemed far away from secret, dark holes in their cellars that Daisy and her friends were told never to talk about. But what harm could there be at the beach to ask her friend, Doris Blair, if they had a secret hiding place at home?

"Yes, we do," her friend whispered and then laughed, that she did not have to hide this while making castles in the warm sand. "Last fall, we had several groups to hide in our deep hole in the cellar. One time, there were three men and one lady in the cellar waiting for the rain to stop, and my mother had her come up to the kitchen to get warmed by the hot stove. She asked if she could bake something special for our family, like a chocolate cake! So Mama set out all she asked for, and the slave lady said there was enough left over to make a pie. Then the rain stopped, so they left that night—not walking, as my father had a big farm wagon for them to hide in for the trip to Canada. Mama cut that great cake in half for them to take with them. She said it was better than what she could make herself!"

⚜ ⚜ ⚜

The leisurely days by the sea came to an end one day, with both Frank and Mr. Jackson visiting for a few days of swimming and then getting the trunks packed up again for the return trip home. The regular routine of life began again, and for Daisy, this meant going back to school.

Four separate groups of slaves came through on the railroad in the next month. And twice it was necessary for them to get down into the deep hole while the agents walked through the house. Their house was most definitely under suspicion. So far, no children had been among the fugitive groups that had come their way.

The days began to get shorter, and a chill was in the air once again. The blanket chest was emptied of all the clothes, and the sewing circle kept working steadily to replenish it. The leaves were starting to turn, and one morning they were ablaze with fiery shades of red, yellow, and orange. A New England autumn had returned again. And as the days passed, the growing excitement of rustling leaves underfoot and dried cornstalks and pumpkins in the fields all led up to the coming climax of Halloween!

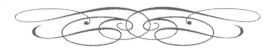

Chapter Ten

A Special Friendship Begins

At every railroad stop, the eight weary runaways were urged to hurry along and keep ahead of the cold weather to come. Taffy was being carried for longer periods of time. But in spite of this, she was always tired. The kindly faces and helping hands that secretly fed them and gave them a peaceful rest all blurred together in her mind. Too tired now to even eat more than a few nibbles of hot food, she wanted only to wrap herself in the puffy comforters and fall instantly asleep. Never before had she ever felt such comfort as she did being wrapped in these light but oh-so-warm, goose down-filled quilts!

As they entered southern New England, the tangled underbrush and woodlands burst into a blaze of autumn colors. It was everywhere—under their feet, flying through the air, and shimmering on the tall trees—yellow, gold, rust, orange, red, and purples. They had never seen anything like it! There was a crispness in the air and the invigorating scent of the late harvest. Juicy apples were tucked into their parcels at every stop. The sun shone every day in a bright, blue sky. Everyone felt more alert again. And even Taffy found she could walk for longer periods of time before the weak, trembling sensation came over her again.

One sunny afternoon, staying within the woods, they followed alongside a river until twilight. Sam announced they must stop and rest until it was dark. The map and instructions indicated they were approaching the outskirts of a large town and must wait until dark to continue on to the waterfalls. Here they would wait again, for as long as it took for railroad scouting parties to find them.

When darkness fell, they started walking again, following the river, until they eventually heard the thundering sound of a waterfall off in the distance. As they neared the falls, the roar filled the night air.

"This has to be the right place," agreed Sam and George as they returned to the group after scouting around the area.

"The rest of you can take a rest, and we'll keep watch for the railroad men," said Sam.

"How will you know if they are the right people?" Tom wondered.

"Because we were told at the last stop that these men would be walking with sticks or canes, and they would be thumping them on the ground in a certain signal pattern. No one else could know this," replied George.

"I don't see how we can hear anything with the noise the waterfall makes," whispered Susie.

Taffy, Susie, and Julia huddled together against a pine tree and managed to fall into a restless sleep. Clara and Tom settled down at the next tree. John said he would stay alert and help Sam and George keep watch and listen for the thumping signals.

Several hours went by before the men heard the thumping pattern in the woods, coming closer to where they were hidden. George thumped a stick in the same pattern. Then he and Sam walked out into a small clearing and looked around.

Two men appeared suddenly, out of nowhere it seemed. One was short and heavyset, and the other was almost as tall as George.

The tall man spoke first. "How many are you?"

"Eight in all—four women, four men," whispered Sam.

"There are three houses involved tonight, so six will go with Mr. Henderson here. He will leave three of you at one house and take the other three to his house. The remaining two will go with me in a different direction. You can decide how you will divide up. You'll be together again later, when we get you on your way."

"We'll divide up in our recent house grouping," said Sam. "That means that young Tom, John, and Clara go to one house. Julia and George and me, to another. And Susie and Taffy should go to the smallest house, as they are used to sleeping in one bed, if beds are used. We are all used to quilts on the floor though, just fine."

This dividing up plan had begun once they'd started staying overnight in homes, sometimes in large barn lofts or in cellars near the hiding holes when needed. But now all the eight runaways, could now talk softly to each other and share their tragic pasts. Finally in New England, their weary bodies and spirits were uplifted by the bright fall colors, and they began to realize they could have plans of their own choosing ahead of them.

Julia and George both knew they wanted to be in a large town or city to find work, she as a fine seamstress and George in a law office. Sam said he would also like to be with George and suggested that the group make immediate plans together—remaining as a family group of eight. Julia planned to take full charge of Taffy during her growing up years. Both Clara and John shared their love for young Tom and wanted him to have a musical education. Clara knew she could work as a special cook, and John could take care of expensive horses, so they would choose living in a city. Both of them had lost their former mates when young—to the awful word *sold*—and had never planned to marry again. But who knew what a life of freedom would do for their future?

Julia gave Taffy a hug and whispered, "I'll see you in just a day or so. Try to eat more, Taffy. You're getting too thin."

Silently, Susie and Taffy followed the tall man away from the falls, up a wooded hillside, and alongside a broad pasture. They came to a gate between a stone wall that opened into a smaller field that had been plowed under for the winter. In the middle of the field, a strange figure was flapping in the night breeze. For a few minutes, the cloudy sky revealed a half moon. In the pale light, they could see large pumpkins spaced out in the field. At the end of the field, they walked through a trellis and into the backyard of a large white house.

Off to one side was a small barn and a separate shed. The house was dark; not one oil lamp was burning as they followed the man up the back steps and into the kitchen. He went to the kitchen table and lit an oil lamp. The blinds were all shut tightly at the windows, so no one could look in. A big, black kettle was on the still-warm stove, and wonderful aromas were coming from it. On the table was a loaf of bread, ready to slice.

The man lit another, smaller lamp and indicated that Taffy and Susie should follow him down a flight of stairs into the cellar. A rug covered part of the floor, and piles of quilts were on chairs.

The man told them, "It's much later than we thought it would be. We had to scout around a long time before we found you. There's soup still warm on the stove and bread on the table if you want to eat before you sleep. You don't have to worry about anyone coming here tonight. The agents are only allowed to come during the day to search a suspected house.

"But during the day, we are required to let them search because of the Fugitive Slave Law. Now, this house has a special hiding place, big enough for three or four grown-ups, so you don't have to worry in the daytime either. There's a deep, dry well under that old chest, and the minute anyone comes to search this house, that's where you will be hidden. We'll take care of all the details in that event. You just relax and get all the sleep you can. And there's going to be plenty of food to eat whenever you're ready for it."

While he was still talking, Taffy took the top quilt off the chair, wrapped herself in it, lay down on the rug, and promptly fell fast asleep. For the first time, Mr. Jackson noticed that she really was a very young girl, about the size of Daisy.

"This is the first time there has been a child in any group. How old is she? Are you her parents?"

"She's ten years old, sir, and I take care of her. Her mother and father were sold away this past year," answered Susie in a low whisper.

"You can talk out loud down here," Mr. Jackson said, "as you will be told about it before anyone gets inside the front door. Poor little child, how did she ever make this long trip?"

"She was very strong at first, and she has a lot of spunk," said Susie. "But she's been carried most of the time for a long time now. She's very exhausted, and she hasn't been eating enough, either, to keep her strength up."

"Well, the plan is for this group to spend two nights before going on, as we expect a heavy rain tomorrow. So perhaps she can get enough rest to get her strength back to eat well."

Mr. Jackson left them then and said they could leave the small oil lamp on low the rest of the night. The kitchen one he would put off before he went upstairs to bed.

❋ ❋ ❋

The next morning, Daisy was downstairs before Aunt Mary arrived. Her father had put more wood into the kitchen stove and was stirring the oatmeal. Daisy got the milk out of the icebox in the back entryway, and she and her father sat down together to have breakfast. There was only one scrap end of the bread left on the table.

"Who ate all the bread up?" asked Daisy.

"Daisy, we have a new group of runaway slaves in the cellar. They came in very late. We went out two times to look around. And thankfully, we finally found them. You'll be very surprised to know that this time there is a child in the group. Two are at our house, and one is just a little girl about your size and age. Poor child, how she ever survived such a long trip, I cannot imagine. She fell sound asleep before I even got back up the cellar stairs."

Aunt Mary came through the kitchen door, shaking herself. "It's already starting to rain, Mr. Jackson. You better take your umbrella today."

Daisy excitedly told her the news about the slaves' arrival and that one was a girl her own age!

Mr. Jackson got ready to leave, and said, "Mary, it was almost three in the morning before I got them settled in the cellar. I don't think they'll be awake to need anything to eat until late in the day. They did eat the soup and bread last night I notice. And the plan is for them to stay over tonight and leave tomorrow night."

After her father left, Daisy continued talking about the girl her own age hiding in the cellar. "Do you think she'll be afraid to climb down into that dark well?"

"Let's hope no agents come by, and she won't have to, poor little thing."

"I wish I could stay home from school, today, Aunt Mary."

"Well, you know your mama won't allow that. You can see the girl later. They'll be staying one more night, you heard your father say."

The school day seemed very long to Daisy. She wanted so much to tell her best friend that her family was hiding a girl their very own age, but she managed to hold her tongue.

Daisy remembered what Cornelia had told her over and over. "Remember, Daisy, the freedom of slaves is more important than you having the fun of being a blabbermouth for a few minutes."

Daisy didn't stop to chat with anyone on the way home. In fact, she walked a different way home, longer around, so she wouldn't have to be with her friends. While she hurried along, she thought to herself, *Maybe I can take her up to my own bedroom to play with dolls. But what if the agents come while she is upstairs? Then what happens? She would have to run quickly down the back stairs to the kitchen, and down to the cellar.* These thoughts ran through her mind as she approached the corner of her own street.

Two men came from around the corner and walked by her. They looked vaguely familiar. Of course, they were the same two Southern agents who had searched the house the last time! They did not seem to notice her or if they did remember she was the same girl who had followed them down to the cellar, they did not acknowledge it by saying anything.

Daisy ran the rest of the way home and burst into the kitchen, calling out, "Where is she? Can she come upstairs to my room?"

Both Aunt Mary and her mother were working together in the kitchen, baking pies and preparing a beef stew. The warm room smelled of apples and cinnamon.

Mrs. Jackson put down the apple she was peeling and put her arm around Daisy.

"I have something very serious to tell you, dear. Poor little Taffy cannot play with you, and she is not in the cellar anymore. She's already upstairs in your room, and she's tucked into your big bed—a very sick little girl. Doctor Shaw came by here just an hour ago. Susie—the young woman with her—told us she was afraid Taffy had a fever. None of them even woke up until early afternoon. That's why we called the doctor right away. He thinks it's just a cold and fatigue, but there is the danger of her getting pneumonia when she's so run-down with exhaustion. But at least, it's not some contagious disease. So you'll have to sleep with Cornelia.

"I thought Taffy would be most comfortable in your room, with all your toys and pretty things to look at. And she'll be next to our bedroom, in case she calls out in the night. Aunt Mary fixed up the spare bedroom off the kitchen for Susie. There's no reason she should sleep in the cellar when we have a spare bed, and Sam may get to come here after dark and can sleep on the cot on the third floor tonight. He wants to see Taffy and Susie they said. It's been a busy afternoon, Daisy, I tell you."

"Her name is Taffy? And she's in my bed—sick?"

The Underground Railroad suddenly came into focus, having a personal meaning for Daisy.

"Can I go upstairs to my room and see her? Can I help take care of her?"

Mrs. Jackson resumed peeling apples and replied, "Yes, you can sit beside her later. She's asleep now. We'll see how her fever is in a while. Put your school bag on the chair and help us peel some vegetables. We've plenty of mouths to feed in the next few days. Taffy cannot leave, so the others will have to wait, too."

After all the vegetables were added to the stew pot, Mrs. Jackson checked the clock.

"Mary, you go on home soon, as usual. Just come a bit earlier tomorrow morning. All right, Daisy, you come upstairs with me now, and we'll see if she's awake. It's about time for her to have more cough medicine the doctor left. My opinion is that she is suffering more from exhaustion and lack of nourishment than anything else. At least, I hope I am right. Such a long trip, all the way from the South up here to New England, is more than any child should endure. It's bad enough for the grown-ups."

Daisy and her mother went up the back stairs together, leaving Mary to get everything organized before she went home.

Taffy was half-awake. Mrs. Jackson felt her forehead. "I do believe she's a bit cooler now. She was so hot earlier today; it really had me worried!"

She held Taffy's head up and urged her to take a few sips of juice after the cough medicine.

Daisy looked at the little girl solemnly. It was never fun to be sick. "Is she really the same age as me? She looks so tiny, lying there. What pretty, black, curly hair she has."

"I'm ten years old," whispered Taffy in a weak little voice "So am I! "When was your birthday?"

"May 28."

"Mine was May 30th! What did you get for your birthday, Taffy?"

"Daisy, shush, That isn't proper to ask anyone!"

"Susie gave me my mama's book and a chocolate cake, and Sam gave me paper and a pencil," came the weak reply from the pillows. Daisy shifted her body up closer to Taffy's pillow, whispering, "I had a chocolate cake, too! Did you make a birthday wish and blow out all your candles?"

"Yes, and it came true right away."

Daisy fluffed up Taffy's pillow, and whisperd,

"It did? My wish took a while, but I helped make it come true."

"So did I," replied Taffy with a weak smile.

"Now that's enough talk for now, Daisy. You'll wear her out. Taffy, dear, you go back to sleep, and maybe you'll enjoy some chicken soup later. We'll be right here when you wake up, and Susie will come in to be with you, too, I promise. And perhaps so will Sam."

Mrs. Jackson turned the oil lamp on low so Taffy wouldn't be in the dark when she woke up. Taffy was already asleep again.

Daisy lingered by the bed, looking down at Taffy. "Mama, she said she received a book for her birthday. Does that mean she can read? You always said slaves weren't allowed to learn to read."

"They aren't, usually. But some do learn, secretly. If it was her mother's book, as she said, then perhaps her own mother could read and taught her daughter."

"Is her mama downstairs in the cellar?"

"No, Daisy, it's a very sad story. She's here with a young woman, hardly more than a young girl herself—the one called Susie, who's going to sleep in the room off the kitchen. Anyhow, it's Susie who cares for her, because Taffy's mother and father were sold last year, and she was left behind at the plantation without them! She's never seen them again. Isn't that awful? That's why slavery is so sinful—that families are willfully separated by the slave masters, as if they had no feelings at all. Even animals can grieve over their young when separated! Now, we are confronted with this terrible fact, right before our very eyes—with Taffy right here in our own home!"

"She's an orphan now, then, isn't she?"

Mrs. Jackson nodded, wiping the tears from her eyes.

Daisy tenderly tucked the blankets closer around Taffy's chin. "Can I sit beside her while she sleeps? I'll get a book to read while I sit here. Then she won't be alone if she wakes up."

✸ ✸ ✸

The next time Taffy woke up her fever was down, but she still was very weak and only sipped a little of the hot chicken soup. "Where is Susie?" she whispered.

Mrs. Jackson brought Susie upstairs. She sat beside the bed, holding Taffy's hand and smoothing her forehead.

Taffy soon dozed off again, without hardly speaking to Susie.

"I can't leave without her. I'm all she has for family. She's all I have for family now her mother and father are gone. I promised her mother I would always take care of her," cried Susie, the tears streaming down her cheeks.

Mrs. Jackson put her arms around Susie and tried to comfort her. "Of course you can't leave without her. You'll just have to stay here until Taffy is well enough to travel, and that is all there is to it," she said, the tears streaming down her own cheeks as well.

Daisy sat there with them, sharing the sympathetic sadness.

Chapter Eleven

Hiding Places

"What are we going to do?" Mrs. Jackson asked her husband. "Susie and Taffy are family to each other. They should never be separated, and Sam is very devoted to both of them."

"How soon do you think Taffy will be able to travel again?"

"Oh, she couldn't possibly get up and go anywhere for at least a week, and it should be longer. She could so easily get pneumonia. I don't see how she can survive more of this terrible journey, especially now that cold weather is almost here."

"That's the problem," said Mr. Jackson, shaking his head. "It's the weather ahead of them. I'm going to see what I can find out about a wagon to get them all the way to Canada, but I doubt one wagon can hide eight people. I think I'll have a talk with Sam. He's the real leader of this group."

Mr. Jackson and Sam sat at the kitchen table, talking late into the night.

"My responsibility is to the group, to get them safely to freedom in Canada as I promised them I would. But I don't want to leave Susie and Taffy behind. I feel like I'm abandoning them—my best friends! If they come along later, with another group, how do I know someone will be willing to carry Taffy? I finally carried her a lot of the time. And so did George. But even so, she still got all worn out," said Sam sorrowfully.

Mr. Jackson told Sam about the idea of getting a wagon for the rest of the journey. "Trouble is, even by wagon, time is soon running out, weather-wise, especially with that many people. Sam, what about George? You say he can read and write, too, and that he helped you in many ways on the trip so far. What if George was willing to stay behind until Taffy can travel? And of course, Susie will stay, too. That way, at least most of you can get started right now. The Hendersons won't mind having George for a longer time. They have a big place."

"Oh, I can trust George completely. He's smarter than I am in every way, and he's also older and stronger. Can we get a message to him, to ask him what he thinks about this?"

"Easily. I'll be seeing Mr. Henderson tomorrow morning. We have a meeting of the directors of our first bank out here, and some bankers are coming out from Boston to advise us on certain matters. Afterward, he and I can get together privately and talk about this. The rest of you really should be getting on the way again."

The weather made an immediate decision for them. The heavy rains did not stop. It just kept on and on until the river was at flood level, and the woodland trails were filled with deep puddles. A few more days went by. Sam was still at the Jacksons home, and the others were still at the other two houses.

Both Aunt Mary and Mrs. Jackson kept a close watch on Taffy. Aunt Mary sat beside her bed, encouraging her to keep on eating the nourishing soups they made for her. Gradually, her appetite was returning, but she was still weak. Her cough persisted, and that made her tired.

"Mary, I don't know what we are going to do about Taffy if the agents come here soon. I just do not want to put that poor child down into that cold well. And for another thing, what if she gets one of those coughing spells down there?"

"There's that big blanket chest in the bedroom off the kitchen, and that room stays warm from the kitchen stove. The agents just give a peek into that near-empty room and never go poking into anything. And you know they never spend any time in the kitchen. They can see right away there's no hiding place there, so they just pass on through to the cellar or outdoors. She wouldn't have to hide in the chest for very long."

Daisy, meanwhile, begged her parents to let her stay home from school and help take care of Taffy.

Surprisingly, her father agreed to the idea and confided to her mother, "Maybe it's a more important lesson right now to help take care of someone in need than to study from a book."

"Perhaps so. Daisy has all her life to study and learn interesting things. She is very concerned about that little girl, and I know Taffy loves having her around. But what happens if the agents come? Do we pretend that Daisy is home sick? That's it, William! Taffy gets hidden in the blanket chest downstairs, and we don't have to put the bed into order, because Daisy will jump into bed and pretend to be the sick one! With the back stairs, it should all work out quickly."

Mrs. Jackson intended to go right upstairs and tell Daisy and Taffy about this plan. But just then, her friend Mrs. Hale came to visit and talk about the sewing projects.

Daisy and Taffy were now spending all their time together, except when Taffy would nap, which was still several times a day. But when she was awake, the two girls played with dolls, dressing them up and making up stories about them. Daisy brought books to the bed and read out loud to Taffy. As Taffy's strength gradually increased, she read out loud to Daisy.

"Daisy, where is the book that belonged to my mother?"

"Susie has everything hidden away in Cornelia's room, but I think I can find it. Cornelia is still at the girls' academy, and Susie is down in the cellar talking to Sam."

Daisy did find the little book and added it to the pile on the bed. There were crayons and paper strewn around on the bed, too, not to mention stuffed animals.

For Taffy, it was all like a beautiful dream—to sit propped up in bed, with puffy pillows and comforters, surrounded by toys, and a special friend to be with.

Mrs. Jackson came into the room, carrying a tray with a bowl of hot soup for Taffy.

"Daisy, you can go get your soup in the kitchen later. But I want Taffy to have something hot every few hours, you know."

"First, another spoonful of cough medicine. I know it tastes terrible, Taffy, but the hot soup will make you forget it." The medicine and spoon were kept on a table beside the bed.

All of a sudden, a heavy knock came at the front door.

"Who could that be, in the middle of the day?"

Aunt Mary came running up the front stairs to say, "I think it's agents at the door. You better get the plan going right away!"

"What plan, Mama?" asked Daisy.

"The plan to put-But there isn't time even for that now. We'll try something else. With so much piled up on this bed, I think it will work." Her sharp eyes darted around the room.

Mrs. Jackson put the tray on the table next to the medicine. "Taffy, slide down, under the comforter and lie just as flat as you can. And don't move and don't cough. Daisy, quick, put on Taffy's bathrobe—there on the chair—and cover up your dress at the neck. Good. Now get into the bed yourself. There … that's good. And I'll just pile another pillow where Taffy is and shove the books and toys around. There, now, put this extra quilt over your shoulders, Daisy, and part of it over Taffy's side. There. What else? The soup, the medicine, that's all right. It's only for one person."

Mrs. Jackson scanned the room for any telltale signs that two girls were in the room, but she saw nothing that looked suspicious.

"Now, I'm going downstairs. I'll get them out of this room just as quickly as I can. Daisy, if you hear Taffy cough, you cough yourself, just as fast as you can!"

Mrs. Jackson went to the front door. Aunt Mary was nowhere in sight, so hopefully she was already hiding Sam and Susie in the dry well in the cellar. And hopefully, there were no telltale clues left around in the cellar, the kitchen, or the spare bedroom—or even in Cornelia's room, for that matter. And the attic, where Sam was sleeping—he had not become careless, she prayed, as she opened the door.

Mr. Carlson was there, looking frustrated, and only one strange man was with him this time. It was not anyone who had been there before. As she always did, Mrs. Jackson indicated that they should follow her up the stairs first. This time, she added, "We'll start you out on the third floor," thinking that if Taffy had to cough from being under the covers, she would get it over with before they entered the room.

Nothing was out of place on the third floor. As she opened the door to Daisy's room, she said, "My little girl is sick in bed."

"I'm sorry, madam, but we must search every room."

The man looked behind the screen, where there was a washbowl and pitcher on a pine commode and some towels and one toothbrush in a glass.

Then he looked at Daisy, all wrapped up right over her chin and her eyes half-closed. "What is she sick with?" he asked politely.

"She has a fever and a sore throat," Mrs. Jackson said.

"I guess you like to read, by the looks of all these books piled over your bed, young lady," the man said, agreeably enough.

Then he touched one of the books and read its title.

Mrs. Jackson looked with horror at the book he was touching.

It was Taffy's own book! The little worn book was so different-looking from all the others on the bed. Worst of all, inside was written Taffy's name, including the last name of Davis.

Did agents know the runaway slaves they were hired to search for by name? They never said anything. But was it possible that they were specifically looking for a cook named Susie and a little helper slave named Taffy?

But the man did not actually pick up the book. Instead, he took a quick peek under the bed, and then he turned and walked out, saying, "I'm sorry to bother your daughter when she is ill. Thank you."

When Mr. Carlson and the man reached the cellar, everything was in order. Aunt Mary was back in the kitchen, bustling around by the stove. Finally, the man went outdoors by the kitchen door. Mr. Carlson lingered to whisper to Mrs. Jackson, "This man is specifically looking for two young slaves. Very valuable to their owners, apparently, because I heard him tell another agent they were offering a lot of money to get them back—that they didn't want to either punish them or sell them. They just wanted them back again because they were almost like family!"

"Slave owners have some peculiar notion of families," said Aunt Mary.

"Do you know if they know their names, Mr. Carlson?"

"They may. It's likely, but I don't know."

The agent appeared, coming out of the barn.

"Well, I'll go out and escort him away so he won't come inside again. If these two slaves he's looking for come through here, you better hide them very well and, if possible, have them stay at separate houses."

Aunt Mary ran back upstairs to tell the girls the search was over. Then she hurried down to the cellar to uncover and unlock the well. Mrs. Jackson was already down there. But it was no use; she simply did not have the strength to move that heavy chest. But Aunt Mary was soon there. And Susie and Sam climbed out and asked what happened. And where did they hide Taffy?

"Come up the back stairs to Daisy's room, both of you. Agents can only come once in a day. It will do you all good to be together and talk about what you just had to do. Mary and I will fix some tea. And we'll bring it up to the room, and we'll all have a little visit together. I'm still so nervous my teeth are chattering!" said Mrs. Jackson.

Cornelia arrived home from school, and she joined the tea party, too.

When Cornelia heard that Daisy had found Taffy's book in her room, she said, "You know, there's something else of Taffy's in that box. It's some kind of a doll. But it's just flat—it has no stuffing. I'll go get it."

Taffy explained how the pioneer family had given her the doll but could not stuff it because they already had enough to carry.

Cornelia said she would get some quilt padding and stuff it right up for Taffy.

Thinking of the first pioneer family, Taffy was reminded of Tom.

"I wish I could write a letter to Tom. Is he still at another railroad house near here?"

"Yes, he is. And Mr. Jackson can easily deliver a message or a written letter over there. Can Tom read and write, too?" asked Mrs. Jackson.

"He told me he could. He sure can play that flute my father made for him," said Taffy, thinking about her friend and the long trip they'd shared together.

Cornelia wanted to know all about how Taffy's father had come to make musical instruments, and they all listened while Taffy told them something about her mother and her father and their life together on the Davis plantation. She also told them about Louise's visit and how she had turned out to be not only a cousin, but also a spy for the Underground Railroad!

All the excitement of the afternoon made Taffy tired early, so Mrs. Jackson saw that she had an early supper and then was tucked in for the night. That meant that both Susie and Sam went up to sit beside her for a while. Later, when the family sat down for their evening meal, Susie and Sam ate with them. Since agents were not allowed to come searching in the evening, it seemed safe enough, but they made sure all the blinds and curtains were drawn across the windows.

Mr. Jackson was filled in on the details of the afternoon by both his wife and by Daisy.

"Taffy never coughed at all, and she didn't move one tiny bit," said Daisy. "Did I look sick, Mama, with my eyes half-closed?"

"Yes, you did just fine. But oh, I was terrified when he looked at that book with Taffy's name inside. We'll tuck that away in a hiding place again."

Cornelia was sitting there, looking very thoughtful. And then she said, "You know, what Taffy had to say to us this afternoon about her family and her life as a slave child was very sad, but it was also very interesting. Susie, you must have your own story to tell. And, Sam, so must you. I've been thinking I would like to write down your stories as you tell them to me. Someday, people will find them a special insight into the history of this country. You can write, I know, but you haven't time to write your own stories. But could I try to do it while you are still staying with us?" Her eyes shone with excitement, considering her plan.

"I don't have much of a story to tell," said Susie.

"Yes, you do, Susie! And you can tell about Taffy's mother and how she meant so much to you. That's a story in itself. And then there's Julia and her story and how she just accidentally showed up at the Davis plantation, and you found out she was Della's long-lost sister, making her Taffy's aunt! That's an amazing story, right there," said Sam, his face brightening with this idea.

"What do you mean Taffy's aunt? Who is Taffy's aunt?" asked Cornelia.

"Tell her, Susie. You tell her," said Sam.

Susie still felt strange, sitting at the table and talking with white people. But this family was making her feel more at ease with each passing day, so she took a deep breath and managed to tell the Jacksons how it had all happened and how she had felt this strange sense of having met Julia before.

"And that's the same Julia who is over at the other house?" asked Mrs. Jackson.

"And Taffy doesn't know that Julia is her aunt?"

"No, we all—that is, Sam and Julia and I—decided we should not tell Taffy. She would get too attached to her while she was still at the plantation sewing, and then she would have to leave, and it would just make Taffy sad all over again. She was very upset for a long time after she lost her parents, but she had finally begun to be her cheerful self again after she got so excited about learning to read and write."

Everyone was silent for a few moments, taking it all in.

"I think you did the right thing, not to tell her yet. There's time enough for that when you are safely free," said Mrs. Jackson.

"That does explain something," said Mr. Jackson. "I did tell Mr. Henderson to ask George what he thought about staying behind until Taffy was well enough to travel. I said that Susie would stay, too, of course. Today I got the answer. He will stay, but he asked if Julia could also wait for Taffy. Mr. Henderson said it was all right with them, and that was all that was said about it."

Sam shook his head and said, "Julia was very frightened about making the escape. I don't think she would have had the courage to go through with it except for wanting so much to be with Taffy. For a slave, she had grown up in a very protected way. And then losing her older sister, as well as the only home she had ever known, made her very fearful and timid."

Susie added, "She and George have become good friends, and I think she depends on him a lot."

"Well, it all makes sense then, doesn't it? Another tragic slave story for your collection, Cornelia." Mrs. Jackson sighed. "If only you could talk to her about it. That's it! You can talk to her! With Sam leaving, we can make room for Julia over here until Taffy is strong enough to leave. Also, it's easy for us to take in another woman as far as sleeping arrangements go."

"I'll tell Mr. Henderson our plans. With only George left over there, they can still hide any other slaves that come through. There won't be many any more. It's getting too late to expect to walk to Canada before snow falls in northern New England."

The next night, Mr. Jackson came home with the news that all the plans had been made.

"We have the wagon ready, and it's large enough for the five of them plus the driver. They'll be starting out at the Blair farm, as that is right on the edge of the open country and the road north. Not apt to be any agents hanging around out there like they are here, right in the town. I'll walk with Sam late tonight over to the Hendersons, and he'll walk with them over to the Blairs. Let's see, now, Sam, it's the older man who will be leaving from Hendersons. And what are the names of the last group?"

"There's Clara, young Tom, and John."

"Of course—the young boy. I almost forgot I have a message from him to Taffy. Mr. Henderson did a thoughtful thing when I was over there today. He sent his son right over to the Blair farm and had him wait while Tom wrote out a short message to Taffy. It seems he can write quite well; didn't take him long at all. It is amazing how most everyone in this group can read and write!"

He gave the piece of paper to Sam, and both Susie and Sam went upstairs to be with Taffy for a while before she fell asleep.

Sam handed her the note. "Do you want to read it out loud to us, Taffy?"

"He really can write," Taffy exclaimed. "I was going to write to him, and now he's done it first!"

Taffy read out loud:

Dear Taffy,

This is our last day here. We start leaving tonight for Canada, but we don't have to walk all the way. There's a wagon waiting for us at the farm. I've got my flute packed safe in my bag. I'll see you in Canada, when you get better.

Your friend, Tom Blair. This family was so good to us, John said we should take their name from now on.

"That means you are going, too, Sam, doesn't it? Susie, you aren't going, are you?"

"No, no, Taffy. George and Julia are going to wait until you are strong enough to travel, and the four of us will leave together," said Susie.

Susie tried to keep from crying at the thought of being separated from Sam, but the tears started falling down her cheeks.

"Everything always ends up in good-byes. I'm so afraid we won't find you ever again," cried Susie.

Sam felt like crying, too. Susie and Taffy were the closest people to family he had ever known in his life. He certainly didn't intend to lose them now.

"Look, Susie, Taffy. You have to believe we will get together again in Canada, and we will! You know why? Because we can read and write, all of us! We can leave messages where we are, and we will find each other. Anything is possible when you can read and write. You know that!"

"Will you write to us, Sam, as soon as you get to Canada?" asked Taffy, the tears starting down her cheeks, too.

"Right away. But it is possible you may not be here much longer yourselves. Mrs. Jackson says you are getting much stronger every day now, Taffy."

Sam hugged Taffy good-bye, and Susie walked out into the upstairs hall with him.

"I'll say good-bye right here," said Susie, "because I don't want to cry in front of everyone."

"Good idea, Susie. Neither do I."

They hugged each other tightly for a long time, and then Sam hurried down the back stairs to the kitchen where the family was waiting.

Susie went back to sit beside Taffy, but now she really burst into tears. And she cried and cried for a long time.

Taffy put her arms around Susie and tried to comfort her. "Remember, Susie, it used to be me that cried, and you held me and rocked me."

"I remember only too well that sad time. Sometimes I wonder if it will ever be any different for us."

Susie finally wiped away her tears and said, "Now I've cried so much my throat is sore."

The next morning, Susie's throat was still sore, and she had a fever, too.

"Do you still want Julia to come here late tonight?" asked Mr. Jackson before he left for the factory and a meeting with Mr. Henderson.

"Yes, we can manage," replied Mrs. Jackson. "I do want to meet Taffy's own mother's sister, and it will be good for the three to be together again. It may be a little longer than we thought, now that Susie has come down with a cold. I hope it's not as bad as what Taffy had. She could so easily have slipped into pneumonia."

"It all that good chicken and beef broth that did it, Mrs. Jackson, and all that lovin' attention she got with it," said Aunt Mary. "I sure am eager to meet Taffy's aunt."

"We'll just change the sleeping plan I had. I was going to put Susie in with Taffy now she doesn't cough at night. But now Susie better stay by herself off the kitchen. Daisy can stay in with Taffy, if they'll promise not to giggle half the night. And Julia can sleep in Cornelia's room. That way, there're no extra beds set up to look different if the same agents return here."

"We just better make sure Daisy doesn't leave any telltale signs around to look like there's two people using that room. She better keep her toothbrush down here in the kitchen from now on, for instance, and Cornelia, the same."

"There's something else Daisy has to do, too. She has to start going to school again! I don't know what's gotten into me, letting her stay home so long when she's not sick!"

Daisy came downstairs in her bathrobe just then.

"I think you'd better get dressed and go to school today," said her mother.

"Oh, Mama, Not today! Taffy and I want to make a jack-o'-lantern out of a pumpkin today so it will be all ready for tomorrow night. Tomorrow night is Halloween!"

"Daisy, you know if you don't show up at school, then you can't go outdoors tomorrow night either."

"I don't care. Taffy can't go outside. I wouldn't go outdoors with my friends anyway. I just want to be with Taffy." She looked at her mother pleadingly with a loud sigh.

"All right. Today and tomorrow, and then you go to school."

"I promise, I'll go, Mama. But how can Taffy hide in my bed if I'm in school? I mean, if I'm seen going to school, then I can't be in bed sick at the same time, can I?"

"I think Taffy can hide in the well now. She doesn't cough anymore, and she's so much stronger; it won't do her any harm. Now it's Susie I'm worrying about coughing. But Susie is too big to hide in the blanket chest. Mary, we'll have a big towel in the well, so if Susie coughs, she can bury her face in the towel. And she'll have to be on the bottom rung and then Julia and Taffy on the top. But let's hope we don't have to do that."

"Taffy, have you ever made a jack-o'-lantern?" asked Daisy later.

"No. What is it?"

"You'll see. Come on down to the kitchen. Aunt Mary got a big round one from the patch out back."

Together, the two girls drew a face they liked. Aunt Mary insisted on slicing off the top, and then they both scooped out the insides. Aunt Mary gave them a small sharp knife. And taking turns, they cut out the face.

"Now we stick a candle in the bottom," said Daisy, showing Taffy how it was done. Sometimes, Daisy felt like an older sister to Taffy; there were so many things Taffy had never done.

But there were other things that Taffy was better at, and one of them was baking.

"Aunt Mary, do you know that Taffy can make a chocolate cake all by herself? Can we make one together today? We can pretend it's Susie's birthday and put candles on it to make her feel better."

"If your mama says so, you can."

Taffy and Daisy got along so well together. It was hard to resist Daisy's ideas for interesting projects to do inside the house, since, of course, they could not go outdoors.

Aunt Mary set out the ingredients on the table in the center of the room and gave the girls three round pans for a triple-layer cake.

"You might as well make a big one so there'll be enough for everyone. And be sure to save a piece for Julia tomorrow."

"Is she really coming here tonight, Aunt Mary?" asked Taffy, starting to break eggs into a big bowl.

"This very night, but you two will already be in bed before she gets here, and mind, you both go to sleep right away."

"It's just like having a sister my own age." Daisy sighed contentedly, watching Taffy mix sugar into the eggs.

"Same for me," said Aunt Mary, getting out a small pan to melt chocolate in. "It's having two honey lambs instead of one."

It turned dark early now, but Aunt Mary had already shut the blinds and pulled the curtains together, which she always did if the two girls were going to be in the kitchen.

After the cake was placed in the oven, Aunt Mary handed Daisy a long match. And Daisy lit the jack-o'-lantern on the center of the table. Elbows propped on the table, chins cupped in hands, the girls sat quietly for a while, admiring their joint handiwork.

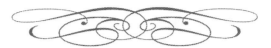

Chapter Twelve

The Failed Escape

The day after Halloween, Daisy went back to school.

"I just wish Taffy could go along with me." Daisy sighed.

"We all wish that, Daisy. School is where a bright girl like Taffy belongs," said her mother. "Now, don't complain. You've had a very special kind of vacation that you will never forget."

"I'm coming straight home from school to be with Taffy," said Daisy, reaching up to a kitchen hook for her book bag.

"Yes, and remember, if any of your friends wonder why they cannot come over here after school, you just say that you are supposed to take a rest when you get home—your mother's orders! That's all you need to say."

Taffy was still upstairs. From the sewing room window, she watched her friend until she disappeared from view. "Good-bye, Daisy," she whispered. "I wish I could go with you."

Taffy might have felt sad and lonely on this day, except for the excitement of knowing that Julia was asleep in the very next room! At least, she hoped she was.

Taffy ran down to the kitchen.

Mrs. Jackson was having a second cup of coffee and discussing food plans with Aunt Mary.

"Did she come last night?" Taffy asked them right away.

"Oh yes, she got here all right. Mr. Jackson saw to that. She didn't come alone. I'm sure she is tired, so we'll let her sleep late. Then you and I will go wake her. Taffy, what do you say we treat Julia to breakfast in bed this morning when she wakes up?"

The next hour or so dragged by for Taffy.

"Can I just peek in and see if she is awake yet?" she asked Mrs. Jackson.

"All right, dear, go ahead," said Mrs. Jackson with a laugh.

Taffy peeked in, but Julia's face was turned away from view. So Taffy tiptoed over to the bed and stood there, looking down at her. Julia sighed, turned over, and looked straight up at Taffy.

"Taffy, Taffy, Is it really you?"

Julia sat straight up in a flash and reached out her arms and hugged Taffy close to her, her face beaming into a wide smile. How good it felt to feel Julia's warm embrace again! Whenever Julia hugged her, she was always reminded of her own mother. Taffy sat down on the bed and happily snuggled up to Julia.

They talked for a long time until Taffy remembered about breakfast. "Julia, stay right here in bed! I'll be right back with a surprise for you!"

Taffy ran back downstairs to the kitchen. "She's awake! Can we bring up her breakfast now?"

"Yes. You wait here while Aunt Mary warms up the muffins, and I'll just run up and say good morning and see if she wants coffee or tea," said Mrs. Jackson. "I haven't even met her yet, you know. I fell asleep before they got here last night."

Mrs. Jackson went upstairs and welcomed Julia. She told her that clean clothes had been laid out for her and showed her where everything was in the room.

Then she half whispered to Julia, "We know that you are Taffy's real aunt, her own mother's younger sister. Susie told us all about it but not in front of Taffy. She still knows nothing of this."

"It's just as well, at least for now," said Julia.

How beautiful she is, observed Mrs. Jackson, taking in her milk chocolate complexion and widely set brown eyes.

"How is Susie? Is she better? I was so worried when we got the message Taffy was so sick, and I suppose Susie caught it from her."

"Susie is going to be fine, just like Taffy. But we have to be cautious; you have all been exhausted by the ordeal of your awful trip. Pneumonia setting in is the big worry, you know."

Taffy came walking ever so slowly into the room, carrying the breakfast tray.

Later, Julia dressed and went downstairs to sit beside Susie, who was still resting in bed, where she would stay most of the day.

From the moment Susie was reunited with Julia, she perked up. While sick, she had worried constantly that all the plans could go wrong. What if she never found Sam again? What if he was captured and sent back? What if George and Julia could not wait any longer for her to get well? What if the agents found her and Taffy and they were sent back and then separated forever? The *what-ifs* went on and on as she lay there sick. Sometimes the burden of her basic loneliness was too much to overcome.

But now, spending the long days with Julia right there restored her spirit. After missing Sam so desperately, Susie found Julia's presence a deep comfort. Was it because some quality in Julia really did remind her of Della? Julia had admitted back in the cabin that her older sister had more courage than she did. But still, there was a mature, quiet strength about Julia that was healing to Susie.

Susie started getting dressed in the morning and staying up longer and coming to the dining room table at night instead of just nibbling at her meals, alone in her room. Julia was more accustomed to gracious ways of dining from her childhood, but Susie tried her best to gain courage from having Julia there beside her. Everyone talked and laughed at the table, and no one seemed to notice if Susie was quiet.

"How long do you think it will be before Susie is strong enough to travel?" Mr. Jackson asked his wife.

"I think about a week more is all she needs if she continues to eat well," said Mrs. Jackson, passing the rolls to Susie.

The remaining days were a precious interlude for them all, both for the runaway slaves and for the Jackson family. Time seemed suspended in the present. They had no past experiences in common, and they would share no future together. Yet, they did share this dramatic time in their lives, united by the tragedy of slavery. And beyond that historical bond, real trust and affection had blossomed. For this brief time in their lives, they were like one family, with its variety of personal relationships.

Mrs. Jackson summed it all up when she sighed and remarked to Aunt Mary, "It's the same feeling I had when all the children were home—everyone under one roof, pursuing their own special interests. That's what I like best."

"That's right," agreed Aunt Mary. "That's how I like it, too—just cooking up a storm and knowin' everyone is going to be here to enjoy it."

For Taffy, being here allowed the release of her naturally buoyant spirit, instead of that tight, closed-in feeling in her chest she had come to experience more and more after her parents disappeared. If she ran downstairs, she was bound to be hugged by someone—maybe Aunt Mary in the kitchen or Mrs. Jackson in the dining room. And on weekends, when Frank was home from Harvard, he, too, would take time to chat with Taffy. When Mr. Jackson came home, he would ask Taffy, as well as Daisy, what she had been up to all day.

Best of all, however, was the constant joy of being with Daisy. The two girls were never bored together; they moved from reading together to baking something in the kitchen to playing with dolls and making up stories for them to drawing pictures or just giggling over nothing in particular. At night, after being tucked into bed and promising they would go right to sleep, the whispering and giggling still went on under the puffy comforters.

Mrs. Jackson and Julia found they shared their dressmaking expertise. Julia showed Mrs. Jackson the secret freedom skirts that neither Taffy nor Susie yet knew existed.

"They are handsome, Julia," Mrs. Jackson said, admiring the work. "Let me see if I can find some fabric that would make up into blouses for them." She rummaged around in some boxes and found plenty of silky material, some in white and some in ivory.

"If we make them very simple, I think between us, we could complete three before you leave," she said.

After that, the two of them became pleasantly engrossed for a few hours each day, still keeping the project a secret behind the closed sewing room door.

One night, after Taffy and Daisy were tucked into bed, Cornelia asked Julia if she would "tell her story" while she took down notes. Julia agreed, and Mr. and Mrs. Jackson asked if they could "listen in." Susie joined them.

Mr. Jackson set a large oil lamp in the middle of the dining room table and turned it up high. Over a pot of tea and cookies, they sat there, occasionally asking questions, as Julia spoke calmly in her soft voice, except when she reached the part where she and Della were separated. Then her voice broke, and tears brimmed over in her eyes.

"I was sixteen, and she was nineteen. No matter what else ever happens to me, that will remain the saddest day of my life."

"And how old are you now, Julia?" asked Mrs. Jackson.

"I'm thirty."

"Then Della is now thirty-three. Do you look alike?" she asked, forgetting that Susie could also answer that question.

"Hmm … Our eyes, maybe, and we have the same color of skin. But at seventeen, I was tall and very skinny, and Della was shorter. What do you think, Susie?"

Susie just nodded without speaking. The tears came to her eyes, too, at the talk about Della. She was very fond of Julia, but no one could ever replace Della in her heart. Susie wiped her eyes and managed to say, "I knew there was something vaguely familiar about Julia from the first time I saw her, and it just got stronger and stronger, until I just had to try and find out."

"What about Taffy? Who does she most take after?" asked Cornelia.

Julia nodded at Susie. "What do you think?"

"Taffy seemed just like her mother—the same bouncy, the same cheerful way about her all the time. But after she lost her parents, that disappeared. After a while, she cheered up again, with learning to read and learning so much about cooking. But she was still much more quiet after that."

Julia added, "There was just something about Taffy that drew me to her. But of course, in my wildest dreams, I could never have guessed why."

"It really is a strange coincidence that you were brought together," mused Cornelia. "Perhaps another wild dream would be possible—that Della might be a fugitive slave and get to Canada, and you will all be reunited someday."

"It's not entirely a wild notion," said Mr. Jackson. "It's very likely that Lincoln will win the election, and I wouldn't be surprised if that means the end of slavery someday."

Mr. Jackson rose from the table, adding, "I think we've asked Julia enough questions for one night. We'd better all get up to bed. Tomorrow is the big day, you know—Election Day.

"I hope we have cause for celebration after all the counting is over," he added.

"If only the women could cast their vote, too," said Mrs. Jackson.

"If Lincoln wins, will it mean war, Father?"

"I'm afraid it will come to that eventually. There's talk that South Carolina will secede in protest if Lincoln is elected. And who knows what the other Southern states will do if one goes?"

"Well, if it comes to a war, I shall leave school and study to be a nurse right away," said Cornelia.

"You're too young," said her mother.

"I won't be when I'm all trained."

"By then, the war will be long over," said her father. "The South will not be able to hold out long if it comes to war. It's the North that has all the steel to make guns and equipment for a war. The South will have to buy everything from France and England if we go to war. They don't have half as many miles of railroad track, either. And the Northern ships will blockade all the Southern ports. It won't be a long war."

In his heart, Mr. Jackson hoped his views were right. He certainly did not want a war between the states. The country divided against itself? Americans fighting each other? It did not seem possible. Still, he did not want to see slavery allowed to exist in the expanding western territories. There were no easy answers. But he knew he would cast his vote for Abraham Lincoln tomorrow.

As they cleared the table, Mrs. Jackson asked, "Do you think the Southern agents will disappear if Lincoln is elected?"

"I think they will be leaving anyway as winter sets in. Fewer slaves are coming through our way now, according to our sources. Mr. Henderson had three the other night, though. The Blairs had a few, too.

"That reminds me, we've made arrangements with Mr. Henderson and the Blair farm for the escape plan by wagon. We decided it was not wise to have the wagon start out from this house. Any remaining agents are more likely to be snooping around in these settled parts than out in the open countryside."

Susie asked, "Do you think Sam and the others have reached Canada yet?"

"We could be getting a message soon now. The driver promised to send word as soon as he had them safely across the border. And as far as we know, the weather has been no problem. But that won't last much longer. Once we get close to Thanksgiving Day, snow can be expected in northern New England and even down here."

Upstairs in their own room, Mrs. Jackson sighed and said, "I wish they could stay through Thanksgiving Day. It's only a few weeks away now."

Mr. Jackson shook his head at her and chuckled. "Of course you would, and you would hardly have the Thanksgiving table cleared away, and you would be planning Christmas for them all!"

"Well, they do deserve it. They have all endured enough suffering. I know we have never had runaway groups stay so long before, and that is one reason I have become so attached to them. But it's also because they are all so bright and can read and write. They are ready to begin living a normal, free life and to make their mark in this world. It's a wicked world, indeed, if they are kept from doing it."

"That's why I'm voting for Lincoln tomorrow. He's our best hope for achieving it for them. Cornelia told me that Julia has a better education in literature than she has had at the academy. Julia should be able to go to college. And don't worry about Cornelia becoming an army nurse. It will never come down to that."

The next morning, before he left the house, Mr. Jackson reminded his wife and Aunt Mary, "We can't let up on caution just because there seem to be very few agents, if any, left around here. Remember, Mr. Carlson said there was a lot of money to be made by finding fugitive slaves who are valuable, skilled house workers. Don't let Daisy and Taffy get careless and go outdoors together. And don't let them be in the front of the house unless the windows are covered. Upstairs is different. I've stood outside and looked, and you can't see in."

Mr. Jackson's parting words of caution were like an omen for that very day. It began raining at noontime, and Daisy was soaking wet when she arrived home from school. She changed into dry clothes, but still feeling chilled, she asked Aunt Mary if she and Taffy could make a dessert. It was so nice and warm near the kitchen stove, and the oven was already hot.

"How about a chocolate bread pudding?" suggested Aunt Mary. "There's plenty of milk and stale bread."

Cornelia was also home from school, and she went into the front hall to get something. As she passed through the parlor, she glanced out the front windows and saw Mr. Carlson and two agents already turning up the walkway to the front door.

Cornelia ran to the front stairs and shouted up, "Mother! Daisy! Taffy! Where are you all! It's two agents at the door! One was here the last time alone."

There was no response from upstairs. Cornelia ran up the stairs, calling out, "Mother, where are you? It's agents at the door right now!"

Mrs. Jackson came out of the sewing room, where she and Julia were working away behind the closed door.

"Cornelia, I hear you. Run to the kitchen and warn Mary. Then let them in, but try to keep them in the front hall for just a few minutes."

"Julia, run down the kitchen stairs, quick."

Then Mrs. Jackson looked in Daisy's room.

Taffy was there alone, changing her clothes.

"I'm sorry, Mrs. Jackson, but I spilled milk all down the front of my dress, so I'm putting on a bathrobe for now."

"Where's Daisy?"

"She's in the kitchen, mopping up the floor where we spilled the milk for the pudding."

"Is Susie downstairs, too?"

"She's taking a nap in her room."

"Quick, Taffy, there's no time to spare. Put on a bed cap … Where is it …? Here it is. And get under the bed covers. Pull the bathrobe way up around your neck … there. And bury your face in the pillow. Now, I'll pull the quilt way up. What are these damp clothes on the chair? Oh dear, they are Daisy's school clothes that got wet. I'll hide them in the blanket chest in the sewing room. Don't move or breathe, Taffy. They won't be in here long."

Mrs. Jackson stashed the clothes in the chest and then flew down the back stairs to the kitchen. She could hear the front door opening and the men's voices as they entered.

Susie was up from her nap, mopping the floor with Daisy. Aunt Mary and Julia were already down the cellar stairs, pulling the old sea chest away from the well cover.

"Never mind the floor, Susie. Get to the cellar, now! You too, Daisy. You can't be in two places at the same time, and Taffy is already in bed, being you. Hurry! Go!"

She could hear the sound of heavy feet already going up the front stairs. Mrs. Jackson ran back up the kitchen stairway, and met the men, following Cornelia in the upstairs front hall.

"Please be quiet in my daughter's bedroom. She's taking a nap," said Mrs. Jackson crisply.

"I thought she was all better. I saw her coming home from school just the other day," said one of the agents.

"Well, she's well enough to go to school, but she's still rather weak. So I'm trying to be careful and see that she rests when she gets home. There's a lot of pneumonia going around these damp days, you know."

The agents nodded and walked quietly around the room, peering behind the screen and under the bed as they had done before. There was no movement in the bed. Only the top of a white embroidered bed cap could be seen from the fluffy pillows.

After that, Mrs. Jackson suggested they go on up to the third floor to search and then finish the other bedrooms on the way down. *That should give them time to get the cellar organized*, she thought. Cornelia left them at that point and went down to the kitchen. No one was in sight. She hurried down the cellar stairs.

Julia was already standing at the bottom of the well, with Susie on the lower rung. Daisy was closest to the top, and Aunt Mary was just that minute slamming the cover on tight. Cornelia helped pull the rug over the cover, and then the heavy sea chest was pulled back over the rug. Together, they straightened out the wrinkles in the worn rug and put the three dusty boxes and the lamp back on the sea chest.

As they did this, they had to be careful not to leave fingermarks. Since no slaves had recently been hiding down in the cellar, there were no clues in sight to hide.

Aunt Mary grabbed a basket of apples being kept there, and they both hurried up to the kitchen, shutting the cellar door behind them. Cornelia ran to the bedroom and straightened out Susie's bed. There were no telltale clothes in sight. Everyone had managed to keep on guard against carelessness, and everything had to be constantly kept out of sight in chests or drawers. Agents never went that far in their searching.

Aunt Mary was already peeling apples, looking as peaceful as she could manage, with her heart pounding. Cornelia put on an apron, and finished mopping the kitchen floor, just as the agents came down the back stairs.

As usually happened, the kitchen was of no interest to them, as it offered no hiding places. They poked their heads into the bedroom, and that was all.

"Now, we'd like to check that cellar again," one of them said.

Down the stairs they went, with Mrs. Jackson leading and Cornelia following. This time, they stayed there longer, as if they were suspicious about something down there.

They peered into every corner, as if they were looking for a secret door somewhere. One of the men stood right next to the old sea chest, looking down at it.

Mrs. Jackson and Cornelia held their breath.

No finger marks showing on the chest. It had rope pulls on each end.

❈ ❈ ❈

Julia, Susie, and Daisy barely breathed in the deep well. They could hear the muffled footsteps and voices up above them. Daisy felt as if she would suffocate with fright. Her heart was pounding, and her teeth were chattering. It was damp and cold and black as pitch. For the moment, she forgot she was a white person, safe in her own home! The airless moments went by. Susie put one free arm around her in comfort.

Then it became quiet. After what felt like a long wait, Aunt Mary came down the stairs and began pulling on the rope handles. Finally, the heavy cover was lifted. Light and air appeared above them, and they climbed out.

Aunt Mary, Mrs. Jackson, and Cornelia were waiting for them.

"They have gone now. It's all right. Mr. Carlson took them through the shed and the barn, and then they went down the street."

"And Taffy is safe?" both Susie and Julia asked at once.

"Taffy is probably still hiding in bed, Let's go right upstairs and tell her she can come out from under the covers," said Mrs. Jackson in relief.

Cornelia hugged her little sister. Daisy was still shivering.

"Isn't it strange, Daisy," said Cornelia, "that Taffy has never once had to hide in this secret well, but you are the one who had to use it!"

They all followed Mrs. Jackson up the back stairs to Taffy's room. Taffy's head was still buried deep in the pillows, and there was no movement.

Mrs. Jackson touched her, leaning down close. "I do declare; she's actually fallen asleep through all this fright!"

"Well, it's no wonder, Mother," said Cornelia. "Those two stay awake long after they are tucked in for the night." Cornelia laughed.

"Where are my wet clothes, Mother?" asked Daisy.

"I hid them in the sewing room! Now I think about it, I don't know why it mattered. I just thought there were too many clothes lying about for one little girl!"

They tiptoed out of the room, leaving Taffy to finish her nap.

That night, everyone gathered in the kitchen as soon as Mr. Jackson arrived home. They all began talking at once, telling him all the details of what had happened. But the highlight of the story was that Daisy had had to hide down in the secret well!

Later, Mr. Jackson talked to his wife alone. "We have to get them on their way now. The escape plan is all set, ready to go. The moon is still small, but every night now, it will get brighter. Do you think you could get them ready to leave tomorrow night? I went out to the Hendersons' today, and I talked to George myself. He is certainly a dependable and intelligent fellow, so we have no worry that they will be in good hands. Mr. Henderson wasn't at home; he had to go to Boston. But he's expected back tomorrow afternoon. I figure we should leave here about eight at night, and I will walk them as far as the Hendersons'.

"From there, George knows the way to the Blair farm. It's not far. But there is a big, open field to cross. But it's so out of the way, it seems the best place to start the wagon. They won't need to carry a heavy load of food. There will be stations along the way to take care of that. Just see that they dress warmly."

❊ ❊ ❊

"Taffy's last day is today?" Daisy cried at breakfast, hearing the news from her mother and Aunt Mary in the kitchen. "Why can't we adopt her so she can stay and be my sister?"

"Daisy, she wouldn't be safe here, not even going out to school and just walking about. Both she and Susie are worth a lot of money as fugitive slaves. It's too dangerous here, even now. You saw what happened yesterday. Once they cross over into Canada, they will be free from slavery! That is what is best for Taffy. We have to think of that, no matter how hard it is to say good-bye."

"Please, Mama, don't make me go to school today. Please!"

"It's going to be a long, sad day," moaned Aunt Mary. "I'm going to start cooking right now. At least they'll start off well fed."

Cornelia came downstairs in her bathrobe. "I'm not going to school today, either, Mother. I want to spend the day with Susie and Julia, and I want to be sure Susie packs the clothes I have for her. We are just the same size."

"Then let's begin with a special breakfast, all together in the dining room, girls. You help Aunt Mary and set the table. Perhaps we could have pancakes and syrup," said Mrs. Jackson.

"And bacon," added Daisy.

"Mary, why don't you plan to stay overnight? Then you'll be here when they leave, if that's any comfort to you. Once Susie is all ready, you can fix up the room for yourself again."

Mrs. Jackson could see that her most important task this day would be to keep everyone on an even keel, with some degree of cheerfulness. *After all*, she said to herself, *we're not sending them off into a long and weary walking trip. They will be safe if not warm, all the way by wagon. And there's no reason why this escape should not work."*

Out loud, she said, "I'm going upstairs to the sewing room and get out all the warm scarves, mittens, and the like. And we'll see later today who wants to wear what."

The first thing she did upstairs was put Julia's secret blouses aside for her to pack in her own bundle, along with the freedom skirts.

"We did a fine job together," said Mrs. Jackson sadly, folding the pretty blouses. They had even found time to add lace at the high necks and make velvet bows to attach. *I just wish I could see the three of them wearing these outfits,* she mused to herself. *Perhaps we should have had a party one night and let them get dressed up. But then, these are freedom outfits. And they won't be free as long as they are still in this house.*

Later in the day, Daisy helped Taffy pack her bundle. Daisy went to Cornelia's hidden box and found the pioneer rag doll and Taffy's mother's little worn book.

"Do we have to unstuff the doll?" she asked Cornelia.

"No, Daisy, it's all right this time; they are not walking and carrying their bundle."

Daisy felt worse and worse as the afternoon passed by.

Taffy seemed to be handling the impending departure better.

I guess I really thought Taffy would somehow get to stay here forever, Daisy thought to herself. *After all, isn't that just what happened to Aunt Mary years ago? And she's still here!*

Like her sister, Daisy, too, had some extra clothes to share. But that didn't strike Daisy like much of a farewell gift. It was just secondhand clothes to wear.

All of a sudden, she thought of her beaded bag, put away in its box. After all, since she had stayed home from school, supposedly sick, she'd had to stay home from Sunday school as well, so the beautiful bag had not been used in a while. What was that legend Mr. Draper had told her about? If you gave the bag away, with loving thoughts, the bag would bring good luck and wishes fulfilled to the new owner! That was it! And who else but Taffy needed more good luck and wishes fulfilled as she began her final escape to freedom?

Daisy had once shown the bag to Taffy and told her how she had worked in her father's candle factory to earn it.

"I want you to have my beaded bag as a gift from me, Taffy," she said now.

"But you worked to buy it, Daisy. You better keep it."

"No, I won't be happy keeping it anymore. Remember, I told you how it's supposed to bring good luck if you give it away with loving thoughts? More than anything else, I want you to have good luck. And I also want you to have something to remember me by."

"I don't need anything to remember you by. I'll never forget you, Daisy. I'll give the bag back to you someday."

"No. It's yours forever. We'll be friends forever, too."

Mr. Jackson came home early, and they all sat down together in the dining room. Mrs. Jackson insisted Aunt Mary sit down, too—she had stood all day long in the kitchen, cooking one good dish after another.

At the last minute, Frank arrived home from college for a few days break after exams. He was surprised to discover the runaways were to leave in a matter of hours and said he would accompany them and his father on the walk to the Hendersons'. Before they left the house, Frank walked around the nearby streets and back through the fields to see if anyone was around.

It was finally time to go. The bundles were on the kitchen floor by the door. Susie, Taffy, and Julia were all bundled up in warm clothes and boots. To keep their spirits up, they all kept reassuring each other that they would keep in touch by writing.

"I'll go first," said Mr. Jackson. "When I've crossed the two fields and reach the woods behind the stone wall, the three of you start out together. Give me about ten minutes, and if there is no sound from me, it's all right. And, Frank, you follow behind and keep watch."

The pale quarter moon was suddenly covered by passing clouds. The three figures disappeared into the blackness, followed by Frank. When the pale moonlight shone down again, there was only the flapping scarecrow in the middle of the pumpkin patch to be dimly seen.

Daisy turned from pressing her face against the window and moaned, "They're gone. They're really gone."

Once the five of them reached the woods behind the stone wall, they stopped for a few minutes.

Mr. Jackson whispered, "Now we'll start to walk briskly in single file. Remember, it's about a half hour, all through the woods. There's just a short, open field to the back of the house. George said he would just stand outside and keep watch for you until you get there. Frank and I won't cross over with you—the fewer the better. When we are certain you all are there, we'll turn back."

The moon was in and out as they walked. When they reached the cleared land behind the house and barn, it was deep in clouds once again.

"Good, it's all black. Just walk together now. Go—and God bless you," whispered Mr. Jackson. "There's no deep holes between here and the black shape of the barn up ahead; I checked it out myself."

The men stood there awhile, peering after the women who had become their friends. Without any moonlight it was impossible to tell if they had reached the back of the house. All of a sudden, a weak light shone in a window and then went out again.

"That's the signal, Frank! They are safe inside the house. We can go home now."

When they got back, they found Aunt Mary, Mrs. Jackson, Cornelia, and Daisy sitting at the kitchen table waiting up for them. They had the oil lamp on low, and the teakettle was hissing on the stove.

"We've done all we can do for them now. They are safely inside the Henderson house. George gave us a signal just as he promised he would do. Now it's up to Mr. Henderson to guide them over to the Blair farm and the waiting wagon." said Frank.

It was now ten o'clock p.m. Mr. Jackson banked the fire in the stove for the night. "By now they should be just starting out in the wagon. There's a stiff breeze, but it's not too cold. They'll have plenty of blankets in the bottom of that big wagon, and mounds of hay go over that. The worst problem they'll have is a bumpy ride." His confident words helped everyone feel a little better, and they prepared to go up to bed.

Daisy lingered in the kitchen. "Mama, can I sleep with Aunt Mary tonight? I don't want to be alone in my room, and it's so much warmer next to the kitchen."

"Let her stay," said Aunt Mary. "We'll keep each other company if we can't fall asleep."

❈   ❈   ❈

Mr. Jackson's confident words were not being borne out in the reality of what was happening. For one thing, Mr. Henderson had not returned from his trip to Boston as expected, and his wife was concerned about it.

But George was not daunted. "It isn't necessary for anyone to guide us over to the Blair farm," he said. "I walked part of the way myself, when Sam left, and it's not complicated. The fewer the better. Probably there was some trouble with the carriage, and he's just held up with repairs this time of night."

Again, the runaways set out into the darkness, with occasional glimpses of the moon. After the open field, they were once again hidden in deep woods. The slope of the land changed, however, between the Henderson farm and the Blair farm. The slight path they followed was on the same level with the field to their right side. But to the left, the land dipped down a steep hill into a rocky gully. Once a stream had run its course through there, but it had been long ago been diverted. There were a few large ledges alongside the dried up streambed. After walking about half an hour, they could just barely make out the farm buildings across another open field. They were just black shapes. But it had to be the Blair farm, for there was no other place anywhere near there. They stopped and took a good look at the space they would have to cross to get to the barn and sheds. Two haystacks were fairly close by in the field.

George whispered, "We'll walk to the first haystack and stop and take another look around before we go on to the next one."

They were almost to the first haystack when, suddenly, two black figures jumped out from behind it, shouting, "Stop! We'll shoot!"

In a split second, George grabbed Taffy and lifted her onto his back. At the same time, he whispered to Susie and Julia, "Run! All the way to the bottom of the hill. Find a big ledge and hide for a while. Get all the way back to the Jacksons' later. Don't stop at Hendersons'."

There was no time to discuss any details. For the next minutes, each person was a loner, running for a hiding place. Only George and Taffy were together. Susie was the first, scrambling down to the gully. Where was the bottom? Looming up in front of her was a high and sloping ledge. She touched its steep sides and felt her way along it, until she thought she was on its lower side, nearest the streambed.

Julia was close behind her. She could hear Susie's feet crunching over the twigs and leaves. *Lord, don't let me trip and fall down*, was her only thought. Then she, too, felt the cold sides of the ledge and felt her way, hand over hand, along its side.

"Susie, are you there?" she whispered frantically, wondering where her handholds would lead her.

"Here, keep coming," whispered Susie. And in another minute, Julia bumped into her.

"I think this is the bottom. There's pebbles underfoot." Susie gasped.

They both stopped, breathing hard, and listened for anything coming.

Not one sound did they hear. No twigs breaking underfoot. Nothing. The silence itself was terrifying. Where were George and Taffy?

For a long while, they kept silent. But surely, no one could be close by, searching them out, without their footsteps being heard. The November leaves and twigs were dry and crunchy. Even the occasional rains didn't change all of that. Did they dare to call out to George? Why didn't he call out to them? They still kept their silence.

Finally, Susie said, "Perhaps George has already continued back. Maybe he's waiting further along for us. We couldn't hear his footsteps while we were running downhill, you know. I heard him tell us to go back to the Jacksons', so maybe we should start back now."

"How do we know which way is back?"

"Because uphill is to the right going forward. So going back, uphill should be on our left," said Susie. "Come on. Let's get started. It won't do us any good to stand here all night long."

They followed the small rocks and pebbles along the old streambed.

After they'd walked for quite a long while, Susie said, "I remember that we did follow a streambed, even before we got to the Hendersons', but there was no steep hill on our right; the land was more level along that part of the way. Let's go uphill now and see if we are anywhere near the Henderson farm."

Just as Susie had figured out, the hill was no longer steep. In a few minutes, they were at the edge of the woods, looking across a field. And there, looming up in the dark sky, were the black shapes of the Henderson farm.

"Oh, dear, why can't we cross the field and go in there for safety?" whispered Julia.

"Because that's probably where the agents are waiting for us," whispered Susie. "I think George figured they didn't know we left from the Jackson house in town, so they still are not looking for us to return there. Come on, Julia, we have to keep going. We can't get lost if we follow the very edge of the woods. And when we get to the stone wall, all we have to do is follow that until we come to that gate, and then we'll know where we are."

Susie's sharp instincts were correct. After walking along for what seemed a long time, they came to the stone wall on their left. Another tense way along, and there was the old gate and, through it, the big, open field. And hopefully, beyond that, they'd see the familiar pumpkin patch and the scarecrow.

"We can't wait till morning comes, so let's make a run for it. Let's run just as fast as we can, all the way!"

Across the field, they flew, still hanging onto their bundles—into the pumpkin patch, by the scarecrow, through the trellis, and into the Jacksons' backyard and then the barn and the woodshed. There was the back door to the kitchen, at last, at last!

Susie tapped lightly on the door. No response.

"Mary's window," she gasped. She tapped on the window.

It seemed forever. The door opened a crack.

Susie pushed it open, and they both fell inside, straight into Mary's arms.

"Lord, have mercy! Are you being followed? Do we need to open the well?"

"No," gasped Susie. "But we lost George and Taffy."

In gasps, they both managed to tell her what happened. They half whispered, but Mr. and Mrs. Jackson woke up, heard the low voices, and hurried downstairs. Daisy remained asleep.

"I didn't think there would be any agents roaming around out there. But we can never be sure of anything. They no doubt have their sources and their spies just as the Underground does. I feel terrible. We tried to think of every angle so this escape wouldn't fail. Have you any idea if George and Taffy made it into the woods?"

Julia began sobbing as she spoke. "I saw him pick up Taffy, and I heard his footsteps behind me at first. But when we got into the woods and went skidding down the hill, I could only hear my own feet, tripping over the underbrush. I don't know if George went left or right of where we ended up."

"Agents don't know our dense woodlands and are generally hesitant to get too deep into them. So chances are George may have waited longer, and they'll be along soon. I think the chances are good for that to happen, so try not to worry."

Frank came down the kitchen stairs. "Julia, Susie, I thought I heard your voices! What happened?"

His father explained, again repeating that agents would be unlikely to pursue George and Taffy into such deep woods in the dark.

"But George could get lost himself and be wandering around out there in the wrong direction. I'll get dressed again and head right out to look for them. And you say Taffy was with him?"

"Yes, I saw him just scoop her right up onto his back before I turned and started running for the woods," answered Julia, still shivering.

In the dark kitchen, Mrs. Jackson moved the filled teakettle to the warmest part of the stove.

"I'm going out with you," said Mr. Jackson, grabbing his jacket from the hook. "Don't light any lamps at all, Mother."

"We'll sit right here at the table and wait and have some hot tea in a few more minutes."

Cornelia came downstairs and joined them as, silently, Mrs. Jackson, Mary, Susie, and Julia settled themselves around the table. Daisy slept on. The minutes slowly ticked by.

Finally, Cornelia said, "Let's all join hands and pray silently for their safe return. At least we can do that."

❈ ❈ ❈

George hitched Taffy higher onto his back and held tightly onto her legs. Taffy's arms were clasped tightly around his neck as George sprinted back into the woods and groped his way down the hillside, still half running in long strides. He couldn't see at all what was in front of him or at his feet, and he felt the tangle of underbrush scratch him. *But they can't see anything, either*, he thought.

Suddenly, his feet slid on a rock covered with damp leaves, and he stumbled and went sprawling, rolling over and over down the hill until he reached out and grabbed onto some bushes to break his fall. He pulled himself up to a sitting position and tried to calm his heavy breathing.

Where is Taffy? He reached out all around him in the blackness but felt nothing. *How far up the hill was she tossed off my back when I tripped?* he wondered. He didn't dare call out to her—not yet. *Are the agents still in the woods, listening, but not moving at all?* There was not a sound of leaves or twigs crackling underfoot. That was a good sign. But what of Taffy in the silence? Was she hurt—even unconscious—or was she, too, just being silent, waiting? The thoughts raced through his mind in a jumble of confusion. *How will I ever find her in this darkness without calling out to her?*

Something felt peculiar on his head. He wiped his hand across his hair. A large bump was forming. His hand was wet and sticky. It's bleeding, too, he realized. He tried to squint into the dark for some sense of shapes. He began to focus on a large shape looming up on his right side. He still hadn't tried to stand up. As silently as possible, he crawled in the direction of the shape until he felt the solid, cold side of a ledge. He pulled himself up to standing position. *Good, at least I haven't broken any bones.*

One thing he could tell, and that was downhill from uphill underfoot. Slowly, he felt his way, hand over hand, along the ledge and went back up the hill where the jutting ledge began to level off and become lower, nestled into the sloping hillside. He figured he must now be closer to where Taffy had fallen off. But he forced himself to remain silent and not whisper Taffy's name—not yet, not yet—much as he wanted to call right out to her.

I must be patient, cautious, he told himself. *The agents can't see any better than I can, if they are still around at all. Taffy is smart. She will realize she should be silent for a while, too. If only she is conscious … Please, Lord, let her be all right!* he beseeched.

I'll stay here until daylight if I have to, he determined. *Then I'll be able to find her. But what if she took it upon herself to find her own way back? What then? Would she, could she do that, alone?*

The time dragged by in excruciatingly slow minutes. Still he heard not a sound except the wind rustling through the trees. The moon did not appear at all. Certainly, if two agents were moving around, they would make some kind of sound underfoot. That was the only good sign. George remained standing, leaning against the ledge.

More time dragged by.

Suddenly, the silence was broken. The sound was soft, but there was no mistaking what it was. It was the eerie *who-who* of an owl! Three times in a row the owl hooted softly. Silence again. Then, the owl hooted again. Three times. Silence.

Three times in a row! George said to himself. Hadn't that been the signal Sam had worked out when he'd gone searching for Susie and Taffy the night they'd started out? And when Sam had returned to the group with them, that was the signal he'd given to let them know they should come out from behind the trees and start walking! Up to this moment, he had forgotten all about that. They had never used the signal again.

Bless you, Taffy. You're a smart little girl! He hooted back softly, three times.

From still further uphill, the owl hooted again, three times!

George signaled back and slowly made his way up the hill. He got down on his hands and knees and moved out to the right; he began groping in wide circles with his hands. Suddenly he felt boots and then cloth. There she was, huddled up against a jutting rock—probably the one he had tripped over.

"It's me, George. Are you all right, Taffy?"

"I think so. But I haven't moved at all yet," she whispered back. "I waited as long as I could stand to before I hooted. I haven't heard one footstep or voice at all."

"See if you can get up on my back again. I don't think they are in the woods, and we should move away from here as fast as we can now, before daylight comes."

Thankfully, he felt her thin arms and legs clasped around him as he got himself to a standing position again.

George took a few steps forward, downhill, and then he stopped. He felt dizzy, and something wet rolled down his face.

"Taffy, I think you'll have to walk, at least for a while." He wiped at his face and felt the bump again. No doubt that was what had made him dizzy for a moment.

"I'd rather walk, anyway, George," she whispered back. "I'm afraid, now, being so high up."

Together, they slowly found their way to the bottom of the hill to the pebbles underfoot from the dry streambed.

"Now, we know we turn left and head back," George whispered. "I know I can find the way back from here, all the way to the Jacksons'. Are you all right walking?"

"I'm all right," Taffy whispered, holding onto his hand.

Every now and then, they stopped to listen, but there were no sounds of footsteps behind or above them. Finally they reached the identifying stone wall. And then, suddenly, there were footsteps. George and Taffy froze in place.

After a long silence, they heard thumping sounds. Three very deliberate thumping sounds, like a stick against the ground.

George remembered. Mr. Jackson's stick had made a signal like that when he'd walked into the clearing near the waterfall to find them—a prearranged signal.

George stamped his feet, three times.

Then voices. "It's us. George? Taffy? It's me, Frank, and my father!"

George and Taffy started walking toward the voice, and there they were, bumping into each other in the blackness!

"Quiet now," whispered Mr. Jackson. "We still have to cross the open field to the backyard, and then we're safely home."

Mr. Jackson opened the kitchen door, and the four of them silently entered, closing the door quickly behind them. Mary, Mrs. Jackson, Cornelia, Susie, and Julia were still sitting at the kitchen table, holding hands.

"Oh, Thank God you're both safe, you're safely here," cried Julia, hugging George and Taffy in turn. Then she looked at her wet hand. "Which of you is bleeding?"

"It's just a bump on my head, Julia. I'm all right."

"I'll get some rags, Julia. And you can wash it up for him," said Mrs. Jackson, finding her way in the darkness they were now accustomed to. "What about you, Taffy? Have you any cuts or bumps?"

"I'm all right, but I got thrown right off George's back when we had to run down the hill to escape the agents."

And she and George both began to explain what had happened to them.

"Taffy's one sharp girl. She remembered the secret signal of the owl. She's the one who started it. I didn't even remember it," said George. "You know, Mr. Jackson, I don't think those agents followed us out to the Blair farm. I think they were already out there, for whatever clues or reasons they had. That's why I told Susie and Julia to come all the way back here and not stop at the Henderson farm."

"That's how I see it, too, George."

"There's no use scouting around the neighborhood now. It's so dark. But first thing in daylight, I'll have a look around. There was no one in sight earlier, when you left; I'm sure of that," said Frank.

Aunt Mary helped Taffy off with her coat and boots, almost crying as she repeated, "My poor honey chile. This shouldn't have happened to you—such a terrible fright."

Mrs. Jackson handed her a cup of hot tea. "Drink this, dear child, and then we'll get you tucked into bed right away. Are you sure you're all right? No cuts or scrapes from your fall?"

"Now that I'm back here, I'm all right."

"You sleep just as long as you can. We still shouldn't light the lamp, so everyone try and get some rest. It will be morning soon enough. Julia, you go with Cornelia. Susie, you stay with Taffy. And, Frank, you take care of George. It's just as well we don't stand here talking any longer, just in case anyone is snooping around out there," said Mrs. Jackson.

"Mother is right," agreed Mr. Jackson. "We'll figure out a better plan in the morning when we can think straight again. I won't go to the factory; I'll head out to the Hendersons' and see what I can find out, and then we'll talk with some other Underground folks. We'll find a better escape plan. I promise."

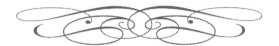

Chapter Thirteen

New Plans

With so much on their minds, Mr. and Mrs. Jackson were down in the kitchen early, in spite of the late night and little sleep. Aunt Mary was already there, stirring up the pot of oatmeal. The door to her room was closed, and Daisy was still there asleep.

"I'm surprised she never woke up in the middle of the night, with all of us out here," said Aunt Mary. "I think she's about worn out from just gettin' through yesterday and sayin' good-bye. I know I am. And now we got to do it all over again!"

"Meanwhile, we still must take all precautions around here. Now we have four fugitives to hide if agents come again to search! It's hard to know if this house is still a major suspect, but we must assume it is." said Mr. Jackson.

Mrs. Jackson looked thoughtful and said to her husband, "You know, I think hiding Taffy in bed with Daisy sitting up in bed, half on top of her, is the best plan. Then, there's only three to hide in the well. And I just hate to think of Taffy having to do that. Daisy said she was frightened out of her mind being down there. So that means Daisy has to play sick again and stay home from school, and we all know she is not going to disagree with this plan! It's all so distressing to her. I think it's risky for her to go to school until this is finally over. She just might say something to a favorite teacher or to a friend, you know, just to relieve the pressure of all this tense secretiveness."

Mr. Jackson had his hand on the kitchen door. "All right then. You know what you have to do. Just see that they all understand exactly what the plans are. I hope I'll have some new ideas when I get back."

Susie, Taffy, Cornelia, and Daisy slept on. Frank also slept late. But George and Julia had too much on their minds to sleep soundly, and they soon appeared in the kitchen. Aunt Mary stirred up a batch of pancakes for them. Mrs. Jackson joined them for a second cup of coffee.

"Now, there's nothing you can do all day until Mr. Jackson comes home. Hopefully, he'll have information about a better escape plan, so you might as well rest all day. Goodness knows, you'll need your strength again, soon enough," said Mrs. Jackson.

George and Julia looked at each other, as if sharing the same thoughts.

George spoke first. "Julia and I need to discuss some important matters privately. That's one thing we can accomplish today. Is there some room in this house where we can do that?"

"Why of course. You can go into the study off the parlor, or you can sit in the parlor. But be sure to close the blinds. The girls always play upstairs; it's safer that way."

After they finished breakfast, George said, "I'll meet you in the study, then, Julia, in about an hour. Is that all right with you?"

Julia nodded and hurried back upstairs.

"Mary, what do you make of George? We don't know anything about his own story as yet, but his manner seems closer to that of an educated man than a slave," said Mrs. Jackson.

"Well, slaves in the 'big house' can have a variety of experiences and jobs. Look at Julia. She was brought up more like an educated white lady than a slave, at least in some ways."

"You're right, Mary. Perhaps that is why Julia and George seem to have so much in common. I just sensed a strong bond between those two at breakfast this morning."

"Just that awful Underground trip is bond enough for anybody. Don't you think so?"

"Of course it is. But I still feel there is something deeper than that between them."

"Maybe Cornelia will find time to write down his story before they have to leave. That's a mighty fine thing she is doing, writing down these stories about runaway slaves."

Daisy emerged from the bedroom, looking blurry eyed. "What time is it? Will I be late for school?"

"Daisy, I have both good and bad news to tell you. You must stay home from school again, perhaps for a few days. And the reason is both good and bad, depending on how you see it."

"But I don't want to stay home from school, now that Taffy is gone. It will be too lonesome."

"Taffy is sound asleep—upstairs, in your bed! And so is Susie! They all had to return here in the middle of the night. The escape plan didn't work, and they were close to getting caught by agents! Don't wake them yet. They need their rest after the fright of last night."

While Daisy ate the last pancakes, her mother told her the details of how the foursome had managed to hide and safely return, but separately, with Taffy being carried on George's back.

"Poor Taffy. She must have been so scared. What if agents come searching the house again? I'll hide in the well so Taffy can hide in bed."

"No, you both stay up in bed. That's the plan we decided on at breakfast. There're three grown-ups now to get down in the well. You'll have to pretend to be sick again. That's why you can't go to school. So just stay in your bathrobe today, and you can both play upstairs. And have all your books and toys on the bed as you did before."

No agents came that day however. The runaway bundles were all safely hidden away, and the warm clothes were hidden as well in the sewing room. Nothing was out of place to cause suspicion, and everyone knew precisely what to quickly do in this emergency.

In the meantime, Mary made plans to cook and bake all day long, with both Susie and Mrs. Jackson also working in the kitchen. Cornelia decided to stay home again. She hoped she'd be able to write down George's story. Frank went down to the candle factory to help out with something, since Mr. Jackson was going to be spending the day on escape plans.

"Mother, are George and Julia going to spend all day talking in the study?" asked Cornelia. "What do you suppose they are talking about so long?"

"I haven't any idea at all. Perhaps they didn't have much chance to talk privately over at the Hendersons'. I don't know. Whatever it is they want privacy for, they deserve to have it."

"Of course they do. I do hope I can hear George's story, though. He said he was willing to tell it. Then I will have them all—Susie, Sam, Taffy, Julia, and George."

"I tell you what you can do, Cornelia," said Aunt Mary with a chuckle. "You wait a little longer. Then you go knock on the study door and tell them that the raisin cake is coming out of the oven and that they can have lunch whenever they please."

"This whole house is going to smell more wonderful as each hour passes," said Mrs. Jackson, peeling apples for a pie. "At least baking does help relieve some of the tense pressure we're under."

"Baking for friends is much nicer than baking for slave masters," observed Susie, rolling out the piecrust.

By the time Mr. Jackson and Frank returned, wonderful aromas did indeed fill the house. But Cornelia still had not been able to write down George's story, because after he and Julia had emerged for lunch, they'd returned to the study to talk again. Then, later in the afternoon, each had gone upstairs to their respective rooms until it was time for the evening meal.

Once they were all seated at the dining room table, Mr. Jackson announced, "I have some good news. It looks like Abraham Lincoln will be our next president! Some votes from distant places are still not in yet, but he's far enough ahead now, I think it's a certainty."

After they had talked about the election for a while, Mr. Jackson told them what he had accomplished during the day.

"First of all, I went out to see if Mr. Henderson got back from his trip to Boston. He did have trouble with a wheel on the carriage, and it was late at night before he got home. He said a carriage passed by him on the road coming from the direction of the Blair farm, and it was not a horse and buggy that he recognized. He thought there were two men inside. Other than that, we have no clues as to who those agents were hiding behind the haystack or what their knowledge might be of any of our plans. We don't dare use that route now, in any event."

"Did you talk to anyone else today, Father?" asked Frank.

"I certainly did. I met with a banker from Philadelphia and he had some very interesting ideas to tell me about. At first, I was skeptical of such a plan, but the more I thought about it, the more I concluded it could work. So I went to see Mr. Hale, and we talked in private; he said he would help with this plan if we decide to go through with it. It will involve quite a lot of people—that is, people who are involved in the Underground Railroad already. No one else, of course. And it will take the help and imagination of every single member of this family plus the rest of you. It's complicated, I admit, but it's clever, and it should work!"

Everyone stopped eating, and looked at him, waiting to hear what this remarkable escape plan could be!

"Where is Aunt Mary tonight?" asked Mr. Jackson. "She'll be involved, too."

"I told her to go home early and have some time with her husband. She'll be back early in the morning."

"Will I be in the plan, too, Father?" asked Daisy.

"Indeed you will, my child. Indeed you will. It will take the wits of all of us to pull this one off!"

"We're waiting to hear it, William. Go ahead now and tell us," said Mrs. Jackson.

"This is what they did at an Underground station at a house right in the city of Philadelphia. To be sure, this was to help just one slave escape. But it could work for four with the right planning. They knew there were agents spying on the house all the time. There seemed to be no way to sneak this woman out of the house, even in the middle of the night. So they disguised her as a white woman. In fact, she was supposed to be the grandmother of the children living there! On the arm of the man supposed to be her own son, she walked right down the front steps, in broad daylight, and stepped into a waiting carriage! What do you think of that?"

Right away, Mr. Jackson's own family had questions to put to him.

Cornelia asked, "How did she get safely into the house in the first place?"

"As I understood it, he said it was after she was already there that the word came that a particularly valuable slave was somewhere in the city of Philadelphia, and this was a prime suspect house."

"How do you make such a disguise so it's convincing?" asked his wife.

"It was quite simple—a veil over her face and the appropriate clothes that a wealthy grandmother would wear. When she appeared on the front steps, her grandchildren came out, too, and they all hugged and kissed good-bye. The agents don't stand right by the steps, you know. They were likely to be across the street somewhere."

"Well, in our situation, wouldn't we have to somehow get four people *into* our house before we could have four people later leaving the house in full view of the street?" asked Frank, looking puzzled.

"Who are those four people going to be? And how do we get rid of them later?" asked Mrs. Jackson.

"I met with Mr. Hale in the afternoon, and we went to my office at the factory. We discussed several possible plans, and I do believe we came up with one that works."

"I know, Father. I know how we could do it!" cried Daisy excitedly.

"All right, Daisy, you tell us how!"

"We have a make-believe birthday party, and we invite lots of people. And then Susie, Taffy, Julia, and George get all dressed up in our clothes and leave in the carriages!"

"You guessed it, Daisy! That is basically what the plan is all about. There are several variations on this escape plan. And here's what Mr. Hale and I decided was the best one. But if you have other ideas about it, we'll talk about them all until we know we have the safest plan.

"Having a party is just what we decided on!" he continued. "It will be dark and, hopefully, confusing in terms of just how many people are invited. Two or even three carriages can arrive. One can let guests out at the front, and the other one or two will turn into the driveway to the barn and pull up as closely as possible to the walkway to the kitchen door."

"Who gets invited, Father?"

"Mr. Hale says his family will do it. There's Mrs. Hale; their son who's about Frank's size; their daughter, your age, Cornelia; and the youngest is Taffy's size. We don't need to match people up exactly, as no one will know how many, are here in the first place!"

Frank said, "I could invite a couple of friends from college whose families I know are conductors on the Underground Railroad. They could stay overnight, wait till it's dark the next night, and sneak off by the back fields."

"Right there, then, we have more than enough along with the Hales, unless you think of someone else to ask."

"Let me think awhile, and we'll decide who else to invite," said Mrs. Jackson. "We'll have all the downstairs blinds and curtains closed but lamps on all over the house so it will look festive."

"Can we really make it a birthday party?" asked Daisy.

Her father replied, "You ladies can dream up any kind of party you want. That's your choice."

"What do you think about this, George? We haven't heard a word from any of you yet. And no wonder; we've all been talking at once it seems!"

"I think I can speak for all four of us—that we are overcome with gratitude at the trouble you are willing to go to in order to help us reach freedom."

Frank spoke up again. "Father, do you have a plan yet for leaving the house? Where will the carriages go when they leave here? I have an idea about that!"

"Let's hear it then. We had several thoughts, but we didn't resolve that part."

"They will be all dressed up in their party clothes when they leave. They'll have to get inside somewhere to take them off and put on their warm clothes. I was down in the shipping room of the factory today. You know, wagons at the rear end of the building can go right inside down there when we load them up. Why can't the carriages go there? The clothes can be hidden there, and the wagon can be waiting there for them. I don't think agents would ever think to be spying on the back of our factory building, do you?"

"Frank, that's the best idea I've heard about that phase of the escape!

"Something else, too. We have to be certain there is no buggy following the carriages after they leave here. I could already be in a buggy waiting down the street somewhere, and I'll trail along and make sure no one is following. If there is, I'll stop them and hold them up long enough so they don't know where the carriages go. I'll say I need help—something wrong with my horse, or I'm sick. I'll think of something by then."

"Susie, Julia, and Taffy, are you willing to try this?" Mr. Jackson asked them seriously, but still smiling at them.

The three of them nodded their heads in solemn agreement.

There was no doubt about it. George had expressed for them exactly what they were feeling; it was very overwhelming what these people were willing to do.

"It's decided then. This is the plan we'll use," said Mr. Jackson. "Frank, you and I will take care of the details about the carriages and son on. And, Mother, you take care of the party and the clothes. We'll get the word over to the Hales' house. Now, when should we do this? We must not wait much longer. It's getting colder weather all the time."

Mrs. Jackson replied, "We can be ready tomorrow night if we have to. But I'd rather wait just one more day if that's all right. I think everyone is still worn out from last night's ordeal. I know I am, and I wasn't the one who had to hide and run in the night air."

"We'll arrange everything for the night after tomorrow then." Mr. Jackson pushed his chair back to stand up, but he waited as George spoke up just then.

"There's something else. Uh, Julia and I would like to speak to you and Mrs. Jackson privately, if we could, for a few minutes tonight?"

"Of course … we can talk in the study."

Mrs. Jackson closed the study door behind them. Something clicked in her mind, and she had a premonition of what was about to be discussed. Or perhaps, the appropriate word was *announced*?

George did the talking.

"Julia and I have been talking about this today. That is, we have talked about part of it before, at the Hendersons'. But now we have come to a different conclusion. What I'm trying to say is that Julia and I have become very devoted to each other over the long trip, and we decided that we want to get married someday. We figured we would get married when we reach freedom in Canada. That seemed to be the only possible plan. But now, we feel differently—especially after last night."

"After last night, we came to realize that we are still in so much danger and that we might never even get to Canada and freedom," Julia added. "So now, we would like to be officially married before we leave here, if that is at all possible."

"Yes, as Julia says, we want to begin our new life already married—as a real family. I know about Julia being Taffy's own aunt, and we want to be a real family for Taffy, right from the beginning. For Susie, too, if she wants to be with us until she's older."

"George has many skills he hopes to put to use right away. But eventually, he wants to study to become a lawyer, so he can help other fugitives," said Julia.

All Mrs. Jackson's vague thoughts came into focus. She had not allowed herself to dwell upon them, but now the reality was right before her eyes and ears!

She kissed Julia and patted George on the arm. "A wedding! Our escape party is going to be a wedding!"

"Oh, no, Mrs. Jackson, it's not a wedding we're asking for. We just thought, if there's time, we could be legally married," said Julia.

"We thought you probably would know some legal official you could call upon to come over here to marry us," said George.

"Indeed we do," said Mr. Jackson. "And we also have a preacher friend, too, and they are both abolitionists to the core."

"So now we have two more guests for our wedding party," said Mrs. Jackson. "Let's see, that's, um, nine guests total, and we are five, and Aunt Mary and her husband make sixteen. And then there's the bride and groom, plus Susie and Taffy, making a grand total of twenty people. Why, that's an easy number to plan for in one day plus!"

"There's no use arguing with her, Julia and George," Mr. Jackson said, beaming, before either could reply. "Just accept it, and enjoy it! Mrs. Jackson is already totally involved in planning for your wedding!"

"We must tell the others right away. We shall all have to pitch in and help." Mrs. Jackson opened the study door and hurried to the kitchen where the others were.

Mrs. Jackson called everyone back to the dining room table. "Cornelia, please bring those special cordial glasses to the table. And Frank, go to the cellar and bring up a bottle of that elderberry wine we made last year."

When they were all seated again and the sparkling, engraved glasses were placed on the table along with the opened bottle of wine, Mrs. Jackson announced, "We are going to drink a toast to the success of this unusual escape plan. And then we are also going to make a special announcement. Go ahead, dear."

Mr. Jackson stood up and said, "May the Good Lord, in His Mercy, bless this escape plan and ensure the safe arrival of our dear friends in Canada, to live in freedom from slavery, forever after."

The dim light from the oil lamps illuminated their serious faces, white and black, as they sipped from the tiny glasses. Daisy and Taffy were allowed to participate, their eyes wide and shining with the importance of this solemn occasion.

Next, Mr. Jackson said, "Now, I have the pleasure of making a special announcement—one I have made only once before, almost two years ago. Daisy, Cornelia, Frank, do you remember when we announced your sister Alice's engagement at a party here? Now, I wish to announce the engagement and the soon to be wedding of Julia and George."

Mr. and Mrs. Jackson lifted their glasses and smiled at the couple, and the rest of the group, mesmerized into silence, did the same.

Susie was the first one to speak. "Julia, George! I knew it! I knew it! But I didn't know it would happen now." Susie jumped up and hugged them both in turn. "Oh, if only Sam was here tonight! I wish we would hear from him before we leave. I want to write and tell him the news right away."

"Susie, you may be telling him in person before long. You will be entering Canada at the same location they entered. You'll find him!" said Mr. Jackson.

"I certainly am going to have a lot to write about," said Cornelia. "Julia, when I took down your story, you barely mentioned George! Now, I want to know when your romance first began."

"I must confess, I am just as curious as Cornelia!" said Mrs. Jackson.

"I can tell you," spoke up Susie, her face beaming with pleasure. "It began the night they met at the swamp dance."

"The swamp dance!" said Cornelia, "You never even mentioned that, Julia!"

"She didn't want to go at all," said Susie. "But I guess I just nagged her into it. Julia wasn't used to mingling with slaves she didn't know, especially field slaves. Sam was involved with George by then in our plan to escape, and George had to walk a long distance to come to our swamp dance to talk to Sam. George, you didn't want to come inside and dance. But after you met Julia, you stayed and danced all night long, and then you both sat on the side and talked and talked." Susie gasped with surprise she could bravely say that much at once!

After that, everyone began to talk and ask questions at once!

Chapter Fourteen

Three Things to Celebrate

Mr. and Mrs. Jackson were already downstairs in the kitchen the next morning when Aunt Mary arrived. When she heard the news she said, "Well, I do declare, you had a feeling about those two, and you were right as usual, Mrs. Jackson!" "I think it's a wonderful beginning for them, and it is also good for Taffy and Susie. It will give them a sense of stability and family in a new land. It's going to be good for us, too, to have this extra excitement to plan for. It will help relieve the tension of what we are actually doing, which is planning a dangerous escape!"

Together, Mrs. Jackson and Aunt Mary made out a list for Mr. Jackson to leave off at the grocer's, telling what was to be delivered later in the morning.

Mr. Jackson warned, "Remember, do not order anything that identifies this party as a wedding celebration. You can call it a birthday, if you wish. But the less said, the better.

"We had a wedding reception here just a year ago, so we still have lots of leftover items we can use. I wish Alice and Robert could come. If only they didn't live so far away from us!" sighed Mrs. Jackson. She firmly continued on with plans.

"We'll set up the extra table in the dining room. That way, we can all sit down. It will be elbow to elbow, but it's nicer that way—all together. We'll all help you, Mary. The girls will clean and iron tablecloths. You tell them whatever you want done. You know, I cannot ask one of the factory workers to come over here to clean and iron as I normally would do. It's just too dangerous, having people in this house now. We can never be certain how others really think. We'll all work hard, all day long. And, hopefully, tomorrow we'll have some extra time to think about special touches to make this a real wedding.

"Right now, I'm going to be in the sewing room for a while. I must figure out the clothes, both for the final escape from the factory and for the party. Getting four people all decked out for two such different occasions is going to take some figuring out!"

First, Mrs. Jackson looked in on Daisy and Taffy. The two girls were sitting up in bed, playing with dolls and chattering away with their imaginary stories. She sat down on the bed and asked them to listen to her carefully.

"After you have breakfast, I want you to do whatever Aunt Mary asks you to do. I made out a list of things, and I know there are some silver pieces that need polishing. We are all going to work hard today, so we can have a beautiful wedding party tomorrow night for Julia and George. But we still have to remember to be careful, as usual, about leaving too many clothes around and things like that.

"We have to stay on guard, so I want you to leave the toys on the bed and your bathrobes close by. If any agents come by, it's the same plan. Taffy hides under the covers, and you, Daisy, are sitting up, sick with a cold. I'm going to put the cough syrup beside the bed with a glass and spoon."

Mrs. Jackson knocked on Cornelia's door next. She and Julia were dressed and about to go downstairs.

"Mother, Julia and I were just talking about my writing down the fugitive slave stories. She thinks it's a good thing for me to do this—that it will be part of an important record someday. Julia is interested in writing, too. She says I must find time today or tomorrow to write down George's story. She says I'll be surprised to discover that parts of his story are similar to Julia's! When I listened to your own story, Julia, why didn't you mention your romance with George?"

"Well, you wanted my story, and that's what I told you. Our story as a couple I felt was too uncertain to mention."

"Mother, what about clothes for Julia, Susie, and Taffy to wear at the wedding party tomorrow night? Do you want me to find dresses of mine for Julia and Susie? Oh dear, Julia is quite a lot taller than I am."

"I'm going into my sewing room right now to think about all of this, and then I will let you know. I have some ideas. I just need to be alone for a while to figure it out. After you have breakfast, come in and talk with me, Julia, as you may have to help make some decisions. And, Cornelia, you'll have to help Aunt Mary today. Susie can do some baking, too. And tell Frank and George to get the extra table and chairs from the cellar and clean them off. Remind Frank he said he'll invite his two friends. I think it's a good idea to have plenty of people arriving here. It just helps to create as much confusion as possible. Then, there's the proper clothes for George. Tell Frank he can work on that, too."

Thank goodness Frank is home these few days, thought Mrs. Jackson as she sat down in the sewing room to think.

Then she opened the large blanket chest and lifted out a comforter on top and, underneath that, folded-up fabric. The next layer included a long, shallow box and a soft bundle wrapped in a white sheet and tied with white ribbon. Safely hidden on the bottom were the bundles that Susie, Julia, and Taffy had carried the night of the failed escape. She lifted out Julia's but left the other ones there.

"I must be so careful not to leave anything telltale lying around," she reminded herself as she undid Julia's bundle. She took out the three freedom skirts and the blouses they had made for them.

It should be safe enough to have these hanging up so the wrinkles fall out, she thought. *After all, we are a family of several girls. I could be just rearranging things.*

She pulled another box out from under the sewing table and made certain all the warm escape clothes were where she had hurriedly placed them the night they returned.

Now for the bonnets and veils. She went into her own room and chose two that looked amply brimmed to partially shade their faces. *In the dark, the veils will just be an extra precaution*, she thought and carried them all back to the sewing room.

She went to Daisy's room to find a bonnet for Taffy to wear. The two girls were gone, but two bathrobes were on the chair, and the big bed was heaped with pillows, toys, books, and paper. *Quite a mess, but for once, I'm not asking to have it all cleared away and the bed made!*

Back in the sewing room, she attended to something else on her mind, and then she placed the remainder of Julia's bundle back on the bottom, laid the fabric and the comforter on top, and closed the lid.

Julia knocked on the closed door.

"If it's you, Julia, come right in!

"First of all, Julia, try on a bonnet and let me see how it works … There, so." Now, cloaks or coats are all downstairs, and they can just stay where they are until needed tomorrow night.

Mrs. Jackson removed the cloth she had draped over the hanging freedom outfits. "I hope you don't mind. I opened your bundle so I could take out the freedom skirts and blouses. What do you say we use them in advance of their original purpose? They can be worn at the party and then packed away. You can help me sew on those velvet bows we made for the blouses."

"Imagine. My freedom outfit is going to become my wedding gown! Back at the plantation, when I was making those skirts, who could ever have dreamed of anything so unlikely!" said Julia.

"Well, Julia, you have a choice as it turns out. You can wear your freedom skirt if you prefer. But here is another choice for you." And as she said that, Mrs. Jackson uncovered a white sheet spread across something on the sewing table. She held it up for Julia to see. It was her oldest daughter's wedding gown! Lying next to it on the table was the filmy white veil and a pair of white gloves.

"I do believe it will fit you. You may be somewhat thinner than Alice, but she is also tall. Let's see," Mrs. Jackson said as she held the gown against Julia's shoulders.

"Try it on, dear!"

Before Julia could protest, Mrs. Jackson was helping unbutton her dress in the back.

"There's a special white petticoat for it, too," she said and handed that to her.

Before Julia knew what she was doing, Mrs. Jackson had her into the gown and was hooking it up the back.

"Now, the veil," she said happily and adjusted it on Julia's head. "There! Now have a look in the big mirror behind you!"

Julia surveyed herself in the mirror.

"I must be dreaming!" was all she could manage to say.

"It's almost perfect!" said Mrs. Jackson, getting a few pins and quickly tucking in a little on each side of the waistline.

"Oh, I shouldn't wear this. You must keep it for Cornelia. It should just be for your own girls, not for me—"

"Nonsense! You're not going to wear it to Canada! It may never be worn by Cornelia or Daisy. They will probably have their own ideas, or fashions will change by then. But, of course, it is up to you. Whatever you wish to do."

Mrs. Jackson looked so happy and glowing, admiring Julia in the wedding gown, that Julia could not resist pleasing her. And she had to admit to herself that the beautiful gown did look well on her tall figure. "I would be honored to wear your daughter's wedding gown," she said in a whisper.

Mrs. Jackson helped her off with the gown and hung it up, covering it completely with the white sheet.

"You'll be wearing the warm skirt when you leave. Julia, maybe we should wait until later or even tomorrow morning to tell Susie and Taffy about their surprise outfits. We really do need to get all we can accomplished today, and right now they are all working at different tasks for Aunt Mary. Daisy and Cornelia have party gowns they can wear. That's no problem. We'll show them the wedding gown later, too. They will all be so excited, we'll never get another lick of work out of them the rest of the day!"

Julia and Mrs. Jackson sat down to sew on the velvet bows, and Mrs. Jackson also made the alterations in the wedding gown.

"Julia, there's something I was thinking about when I was alone in here earlier today. I would like to know your opinion of this. You know, your wedding is going to be an event that Taffy will remember all her life. I was just wondering if you have any thoughts about whether it would be nice for Taffy to know that you are her aunt, a real relative—her own dear mother's sister! I was wondering if, someday, when you do tell her, she will wish she had known it on your wedding day. What do you think?"

"It's strange you should bring it up. You know, I couldn't help thinking about it myself. One usually has a family member as part of the wedding, and here I do have one—my very own beloved niece! It struck me as sad that we could not share that knowledge together. I felt it was for Taffy's sake that we kept it from her, just in case we were separated. I didn't want to give her any more grief over the loss of family. Perhaps I should be more optimistic, now that we are almost there—almost to freedom!"

"Do you want to talk it over with George?"

"I did mention it to him, yesterday in the study. He said it was up to me, whatever I thought best. But then I tried to put it out of mind again."

"You think about it today, and if you decide you want to tell her, let me know. I'll see that you have privacy somewhere in this busy house!"

In the afternoon, Mrs. Jackson was in the kitchen going over the morning's accomplishments with Aunt Mary.

"We seem to be coming along well, Mary. Taffy and Daisy are going to polish some more silver, and Cornelia set out the china and crystal on the sideboard and ironed the big lace tablecloths and the white napkins before she went out to do some errands for me downtown. And you have the food coming along just fine. What about a wedding cake? Have you started that yet?"

"I'm starting to mix the batter for that right now, Mrs. Jackson," said Susie from the pantry. "I'm collecting spices and raisins right now from the shelves."

"Both Julia and George loved that raisin cake she made yesterday, so we decided to repeat that for their wedding cake. It will stay moist, and they can all take a piece along with them," said Aunt Mary.

"We're going to let Taffy and Daisy frost the cake tomorrow morning," said Susie, bringing her supplies to the worktable.

"What is that noise coming from the cellar?"

"Oh, that's George down there. He's repairing some of those chairs we need up here."

Mrs. Jackson went back upstairs to look in some boxes for the leftover white ribbons they had used at Alice's wedding. Perhaps she would even find some rice and some rose petals in a box.

Hearing voices from Daisy's room, she peeked in. The two girls were sitting on the bed, drawing pictures.

"We'll polish the rest of the silver, Mama," Daisy reassured her. "But we want to make some decorations for the table, and Cornelia gave us some good ideas."

"Taffy, you are happy about this wedding, aren't you?"

"Oh yes," said Taffy, keeping on with her drawing of hearts and flowers.

"You and Julia and George will be a real family together when you get to Canada now."

"Susie will live with us, too, won't she?"

"I'm sure she'll want to do that."

"Susie is like my big sister, like Cornelia is to Daisy. But I don't have a family anymore—not like Daisy does. Susie says that someday we may find my mother and father in Canada, because maybe they have already escaped. So maybe someday, I will have a real family again."

"Yes. You hold onto that thought, and it may happen one day. Tell me, Taffy, do you think of your parents often?"

"I always think of them before I fall asleep at night, and I pray for them. But I don't cry anymore, like I did at first."

"You're a brave little girl, Taffy. And we all love you very much," whispered Mrs. Jackson, bending over to give her a hug.

Mrs. Jackson left them and stood at Cornelia's door for a moment. There was no sound at all from within. Perhaps Julia was taking a nap. She returned to the kitchen and asked them if she was upstairs sleeping.

Susie laughed. "My no, she's down in the cellar, keeping George company!" Susie was just starting to pour the rich spicy batter into three separate pans.

"You really are happy when you are cooking and baking, aren't you, Susie?"

"It's what I love to do best. I learned how to make this raisin cake from Taffy's mother, you know. I keep thinking about her all the time today. How she would love to be here, helping us get ready for Julia's wedding."

"Susie, I'm thinking we should tell Taffy that Julia is her mother's sister. This wedding would have more special meaning for her if she knew that. It would be nice for you and Taffy to be able to share that knowledge together also. What do you think?"

Susie put down the big bowl of batter and put her hands on her hips. "Do you really think we should? I was always so afraid it would make Taffy so terribly sad all over again if anything happened to Julia—you know, if we were to get caught and sent back or just separated. But I don't feel so scared all the time now. In spite of what we have to still do tomorrow night, after the wedding is all over, I guess I really believe we are going to make it this time. And I'll really see Sam again, too! If we tell Taffy, who should do the telling? Julia?"

"Perhaps both of you should tell her, together. Taffy was just telling me how you are just like a big sister to her. I'll go down to the cellar and see what Julia thinks."

George was still working on the chairs, and Julia was sitting on one that was completed, a pencil and paper in her lap.

"I'm afraid Cornelia won't find time to get George's story written, and I think it is very important that she have these notes, so I'm writing what I know and asking George to fill me in on the parts I don't know."

"Julia, I've been thinking about our conversation this morning, and I've just spoken to Susie. I've also been talking to Taffy, and I now feel that it is a good idea to tell Taffy that you are her aunt. Have you thought any more about it?"

"George and I talked about it again. He thinks Taffy is ready to hear this—that she is very strong for a little girl. I think I'm the weak one! I'm afraid I will just break down and cry telling her!"

"Well, there's nothing wrong with crying. There's enough going on around here right now that is cheerful that the crying will soon be followed by laughter again. I tell you what. If you decide to tell her, why don't you take Susie upstairs with you, and the three of you can go to the sewing room and have privacy for as long as you want. And, Julia, then you can show both Susie and Taffy the surprise freedom outfits! That will make you all cheerful again! They don't know about the wedding gown, either. No one does yet, and I think that Susie and Taffy should share this with you first. You can try it on for them! And they can try on their freedom clothes."

Mrs. Jackson started up the stairs saying over her shoulder, "Of course, when you get to that stage of trying on the clothes, I wouldn't object to being called in for a peek!"

Julia made up her mind to tell Taffy.

Mrs. Jackson told Taffy, "Julia and Susie want to have some time to spend with you, just the three of you together. So run along to the sewing room, Taffy. They are waiting for you now."

Then she went back down to the kitchen and helped Mary with the cooking.

In a little while, Mr. Jackson and Frank came through the kitchen door, followed by another young man.

"This is my friend, Howard Thompson, Mother. Our other pal is coming tomorrow, but Howard had no place to go on this time off. He's from New Jersey. So I thought he could help me make carriage arrangements and whatever else needs to be done tomorrow. Also, we thought it best to get the clothes to George right now. You can see that Howard is tall, like George! Howard is studying law. He is interested to get to talk to a slave who wants to become a lawyer. And he's brought a book along for George!"

Mr. Jackson hung his coat on the kitchen hook, saying, "The wagon is already hidden inside the factory down at the shipping department, and tomorrow the boys can take the escape clothes down there to hide. The Hale family will all be here tomorrow night. That's taken care of. And I've talked to our friend Judge Cotswell. He will come over here tomorrow morning to have them sign papers, and he'll also be a guest at night. But Reverend Southwick will perform the marriage ceremony. They both asked me what George's last name is, and I couldn't tell them—not Julia's, either."

"George is upstairs in his room. Go up and give him the clothes. And make sure he tries them on, in case we have to make any adjustments. He got all those old chairs repaired today and the table fixed, too. Howard can bunk in with you, Frank."

"How are things coming along here, my dear?" asked Mr. Jackson.

"We have so many good cooks in this house, we could open a fancy restaurant! The wedding cake was made by Susie. And let me warn you right now, I don't want anybody sneaking a taste in the pantry! Tomorrow, Daisy and Taffy are going to frost it. Oh, if only this was really just a party to celebrate a wedding, instead of the dark side of it being this dangerous escape plan!" exclaimed Mrs. Jackson. "By the way, did you ask if Mrs. Cotswell will be coming, too?"

"Yes, she will be."

"So it's twenty-one now."

Cornelia was the next one to come in, dumping her shopping bags on the chair. "I suppose you've all heard the news! Abraham Lincoln is now definitely our sixteenth president!"

"We know," said Frank, "but we just hadn't had a chance to tell Mother yet."

Just then, Taffy came running down the kitchen stairs into the kitchen. She ran to Mrs. Jackson, hugged her around the waist, and said, "Mrs. Jackson, guess what I just found out! Julia is my very own aunt! She was, she is my own Mama's sister! Susie didn't know it at first, either, but then she found out one night when Julia was sewing at the plantation!"

"Taffy, that's exciting news!" said Cornelia, giving Taffy a hug and a kiss.

"Come upstairs to the sewing room. Julia and Susie have something to show you right away!"

"Come along, Cornelia," said her mother. "This is very important."

"Julia told me to knock first," said Taffy. "Daisy, are you coming?"

"I'm right here," she said, coming into the hall.

Julia opened the door a crack, saying, "Taffy, you come in alone. And the rest of you wait just a few minutes!"

"What's going on?" asked Daisy.

"Some kind of surprise," said her mother.

"You can come in now!" three voices called out, and the door opened wide.

There they stood—the bride, dressed in her beautiful wedding gown, and Susie and Taffy dressed exactly alike in their mauve-colored freedom skirts and creamy, silk blouses with puffy sleeves and pink, velvet bows and lace at the high-necked collars.

They all talked and laughed inside the small room, the door shut tightly, "Just in case George comes out into the hall," said Mrs. Jackson.

When she had a chance, later, she asked Julia, "Well, how did it go? Did Taffy cry when you told her?"

"No, but I got all teary-eyed, and so did Susie. But then Taffy just threw herself into my arms in that exuberant way she has and was so pleased and excited to find out I was her aunt that we couldn't help but be happy!"

That night at the dining room table, everyone shared the day's projects and news all over again.

"Taffy has a new aunt, and we have a new president. And there's a big wedding cake in the pantry and plenty else going on besides that!" said Mr. Jackson.

An exciting sense of both intrigue and happiness filled the air. The new friends felt closer than ever as they sat and talked together at the big table. The clothes Howard had brought for George did fit him, and the two men were becoming pleasantly acquainted.

"Cornelia, did you get to corner George today and write down his story? Or were you both too busy?"

"No, I didn't find time today, Father. But Julia did take down some notes for me. I've already read them, and it's interesting. But it is also very sad to realize that all of these stories share the same thing in common. George, Sam, Susie, Taffy, and Julia—all of them have suffered the loss of all or part of their families through the cruelty of their slave masters. It was all so unnecessary! No one got sick and died! They were just willfully sold away and separated from their families!"

"Speaking of families, I am reminded that I don't know your last name, George. Both Judge Cotswell and Reverend Southwick asked me that."

"Right now, I don't have a last name, Mr. Jackson. On the Underground Railroad trip, John, the older man in our group of runaways vowed that he would never again speak the last name of his slave master and that, when he got to Canada, he would decide on a new name for himself. I was impressed with that, and I decided I would take a new name someday, too."

"I see. But you will have to write down a name on the marriage certificate. Why not decide right now? There are many good names to choose from."

"I'd like the name to have some personal meaning for both Julia and me. What do you think of my choosing the name of Jackson?" asked George.

"Why, that is wonderful! George Jackson! Julia Jackson!"

"I think that calls for another toast, tonight," said Mrs. Jackson. "New president, new name, new aunt!"

After the warm glow of the toast, the entire group remained at the table talking. Howard wanted to know how George had become interested in the study of law.

"After my parents were sold, I managed to run away," he explained. "I was caught and put on the auction block. I was only fifteen. But fortunately for me, I was bought by a judge who needed a male house servant. He was almost an invalid, and he wanted someone around to drive him to court and wait for him and do errands. Up until then, I had worked in the carpentry shop, like Taffy's father did. I already knew how to read, and in my spare time, I now was able to read many books that the judge owned.

"The judge was failing, and he didn't much notice anymore how I spent most of my time. I almost felt guilty running away. I couldn't help but like him. But I knew I had to leave soon. If the judge suddenly died, I knew I would immediately be sold. And then my chances to escape could be lost. I had met Sam by then, and I knew he had a good escape plan in the planning stage. Then I met Julia, and when I knew she was planning to run away, I had to make up my mind to go, too!"

After that, the talk turned to the election and what it would mean for the country.

"I think we can now count on slavery being abolished sometime in the future," said Mr. Jackson.

"We have to flee to Canada now to secure our freedom. But it could be that, someday, we can return to the United States to live. What do you think of that, Julia?" said George.

"It is something to dream about, and I'm beginning to believe in the most unlikely of dreams! When I first went to the Davis plantation to sew, I didn't believe in anything except that I must keep on being a good seamstress so I would never have to work in the cotton fields. I never thought I would find a relative, such as Taffy. And when I first started making the freedom skirts, I didn't believe they would ever be worn! Last of all, I never expected to get married—ever!"

Chapter Fifteen

The Wedding Day

On her wedding day, Julia was the first one in the household to get up. She had always had a habit of early rising, and today was no different, even though she knew she could rest as long as she pleased. She tiptoed into the sewing room and looked out the window. The sun was rising into a sky filled with low, fast-moving clouds.

The contrast between the bright sun and the dark gray clouds set the scene for this special day—a day that would be filled with emotional contrasts. There would be action and reflection, tension and fear combined with pleasure and joy and sadness.

Right now, for Julia, it was a time for reflection. The sun, moving in and out of the clouds, made long streaks of shadows across the pale field. The woods behind the field were also in and out of deep shadows in shades of rusty orange and red-violet. These were the oak trees that kept their leaves until the winter snowstorms finally sent them to the ground. Here and there, the warm colors were accented with the dark green of tall pines and fir trees. She could see the old gate, half open, between the break in the stone wall bordering the woods.

That field, that gate. Three times in the past week, she had crossed over and gone through the gate in darkness and fear.

What would it be like to just go for a walk out there, with no destination in mind, in broad daylight? Just to walk for the pleasure of feeling the crisp morning air? The irony of it was that, down South, on the plantations, her status as a known slave had made it possible for her to move about freely. She had often arisen early and taken solitary walks before spending the long days indoors sewing. She was reminded of that early morning walk when she had decided she must be brave enough to be a runaway fugitive slave.

Well, here she was, almost to freedom. And yet, it seemed so far away, still. *I wonder if George and I will soon enjoy such simple pleasures together in Canada? Is that too much to expect?*

Considering that, up until now, she had not expected anything beyond a life of existing and dying in slavery, it was an extreme contrast to dream about! But now, miracles seemed to be piling up, and freedom was coming into focus as a possible reality to hope for, to work for. Work! That had never bothered her.

I will work my fingers to the bone to make a good life for us as free people, Julia vowed.

Julia reached out to the worktable and ran her hands across the wedding gown spread out there. This strange day would reach a climax with her actually wearing this beautiful gown! For a few, precious hours, it would be her own wedding gown.

What kind of woman was this Mrs. Jackson who would so graciously let her wear the eldest daughter's wedding gown? It was beyond even kindness. She seemed to have expressed total joy and pleasure seeing the gown fit Julia so well! It was as if Mrs. Jackson was saying, "Nothing is too good for you, Julia—my home, the combined efforts of all my family, our love and our fears, and my daughter's wedding gown!"

Would she and George ever be able to make a life as warm and outgoing as this someday? Julia wondered. "Well, we'll start by sharing whatever home we have with Taffy and Susie."

Taffy woke up early, too. It was so cozy under the puffy quilt; it was always hard to get out of bed. She stayed there, awake and thinking. This was the wedding day! She and Daisy were going to frost that delicious-smelling spice cake this morning. Then Cornelia had promised to help them make fancy white paper cutouts to decorate the lower section of the front stairs, where there was an open bannister. She said there was a box of white ribbons from Alice's wedding they could use, plus a box of rose petals that Taffy and Daisy could toss on the floor in front of the bride. Cornelia knew a lot about weddings. What was it she had said? "Something old, something new, something borrowed, something blue." And the bride was to wear or carry one of each!

The borrowed part is easy, thought Taffy. *But what will the old, new, and blue be?* Probably Mrs. Jackson and Cornelia would figure it out very quickly. *Still, I wish I had something special of my own to give to Julia*, thought Taffy.

Suddenly, it came to her mind, and she quickly jumped out of bed. Where was her packed bundle that she would carry tonight, when it was time to escape? Probably still in the blanket chest in the sewing room. She ran into the sewing room, and there was Julia, looking out the window! Well, she would wait until later to find her bundle.

"Taffy, so you are up early, too! It's going to be such a complicated day and night. I just wanted to be up early and have time to think quietly."

"Do you want me to leave?"

"Of course not, Taffy. Come, sit with me for a while." Julia sat down in the rocking chair, and Taffy nestled onto her lap. As usual, Taffy was always reminded of her mother when she did this. And now she could talk about her mother, knowing Julia knew and loved her, too. She could even ask questions about what her mother had been like as a little girl. It was very comforting as well as interesting to Taffy.

This morning, Julia had questions of her own.

"Are you really happy that George and I are getting married?" she asked.

"Oh yes. We are going to be a real family, you said, and Susie can be part of it, too."

"Of course she can," Julia reassured her.

"Are you going to jump over the broom at the wedding?"

Julia laughed. "I don't think so. That's only a custom that slaves had, because there was no real minister to perform the marriage ceremony."

"Once I went to a wedding at the swamp-dance cabin, and they did that," said Taffy.

"That isn't going to happen tonight, Taffy. There's going to be a real minister to marry us, and we will say all the words written in the Bible. It's going to be a beautiful and dignified wedding." Julia sighed.

"And then you will be Mrs. George Jackson, won't you?"

"Yes. Isn't that a beautiful name? Julia Jackson. Who ever thought I would be getting married at all, and then in this wonderful house and taking their family name as my own? And that reminds me, Taffy. Judge Cotswell is coming later in the morning, and we have to sign a marriage certificate. I think he is bringing some other papers to make the name legal for us. I was wondering, would you like to change your name to Jackson, too? The judge can probably do that for you, too. And then we can start out our life in freedom all sharing the same name. What do you think about that, my dearest one?"

"Will I still belong to my mama and daddy if I find them, if I have a new name?"

"It won't make any difference at all! I know they would like a new name, too, to celebrate being free. And you can decide then which name to use. I don't think they would want to keep the name of Davis. Why should any of you want to be reminded of the people who separated you as a family?"

"Then I'll change my name today, too. Taffy Jackson! Then Daisy and I will almost be related, won't we? Maybe we could say we are cousins!"

Julia laughed out loud. "What a pair of cousins you two will make! But I know one thing. I don't think anyone in this family will object to the idea."

Susie came upstairs to see if Taffy and Julia were up yet and found them together in the sewing room. She sat down on the floor beside them and leaned against Julia's knee. Susie sighed out loud; it was such a comfort to her to be with both of them like this. It was as if a burden of responsibility and loneliness fell away from her shoulders. She was going to live with Julia and George and Taffy. And hopefully, Sam would be nearby to visit. Beyond that dream of freedom, it didn't matter to her what else happened. She would try, of course, to get a job cooking for some family. Imagine, working for pay in a household like this one!

"Do you think there will be white folks like this in Canada?" asked Susie.

"Yes, I do. They don't allow slavery, you know."

"Are you afraid of this escape plan for tonight, Julia?"

"Susie, starting with this day, I shall try hard not to be afraid of anything, if we can all just be free!"

Julia decided she'd better get dressed and go downstairs and have breakfast so she would be sure to be ready when the judge arrived.

After she left the sewing room, Taffy asked Susie to help her get to the bottom of the blanket chest for her bundle. Carefully, they took off each stacked layer until they came to it.

"What is it you want in there, Taffy?"

"I want this," said Taffy, taking out her blue, star-design, beaded bag. "Julia has to have something blue, and I'm going to give her this bag to carry."

"The bag Daisy gave you as a farewell present, the one she worked for herself! Taffy, are you sure you want to give it away so soon?"

"Oh yes, I'm sure. It's going to stay in the same family. We're even going to have the same name, Susie! This morning, Julia is going to have the judge change my name to Jackson!"

"Taffy Jackson! I like the sound of that! Does Daisy know any of this yet?"

"No, but I'll go tell her right now. She should be getting up anyway, so we can frost the wedding cake."

"Taffy Jackson, Taffy Jackson, I really like the way that sounds. I'll just keep mine for a while. Maybe Sam will choose a new name when he gets to Canada, and if I marry him someday, I'll have that name, too. Taffy, I'm going to try on my freedom skirt and blouse just one more time and be sure it doesn't need anymore adjusting. I'm still thinner than I was when Julia made these." Susie patted her front and sighed. "Doesn't that seem a long, long time ago now?"

Daisy was up and came looking for Taffy.

"Aunt Mary said if we came downstairs early this morning, she would make just us a special breakfast. We better hurry!"

It was already too late for that. Frank, George, Howard, and Mr. Jackson were already in the kitchen, waiting and watching as Aunt Mary stirred up batter for pancakes.

Once everyone had finished breakfast, it was time for action. Frank and Howard went to the factory to check on details there. Mr. Jackson said he would come down after the judge had come and gone. Mrs. Jackson and Mary had kitchen details left to do. They told everyone there would be a huge kettle of soup on the stove and plenty of bread, and they were on their own. Mrs. Jackson also announced that now there were too many to sit down at even the two tables pushed together. So the wedding supper would be set out on the sideboard in the dining room, and the guests would help themselves and sit anywhere they pleased.

Cornelia planned to help wherever she could, and Susie the same. As for Julia and George, no one could think of anything useful for them to do, so they went into the study to talk and wait for the judge to arrive.

By midafternoon, the important details had been accomplished. George was now George Jackson, and Taffy was Taffy Jackson. The wedding cake was frosted in white and waiting in the pantry. Frank and Howard returned from the factory. They announced that, as they'd come around the corner in their carriage, they had noticed two men walking slowly by the house.

Mrs. Jackson was dismayed to hear that. "I cannot bear to have Julia and George climb down into that black hole on their wedding day!"

She warned everyone, "We have to stay on guard until five o'clock. Don't decorate with the white ribbons until after that. It will just add to our problems to have to explain a wedding."

Mr. Jackson came home then, and he had good news to tell. Sam and the group had made it safely across the border into Canada! The driver had sent a message to Mr. Henderson.

"There were no problems along the way—no agents and no bad weather! That bodes well for the rest of you starting off tonight. Where is Susie? She'll want to hear this news right away!"

"She's upstairs. We'll go tell her," said both Daisy and Taffy.

Mrs. Jackson suggested that they all had time now to relax for a little while, even take a nap. She had already sent Aunt Mary home to rest and return later, along with her husband.

Before she went upstairs to rest herself, she walked through every downstairs room, inspecting things. The girls had all helped with some light cleaning, dusting, and polishing. But it was not the thorough process she was accustomed to for special occasions.

She reached down and ran her finger along the rung of a chair and found dust!

She shook her head and laughed to herself. *Considering we only had two days notice for this affair and no one from outside to come in and help out, I think we all did well!*

She thought about how different it had all been a year ago when Alice was married. Every detail had seemed so important, and it had taken weeks to achieve the necessary perfection! How fussy she had been, to have everything just right for her eldest daughter's wedding.

This time, there would be no rosettes on the wedding cake, no fancy floral arrangements, and just a simple supper.

"It will be a beautiful wedding, just the same." She sighed, thinking how much she and her family all took for *granted*—their beautiful, old house with its Colonial and Federal period mantels and woodworking; the original land, once a large farm, going back to the 1600s; and all of it under the same name of Jackson. Even their family name they took for granted. And now, this very day, they had given it to people who had not even a name to call their own! And their freedom as citizens—that most of all she was sure they all took for granted. Then there was their safe and secure family life that made even a lifetime seem reasonably predictable, barring sickness or accidents.

"Or war," she added with a shudder.

"What difference does dust in the corners make, after all?"

She walked slowly up the front staircase, thinking, *If we could just get slavery abolished in some peaceful way, without having a civil war.*

Susie was so relieved when she heard the good news about Sam that she put her arms around both Daisy and Taffy and cried.

"I'm only crying because I'm so thankful." She sniffed. "Now I can really enjoy the rest of this day! I think I'll put on my freedom skirt and blouse right away!"

"You better wait, Susie," said Daisy. "Mama said we can't get dressed until it's exactly five o'clock. We have a whole hour to wait."

Cornelia joined them, saying, "It's just a shame that you can never go outside while you are here. We could all go for a nice walk back to the woods while we're waiting for nighttime. In fact, that is where I am going right now, to pick some evergreen boughs and twigs to decorate the stairs with. When I come back, we can attach white bows to clumps of them. And when it's five o'clock we can begin to attach them to the stair railing, and we'll place two large bouquets of greenery at each side of the fireplace in the parlor."

At five o'clock, everyone went into action once again.

"This is it," said Mrs. Jackson, emerging from her own room. "From now on, we'll have our wits about us every minute."

She was already dressed in a taffeta gown of deep blue-violet, which enhanced her deep blue eyes and graying hair. But over it, she had also put on a blue, checked pinafore. She went down to the kitchen where Aunt Mary was just hanging up her cloak. Her husband was out in the barn discussing some repair work with Mr. Jackson, she said. Mary, too, was all dressed up in a black silk dress with a white lace collar, and she now put her pinafore over it to begin getting everything ready for the party.

Cornelia arranged all the fresh-smelling evergreens with help from the girls.

"It almost looks like Christmas," she said, "and it certainly has the same wonderful aroma!"

But once they'd entwined the greenery with white ribbons, it began to look like a wedding party instead.

"Now we better get all ready ourselves," she told Daisy, Taffy, and Susie. "Then I'll help Julia get into her wedding gown, and when we are all ready for a few last details, I'll call you into the room."

The three girls dressed together in the sewing room where the freedom outfits were still hanging. Daisy's dress was a rose taffeta with a white organdy collar, so it blended in well with the mauve skirts and cream-colored blouses.

Cornelia joined them to say that she would bring Julia to the sewing room, too, so she could see herself in the long mirror. They all exclaimed at the sight of the bride, so tall and regal in the long, white gown.

"Daisy, go and tell Mother and Aunt Mary to come up here for a look at Julia. And Mother has the something 'old' for her, and Mary has the something 'new'."

They all crowded into the room, admiring Julia and fussing over her. Mrs. Jackson pinned a pearl brooch at the neck of Julia's gown.

"I've had it a long time, so I think it can be called old," she said.

Aunt Mary gave her a beautiful, lace-trimmed handkerchief that she had bought just the day before. Looking at Taffy, she said "Now, the something borrowed is the dress, the shoes, and so forth. But the something blue—you have that, Taffy?"

Taffy took the blue, beaded bag from its box and gave it to Julia.

"I'll only borrow it, Taffy. You must keep this yourself."

"No, it has to be yours, Julia, because it has special wishes that go with it for good luck."

"All right, then, I will treasure it. It certainly is a lovely design with that blue star."

"We just need to make it look more like something for a bride to carry," said Cornelia. From the table, she picked up an arrangement she had made from tiny evergreen twigs with ivy trailing down from it and tied with a white bow and trailing white silk ribbons. She deftly attached it with more ribbons to the bag.

Meanwhile, Frank's other friend, Carl had arrived, so now there were two covered carriages drawn up close to the back of the house. From the other end of the upstairs, the laughter and voices of the young men could be heard as they helped George get dressed in his borrowed finery. Cornelia walked back there and knocked on the door, but they were all ready to come out. Cornelia looked at them with sparkling eyes, saying "Oh, George, you are a sight to behold in that cutaway black coat and gray pants! Frank, Howard, Carl—you all look splendid, too! Now what about the ring, Did you get a ring for him to give to Julia?" she asked expectantly of her brother. "We have everything under control, Cornelia," said Frank.

"You look lovely, Cornelia," said Carl, admiring her bright and happy face. Cornelia wore the dress she had worn to her sister's wedding, and the green velvet did indeed look well with her dark blond hair piled high on her neck.

"Where is, Julia?" asked George, looking nervous.

"Oh, you can't see her until the ceremony!" said Cornelia.

Mrs. Jackson was coming down the hall to go downstairs again. "Yes, he can, Cornelia! This is no time for such traditional formalities. We only have a few lovely hours all together, so let's just relax and try to enjoy them. Come on down to the kitchen, all of you. Aunt Mary has some special things to keep you all from fainting away before we get around to the wedding supper!"

So everyone gathered in the big kitchen—the blinds all drawn—and talked and laughed as they nibbled on hot cornbread and sliced ham and apple cider. Only the bride and groom sat quietly at the kitchen table, drinking in the sight of each other as if they would never see each other again. And likely it was that they would never again see each other dressed as they now were, in their borrowed finery.

After a while, they heard the cloppety sound of a horse coming down the street. The carriage pulled up by the gate and walkway to the front door, and the Hale family disembarked—all five of them. In a short time, two more carriages arrived, bringing the judge and his wife and Reverend Southwick and his wife, who had decided she did not want to miss this strange party. Now a total of five carriages were parked outside—three along the front and the two between the side of the house and the barn.

Mr. and Mrs. Jackson, followed by Frank and his friends and Cornelia and Daisy, went to the front hall to greet the arriving guests. George and Julia followed after them but went directly into the parlor and stood by the fireplace.

Susie and Taffy lagged behind in the kitchen with Aunt Mary and her husband. All of a sudden, the two girls felt ill at ease. It was one thing to be dressed up in their new freedom outfits, which were truly theirs, and dressy petticoats, shoes, and stockings, which were borrowed, and mingle easily with the family and Frank's young friends. But it was quite another to mingle with strangers.

"Isn't there something we can do for you in the kitchen now, Aunt Mary?" asked Susie.

"You and Cornelia and Daisy can all help set out the food later. But now, you both run along and socialize. Go on out there now, and act like the fine young ladies you really are. You both look the part in those nice gowns, don't they, Joseph?" she asked her husband.

Joseph nodded, and Mary went on talking. "When it's time for the wedding ceremony, we'll be out there, too. But I don't want you hanging 'round this kitchen at all tonight!"

"It's far different from parties at the plantation, isn't it, Taffy?" Susie whispered.

"Remember, Susie, how I wished you could be out on the lawn with all those girls when we made the luncheon party for Louise? She would be happy to see us all dressed up and being part of the guests, wouldn't she?"

"Yes, she would. I want to be friendly, but I get so nervous that I won't do things right or be able to say anything right. Do I really look all right, Taffy?"

"Yes, you do. I bet you would feel better if Sam were here, wouldn't you? Sam could always cheer you up."

"Yes, and I must remember he's safe and he's free! I said I would really be able to be happy knowing that, so let's just try to have a good time, Taffy! There's nothing to be afraid of inside this house, except when agents get in the door!"

Once they were introduced all around, the girls felt more relaxed. Everyone talked at once, and Mrs. Jackson explained to all about the freedom dresses and how they had come to be made and now were being worn for the first time, just a little in advance! A cozy warmth prevailed among them all. Many occasions had been celebrated in these mellow rooms, in the glow of the oil lamps and the three fireplaces, now blazing away. But this time, besides the atmosphere of festivity, there was the bond of shared secrets and intrigue. The burning logs enhanced the woodsy scent of the pines, hemlocks, and fir boughs that Cornelia had arranged in the dining room, sitting room, and parlor. With the white ribbons accenting the greenery, it all looked like a real wedding party. But the thread of tension and fear still remained underneath the gaiety of the guests. It was not a familiar emotion in these gracious rooms, filled with family mementoes and antiques from past generations who had lived here in security.

Mr. Jackson's voice rose above the others, as he announced, "Well, I think it's time we got on with this wedding ceremony. Let's see, now. Do you want Julia and George to stand right here, in front of the fireplace, Mother?"

Before her mother could answer, Cornelia spoke up, "Father, we want to have a procession first! Julia has to come down the front stairs, with Daisy and Taffy walking ahead of her, and dropping rose petals from their baskets. I have it all arranged this way!"

"I see. And do you want me to come down the stairs with her, or do I wait at the bottom?" asked her father.

"Um, you wait at the bottom, Father; there's not much room with the wide skirt. Then, she can take your arm, and you can lead her to the place in front of the mantel, where George and Reverend Southwick must be standing. And, Frank, you and Carl and Howard stand on the other side. There, that's fine. Susie, you come upstairs, too. You must be right in front of Julia. You are the maid of honor!"

"Where will you be, Cornelia?" asked Taffy. "You have to be in it, too!"

"Oh. Well, I'll fill in somewhere." Then Cornelia whisked Julia up the front stairs to the hallway at the top, followed by Daisy and Taffy, leaving the others downstairs, laughingly doing exactly as they were told.

"I'll play the piano," said Mrs. Southwick. "Tell me when to begin."

The Hale family placed themselves beside the piano facing the fireplace. Mrs. Jackson stood next to Carl and Howard, and Aunt Mary and Joseph stood beside her.

When Cornelia called out, "We're ready!" the music began. And Daisy and Taffy came down the stairs and into the parlor, scattering dried rose petals onto the floor as they walked. Both girls were smiling with subdued excitement. They took their places on the opposite side where Reverend Southwick stood with George. Cornelia came down next, carrying a bouquet of evergreens and trailing white ribbons. She walked ever so slowly, smiling broadly, relishing every moment of her planned production. Next came Susie, also carrying an evergreen bouquet created by Cornelia, but her demeanor was shy and hesitant. They stood next to Daisy and Taffy.

Mrs. Southwick had played for many weddings. She paused now, made a few runs and flourishes over the keys, and then began the marching refrain again in strong and measured tones.

"Oh dear!" Cornelia suddenly said, "We should see Julia as she comes down the staircase!" and she rushed out into the front hall where her father already was waiting for the bride. Of course, then they all crowded out into the hallway, even the minister and the bridegroom, and all eyes looked expectantly to the top of the stairs. The staircase was very gradual with shallow risers. And from the landing, it was open the rest of the way down with an attractive railing, which Cornelia had decorated with festoons of greenery and white ribbons. The fluffy skirt of the wedding gown was held out by a crinoline skirt underneath, so that it filled the entire width of the staircase.

There was no doubt about it; Julia was truly a beauty, her glowing dark skin set off by the white gown and veil. For a few moments, they all stood there, transfixed at the beautiful vision.

As she reached the last step, Cornelia led them all back into their assigned positions in the parlor. Julia took Mr. Jackson's arm, and once again, all eyes gazed at the doorway as they entered, and walked slowly to the center of the fireplace. George came forward a few steps to stand beside her, so that they both now faced Reverend Southwick, his Bible open in hand.

The familiar vows were solemnly read and repeated, the voices of the bride and groom soft but firmly eloquent. At the end, Reverend Southwick proclaimed, "May I present Mr. and Mrs. George Jackson!"

George, looking very distinguished with his silvery hair and wearing the formal clothes, kissed the bride, and then the tall and stately couple turned to face their guests. They all clapped and then rushed forward to hug, kiss, and shake hands!

Mary and Joseph soon slipped quietly back to the kitchen. And then Cornelia, Daisy, Susie, and Taffy also joined them to help set out the wedding supper. There were silver platters with sliced turkey, ham, and roast beef; several hot dishes; fluffy, hot biscuits; and all kinds of condiments. Mr. Jackson requested that the reverend say grace before they began, and this was the first time that any reference was made to the eventual finale of this unusual wedding day, for he prayed for their safe arrival in Canada as free people.

How fast the precious time flew by! Mr. Jackson kept a careful watch on the clock. They still had the wedding cake to cut. It was displayed in the center of the table, with silver candlesticks and white candles flickering on each side. Soft hemlock twigs were circled around the cake, with white ribbons and white paper, snowflake design cutouts placed among the branches. After the cake was cut, and extra pieces wrapped up, Mr. Jackson reminded Cornelia, who was enjoying being in charge of the festivities, that it was now time to get ready to leave.

"First the bride must toss her bouquet from the top of the front stairway landing!" said Cornelia, leading the way into the hall. Again, they all crowded below, admiring the beautiful bride, the last they would glimpse of her in her wedding finery. Julia tossed her bouquet over her shoulder. It was easily caught by Susie's outstretched hands, amid laughter and good wishes that she would be the next person among them to become a bride. Susie smiled happily at all the loving attention centered on her.

The ushers and George and the girls followed Julia upstairs, the young men heading to the room at the rear, and the girls to Cornelia's room.

Carefully, Taffy and Susie folded their freedom skirts and blouses into a bundle. Cornelia helped Julia remove her wedding clothes and change into the warm, gray skirt and a winter jacket. When they were ready, Mrs. Jackson came in and adjusted their veils. The long cloaks were downstairs. George, of course, could not be veiled, but the young men had a hat for him. And the plan was that he would walk quickly to one of the side carriages, surrounded closely by his usher friends. Their bundles were all ready at the factory, except for one to hold extra things plus the pearl pin; the lace handkerchief and ribbons from the bouquets; and, oh yes, wrapped-up pieces of wedding cake! And the beaded bag. At the factory, they could further wrap themselves in warm shawls and blankets. George was now wearing a warm suit furnished by the equally tall Howard. Mrs. Jackson insisted they keep the bonnets for the entire trip, just in case it became helpful to wear them again.

The festive aura of the wedding celebration still upon them all helped to dispel the tension and sadness that might otherwise have settled over the group.

"Good-bye, Cousin Daisy," Taffy said as they hugged one final time.

"Good-bye, Cousin Taffy Jackson," replied Daisy. "Write to me right away when you get there. You promise?"

And so it went, all around, farewells and promises that they all knew they would keep.

And then they were out the door and into the various carriages, according to the prearranged plan.

Mr. and Mrs. Hale and their son left by the front entrance, flanking Susie and Taffy. The girls were the same size as the two Hale daughters, who were now left inside, to stay overnight!

Very quickly, they went down the brick walk, through the gate, and stepped up into their waiting carriage.

Judge and Mrs. Cotswell followed after them and walked to their carriage out front. Meanwhile, George was being escorted to the carriage near the side door. And then Julia was escorted out by Mrs. Jackson and Cornelia. Reverend and Mrs. Southwick also went out the side door but walked out to the street where their carriage was waiting. The last carriage to leave from the side of the house only had the ushers inside, and this was the follow-up, just to make sure that the others were not being followed.

In the confusion of so many guests leaving from two doorways in the darkness, it was unlikely that, if agents were watching, they would be able to figure out just who or how many were involved.

In a short while, the last cloppety-clop of the horses was heard rounding the corner at the end of the street.

"They're gone. This time, they are really gone." Daisy sighed.

"Yes. But this time, I am confident they will not be back. They will make it safely to Canada, just as Sam and the others did." Mrs. Jackson sighed as well, weariness finally settling over her.

The two remaining Hale girls returned to the parlor to enjoy playing duets on the piano.

Mrs. Jackson put her arm around Daisy and said, "Come upstairs with me. You too, Cornelia, and help me fold away the wedding gown. Then we'll come downstairs again. By then, your father and Frank and the boys should be back, and we'll have some more to eat. I was too busy and excited before to eat a thing, but now I'm hungry!"

Together, they went upstairs, folded the gown, the crinoline underskirt, and the petticoat. They placed these, along with the white shoes and the veil back in the blanket chest in the sewing room.

"Do you suppose Susie really will be the next bride from the guests at the wedding?" asked Daisy.

"I hope it won't be too soon," her mother said with a laugh. "Susie needs time to just relax and grow up some more."

"She'll probably marry before I do," said Cornelia, folding up the leftover ribbons. "I have so many plans, it will be years before I want to get married. I want to study literature and writing, and I may become a nurse, too!"

"When you do get married, Cornelia, are you going to wear this wedding gown, too?" asked Daisy.

"I don't know. Somehow, I cannot imagine myself looking as beautiful as Julia did—so tall and elegant. I'll never forget her, poised at the top of the stairs waiting to walk down."

"You'll be just as lovely a bride, Cornelia, in your own way and style. But, by then, you may want a dress all your own. And you're shorter, too, than both Alice and Julia. Just don't talk about being an army nurse today, dear. I'm just not up to hearing a word about it."

"All right, Mother. I won't. Maybe we won't have to go to war to end slavery. Besides, I'd rather think about Julia and George the rest of today. They both looked so impressive, and they are both so special. I mean, right now, in spite of their still being slaves, I think of them as becoming important people someday. Do you get that feeling, too, Mother?"

"I do, I must admit. I have a sort of premonition about the two of them. I'm proud of them now, for just the way they are. But I have this dream that, someday, we shall be very proud to say that Alice's wedding gown was worn by Julia Jackson!"

"Did we help make the dream come true, Mama?"

"Just a little bit, Daisy. Just a little bit. They are the ones who had the dream of freedom and the courage to act upon it by becoming runaway fugitive slaves. Until slavery is wiped out from all of the United States forever, the rest of the dreams cannot ever be fulfilled, no matter how much courage anyone has."

"We may have to go to war to make it come true," said Cornelia, already forgetting her promise not to mention the subject again.

"That is my darkest, deepest fear," said Mrs. Jackson. "But we are not going to worry about that today, my dears. We'll just concentrate on one dream at a time coming true and pray for their safe arrival to freedom. Come on, now—let's go down and enjoy the leftovers. I think there's some leftover lemon pie, too, which reminds me I have strange news to tell just to you, Cornelia, and Daisy too, now that the others are on their way. You know that Julia, just this morning of her wedding day, wanted to join us in the kitchen making desserts for the reception. Especially after she saw six lemons in a bowl, she asked if she could make a special kind of lemon pie. When done, it was a wonderful sight just to behold! So did Mrs. Blair think so. But Mrs. Blair had a mysterious story about this pie on our buffet table."

"Hurry up, Mama—tell us so we can go down to eat," said Daisy.

"I'll try," Mrs. Jackson said. "Mrs. Blair said they had three older men and one younger woman in the cold cellar, waiting for heavy rain to let up, so I had her come up to the kitchen and get warm by the hot stove. She asked me if she could bake something nice for me, like a chocolate cake. There were supplies leftover, and when she saw my bowl of fresh lemons, she asked to also make a lemon pie. It was the fancy kind with the white egg topping. I was in and out and never got her name to thank her properly, as the rain let up and they suddenly left. The chocolate cake she baked I did cut in half for them to take with them in the big farm wagon that was to hide and carry them to Canada and freedom. Now I come to your wedding party and see you have a pie just like hers on your table! I'd like the recipe!"

Mrs. Jackson sighed and leaned wearily on a table. Looking at Cornelia, she asked, "What do you make of this mystery? Do you possibly think that it was Taffy's mother?" But Daisy, quickly grabbing hold of her mother, yelled, "Mama, Mama, I know who made that pie for Mrs. Blair! It was Taffy's own mother Della! Taffy told me all about her. She was head cook where they lived, and she taught Susie how to do fancy baking too!" Then Cornelia, jumping out of her chair, also grabbed her mother saying, "It was Della who made the pie, their young owner died suddenly, and their old master sold them all and moved far away!" All at once, the three of them began loudly shouting, and twirling around, "It has to be Della! It has to be Della. She's free! Della is free. She's free at last! She's free at last!" Mr. Jackson, with his son Frank and the two young men helpers, came bounding into the room from downstairs to see what all the noise was about and tried to make sense of what the three were so excitedly trying to tell them.

Cornelia yelled, "Then Taffy's dear mother did become a runaway and was right here in Newton—here on the same street and is now already free in Canada!"

Grasping their story, Mr. Jackson quickly and loudly declared, "Well, we do need to celebrate again! Come right downstairs! It just so happens that Mary went into the pantry and found one more lemon pie tucked away on the shelf under a cover, so Julia made an extra one! This time we'll celebrate with her last special lemon pie!"

Printed in the United States
By Bookmasters